THE
MOTHER
YOU
KNEW

A Novel Based on a True Story

LEILA HILKMANN

Producer & International Distributor
eBookPro Publishing
www.ebook-pro.com

THE MOTHER YOU KNEW
LEILA HILKMANN

Translation: Leila Hilkmann

ISBN 9798388912831

To Mickey and Nooshi
Loves of my life ∽

CONTENTS

INTRODUCTION

My son, Oz, was kidnapped in July 2000 while visiting his father in the States.

My life came to a standstill. My daughter Sevan, who returned to Israel without her brother, was overwhelmed.

The years that have since passed are foggy; events waned alongside mundane chores of daily life, leaving meaningless trails of incidental happenings void of any significance. Overcome with despair and paralyzed emotionally by the pain of my son's disappearance, I merely reacted to my surroundings with indifference. Nothing aroused my interest nor left its imprint on me. Days passed blending into sleepless nights, one long slackened breath that lingered over many years erasing all other reflections in my life.

Throughout the first five years of Oz' disappearance I battled the American legal system tossing between a sense of desperate loss and a childish hope that, maybe, despite all, justice would be found within the courtroom. I clung to hope and refused to let go. I understood that without it I wouldn't be able to go on. Sevan's presence forced me not to give up and urged me to continue living so as not to allow her a motherless existence. Darien, her father, had already given up on her from the start when he decided to sever all ties between both children as part of his sick vengeance against me.

As time went on the days seemed longer. I wished to put an end to the sorrow and frustration that threatened to ignite in me uncontrollable madness, yet I remained passive lacking any courage. My world had shrunk. I merely existed and didn't even consider revenge, though there were moments when my inner storms threatened to spark uncontrollable savagery. I was overwrought with fears of losing my son and longings for him and sometimes I even doubted my sanity. I'd shut my eyes and listen to Oz' voice, afraid that he might be ill or wet in the rain. I feared he'd cry or become overwhelmed with sadness but mostly I worried about the loneliness and isolated existence that was forced upon him and threatened to derail his somewhat frail mind. And the longer time passed the more I wished to guard my memories of him, and hold onto his image that clung to me day and night. I saw him everywhere, in every dimple that crossed my way. His clumsy gait appeared in front of me on sidewalks or odd places; I heard his metal like voice in strange conversations while his laughter flickered from hidden corners. I imagined him walking with his dog along the esplanade and patting it as he listened to music or had his friends over for dinner.

How I wish I could rewrite the events, change the reality that transpired as a result of the kidnapping and recreate a very different one from that which crushed my small family. But my biggest weakness of all, my fear of violence, ultimately won and paralyzed me into passivity by forcing me to freeze in place.

I grew up in a home with little love and the much-needed support for nurturing family ties. What happened in our house reflected my parents' lack of understanding of my sister's mental illness, enabling riots and madness to rule our home. Our sick home sprouted cruelty and distortions that contributed, years past our childhood, to my son's kidnapping. As a child I was scared to breathe or voice my wants and didn't understand how to negotiate situations or reach compromises. My sister Naomi used paralyzing violence to get what she wanted and my parents chose to ignore it. I was terrified of that constant paralysis and of always losing ground to her and carried those fears with me long after I'd left home. Those same frightening emotions also formed the basis of my marriage and accompanied me throughout the divorce proceedings. The price of the divorce was horrific culminating in my son's kidnapping. The brutality of the act and the vicious manner, in which all ties with my son were severed overnight, caused my small family to fall apart and left me crazed with pain and worry.

I'm aware of the enormous fortitude involved with hesitations especially those that decide fates and destinies. Making a choice is never easy because of the difficulty to detect that sharp moment, the precise split-second when indecision turns into a certain choice followed by consequential results that can only be judged in retrospect. And perhaps I'll never be able to tell for certain when that split second occurred or when my indecisions took on the shape of a fatal decision. But what's important is the end result.

The enormous wave of anger stored inside me for so long finally unleashed itself, igniting a gigantic explosion that shattered my paralyzing state of passivity. And I found myself hungry for revenge.

I wanted to take an ax and put an end to Darien's existence just like he had murdered Oz' soul and severed his past. I wanted to cause him tormenting pain and suffering, pulverize every miniscule particle in his body, toss him with great force and unleash my son from his horrid grip. I wished to save what remained of Oz' naive world: life's beauty as it reflected in his slanted eyes and I wanted to hug him to my heart, heal him with love and give him back his happy life.

Twenty-two years have passed since Oz' disappearance from my life, but I'm still holding onto the hope that I'll get to see him. The sheer thought that he doesn't understand why I didn't ensure his return home haunts me, but even more worrisome is my fear that the memory of his existence will dissolve after I'm gone. There won't be anyone left to serve as witness to the story of his disappearance.

Despite all my efforts, I was never given a chance to meet with Oz and explain things to him. It's important that he hear the truth and understand the events that forced him into the reality which he now endures, separated from me and from the rest of his family in Israel.

My family chose to deal with Oz' abrupt disappearance as a secret event worthy of silence and, in so doing, reinforced the act itself. On the internet, however, the detailed case is still being rehashed and debated by lawyers and law makers who use legalese to argue the case adding commentaries, raising countless interpretations and offering various legal opinions. But unfortunately, all their words of wisdom cannot change the cruel reality of my family's situation.

Over the years, the sense of paralysis and powerlessness that was imprisoned inside of me for so long began to dissipate and was replaced by a fierce fury that turned into a formidable force that I no longer wish to restrain.

And so I've made my choice to break the silence and tell the story aided by my own power, the power of a mother's voice.

Truth has many facets. There are words of truth told by the narrator and the words that reflect the reader's understandings of those same words. And in between is the solid truth, fully documented and backed up by facts.

I hope that Oz and Sevan can see the words of solid truth and reach out to me.

CHILDHOOD

Scent memories have a way of carving mysterious souvenirs in exceptional configurations, testimonial imprints hidden within the deepest capillaries of our soul where they remain for eternity; which is why my childhood reminiscences vacillate between fragrant fusions and other odors reeking of missed opportunities, losses and calamities about-to-happen.

Recalling my mother's scent overwhelms me with sadness and fear, though she rarely used Soir de Paris, the perfume given to her by my father at the end of World War II. Its unique smell evoked a floral storm of exotic smells, a heady mixture of jasmine, rose and other exquisite flowers I lack the knowledge to name.

On rare occasions my mother would stand in front of the mirror, a dress hugging her slim waist. She'd balance on high heels that complemented her shapely legs, remove an oval-shaped box from the bathroom shelf, a beautiful little container in royal blue topped with tiny golden stars, and place it carefully next to the sink. From my bed, just a few small steps away, I'd watch her hands push aside the little magic gate, open two miniature doors, take out a small royal bottle and perfume the back of her earlobes. She'd then bend over my bed with a promise to return soon.

When I burst out crying she'd straighten her back.

"Why the tears?! How often do we go out?!"

I was four years old but already paralyzed with fear of Naomi, my older sister.

My father's disappointed face made me swallow my tears and beg. "Just come back quickly...promise you'll come back quickly..."

***

My mother, Rachel, was born in New York, first child to Pearle and Isaac, a small and somewhat gaunt child, with black wise eyes that knew little warmth or love. Grandma Pearle, who was born in Russia and orphaned by her mother at the age of two months, was left with her heartless father who barely survived with his two daughters.

Years later, when she came to America and became a mother, Grandma Pearle drew from her own memories and the cold heartedness upbringing of her father and carried on with the harsh traditional ways she'd known as a child. From a young age she taught my mother to shy away from hugs and kind words which she interpreted as a display of weakness.

At the start of World War I a Zionist movement began forming in New Jersey and New York. Young Jews, who understood the importance of establishing a Jewish state, began organizing Zionist cells that called for the realization of their dream and the immigration to the new land known at the time as Palestine. With the encouragement of Josef Trumpeldor and Ze'ev Jabotinsky who called for the formation of Jewish Brigades, my grandfather volunteered to the regiment of the Mule Drivers, and joined the fighting in Gallipoli. Upon his return to New Jersey, he and Pearle met within the movement, fell in love and married.

As an active Zionist, Grandpa Isaac spent most of his time away from home looking for volunteers to support his vision which he considered more important than his own family.

The vast wealth he'd amassed dealing in real estate following the Great War and the losses incurred by the rich enabled him to realize his dreams. Grandma Pearle, who adored her husband, chose to stand beside him rather than deal with her baby.

And so with her small heart deprived of love and filled with a sense of disappointment and abandonment, my mother was left to the graces of nannies.

When my mother turned three Aunt Abigail was born, a beautiful blue-eyed blond haired sister who resembled Grandma Pearle as though etched by the same artist. Grandma Pearle always raved about her daughter's beauty, yet preferred to continue occupying herself with Grandpa's projects.

Mordechai, my grandparents' third child, was born around my mother's sixth birthday. The short pregnancy lasted eight months producing a nervous little baby whose future was given a grim prediction by the doctors. Uncle Mordechai was afflicted by various ailments and by age one began suffering from severe seizures. My grandparents didn't spare a thing trying to find a remedy for the sick little baby but ultimately felt they had no choice but to declare him a slow and somewhat incompetent child.

In 1931, shortly before my mother's tenth birthday, Grandma Pearle became ill and was forced to have one of her kidneys removed. But nothing deterred Grandpa Isaac from pursuing his dream, not even his wife's frail condition. He packed up his family and moved from his plush New Jersey home to the bare dunes of his dream land. After two weeks in stormy seas they arrived in Palestine and began building the Zionist state.

***

Their first house was built on deserted dunes, a five minute westward walk in the direction of the steep cliffs, sharp eyed sentries cloaked in gray moss that birthed new sunny-faced blossoms at the start of every spring. The yellow lilies with their fleshy, succulent tentacles sprouted golden pearls that carpeted the harsh, stony surface holding their blooms for only a short time before fading against the blazing summer sun. Threateningly tall and harsh looking, their faces molded into colossal misshaped gargoyles etched by millenniums of whirlwinds and salty air, the monstrously grotesque rocks hung above watching in silence the sprawling beaches and waves of the Mediterranean Sea below, a place that remained as steadfast as the days of Genesis.

The Arab residents, whose lands were purchased years earlier by Grandpa Isaac and his Zionist friends, didn't care for the new settlers. Fear ruled the lives of Grandma Pearle and the three children who found themselves, more often than not, alone at home.

The first years were harsh and left their mark on things to come, frenzied, stormy times under the British rule accompanied by violence and bloodshed and a first baby born to my mother Rachel and my father Ariel Baum.

I was born two years later when the British had already left but the situation at home had only worsened. There were long tearful nights spent inside the room we shared, with Naomi's weird ways and the jackals wailing under our window.

Bilha, my younger sister, crowned from birth as 'A Wonder Child' and treated accordingly, landed into the darkness of our home when I was six.

Decades now distance me from my childhood yet my soul remains singed by memories of sadness and fear. I see Naomi's angry face and understand that she was born this way, furious at the world and constantly busy with repulsive evil plans. She was never happy or satisfied with what she had and always demanded everything from everyone. And though her body weight had shriveled to that of a mere walking skeletal, six-feet-tall with hair hanging wildly below her gaunt ass, even then Naomi didn't stop until she'd lost control over her sanity and found herself institutionalized, against her will, in various hospitals and institutions.

After long years of dragging my parents through endless torments and trying to entrap me as well, Naomi decided to marry the man who, years later, was sorry he'd let a split second of weakness tempt him into her tattered bed sheets. The only grace of kindness was the fact that she couldn't bring children into the world but maybe that's why she took revenge and lashed out at me and my children and in doing so found her mission in life.

***

My remembrances, countless metastasized particles, are anything but sequential; most are choppy and disrupted, ruffled at times and somewhat frenzied by virtue of the incidental happenings that took place at home. Some are fragile and thinly spread as they come and go and flutter in between the markings of my life. Naomi's crazed wand ruled over all of us, dictating the atmosphere at home and latching on throughout the days of my child and teenage-hood and beyond.

Naomi and I shared our childhood inside a crowded room in a sand-washed rural community with only a pale blue strip to mark the horizon where the sun dipped at the end of each day. Our small house was planted in the midst of golden sands, virginal dunes that reshaped at the slightest touch of wind and served as our playground. The blue was always with us, above our heads and beyond the kilometer that separated us from the sea. Its calm baby-blue waters chaperoned us during the morning hours and remained with us throughout the day as it turned into a blinding silvering canopy. Night time transformed its purple waters into a sensuous magic delight.

Thirty-nine families lived in our community and on Friday nights we'd all gather together: Naomi with her class mates and I with mine. We were a small group, and everyone knew Naomi.

On Friday nights we'd congregate under the giant Mulberry tree that formed the center piece of the school playground and chat or play games. We entrusted our secrets to the tree and chiseled our names on its thick trunk. I never went out with Naomi and she didn't go out with me but at the end we all shared the same places and the same trees. But our fears were different: I was afraid of returning home and finding Naomi in one of her strange moods with our room all messed up and tattered and my things shoved into strange corners.

Every morning mother would see us out the front door with a cigarette stuck between her long fingers. After sucking deeply she's sweep away the smoke with her hand and turn to Naomi.

"Your hair is nice this morning".

Naomi just stood there, her black eyes staring into the distance through thick heavy lenses.

"Don't fight with your sister, Tara. And remember to wait for Naomi".

I knew I had to watch over Naomi but I didn't like walking home the spoiled face that threatened to explode with anger, a sour discontented shape that knew how to change its expression and turn into something else within a split second. The other children also never knew if Naomi really meant the bad things she said or if she was only joking; maybe that's why they treated her meanly. Or maybe they simply didn't like the bad smells she carried with her, a heavy stench of moldy perspiration mixed with a lemony rot that sprang out of her mouth and caused them to run away.

An enormous carob tree stood on the main path that served, over the years, as the main street of Bo-Acha Yam. Its long branches pointed in the direction of a narrow passageway that led to the grocery store, a place that was more than just a store to us. We'd climb its heavy concrete steps before and after school, huddled together trying to appreciate new colors and tastes and how to get along in life. Those who didn't push and didn't shove remained in line forever.

The dusty place packed with open wooden stands and heaped with fruits and vegetables, stank of strange mixtures. Anyone wanting a healthy peach or a plum had to rummage carefully and refrain from touching anything that was wet.

A long, open mouthed shelf separated the shoppers from the two salesmen and from Ester Sheine, the owner of the store who used the shelf as her own personal refrigerator to store half eaten sandwiches and yoghurts or any other leftover foods that found their way next to the stinking cheeses. The yellow ones survived the less-than-cool shelf but the danger lay with the white cheeses, those frequently dotted with green or black specs. That same shelf also served as a support wall for the bloated barrels that threatened to explode from all the pickled goods squashed inside. There were olives, black and green next to pickled peppers and tiny spicy tomatoes, sour pickles mixed with dill and carrots all dotted copiously with Ester's self brewed hot paprika. She matched carrots with baby cauliflower heads, blended onion rings with beets and radishes, marinated cabbage leaves with lemon and orange peels and every so often forced on odd kumquat or two into hidden corners.

Smoked fish with wide open eyes and sliced bodies just waiting to be weighed also lay on the shelf. Their strong smell attracted the cats congregating outside in hope of catching leftovers. Ester Sheine's troupe of cats loved licking the droplets off the empty fish barrels where the pickled herrings once sat, their smallness wrapped in onion rings with carrot slices and bay leaves.

The rectangular room was always crowded with endless arguments about who's next in line, what's allowed and what's not, how much everyone owed, and mistakes in the pricing. But there wasn't another grocery store within a radius of three kilometers, a fact which helped sustain Ester's store.

Sometimes, on the way home, when I didn't have to wait for Naomi, I'd stop by the store, stand next to the open barrels and send a quick hand to the olives and fish. If I were lucky I'd find a place near the pickles which I loved more than anything else.

Naomi never stopped by the grocery store.

The path leading from the store to the school passed next to Ester Sheine's house with its overloaded yard, a sure explosion given the countless trees that threatened to strangle each other. Orange trees partied with clementines, lemons, grapefruits and pomelas trying to overshadow the guavas and the mangos sitting across from the anona trees, an out of control corral that constantly tangled with the Bougainvillea bushes surrounding it. It was a known secret that Moishe was born to the widowed Ester with the courteous assistance of Mr. Weiss, the strange bachelor who barely survived the Holocaust. Though no one actually spoke about it out loud, everyone referred to the small child with a wink.

Mr. Weiss, a tall, bald headed cypress tree who dragged along his stooping stomach always wore a tie. Even in the midst of summer when the catatonic air threatened to turn into a furnace, even then Mr. Weiss guarded his light blue tie, the one with the gray stripes that were erased from exhaustion.

Every day he'd visit the grocery store to purchase a loaf of black bread, yellow cheese and a small bottle of milk which he'd hug tightly to his body.

He mumbled as he walked and moved his lips, with head bobbing up and down. Though sometimes he'd nod sideways.

Mr. Weiss had a special way with his small herd of cows and treated them gently. He'd take them on a daily walk, speak to them, and pat their flat faces with both hands making sure they stayed clean of any muddy crumbs. I loved their big sad eyes but kept it a secret.

One day I knocked on his door.

"Mr. Weiss, I love your cows. Can I please take them out for a walk?"

Mr. Weiss' head went up and down and with it his small

moustache. I waited for his answer but he only released a meaning-less grunt.

"Please Mr. Weiss, please, I promise to take good care of them..."

I couldn't understand his silence. His bleary eyes wandered some-where high above my head. I turned around and ran back home.

The following day I saw him near the school gate, his hands crossed behind his back like an angry teacher. When I passed near him he extended a stick in my direction.

"Take it!"

"Thank you Mr. Weiss, thank you."

I held the treasure to my chest and repeated the names of all the cows. Mr. Weiss cleared his throat and spat.

I never knew ahead of time when he'd take them out but some-times I'd get lucky and then I'd have to get mother's permission because there was no one else to wait for Naomi after school.

Goulman too had an interest in Mr. Weiss' cows. His big yard bor-dered with the school allowing his chickens to roam freely next to Mr. Weiss' cows. Goulman believed that cow manure enriches the soil so he added clover and vetch and reached certain understand-ings with Mr. Weiss.

On the way to school I'd pass slowly near Mr. Weiss's house hop-ing to hear his flat voice call out.

"Come to Goulman after school."

He didn't have to say anything else to make me happy. At the end of school, I'd shoot through the school gate, enter Goulman's yard and make sure to return the small herd to its barn.

***

School was a kilometer away from our house but only when it didn't rain. The snaky trail remained dusty throughout the long summer months turning into a thick muddy pass in winter. The rain forced us to find alternative routes and skip over nettles and vegetation to avoid the puddles that took over the path. It lengthened the way and served as an excuse to be late for school especially on beautiful sunny days in the midst of winter.

I loved studying and drawing flowers, trees and maps using a fountain pen dipped in tiny bottles of colorful dyes but I didn't like waiting for Naomi after school. There were always problems bringing her home but mother refused to hear excuses and demanded we return home together.

I had no choice.

I tried to do what mother told me even when her words confused me. She'd put a finger to her mouth take me to the back porch and whisper words in my ears, words she was afraid to say out loud to Naomi. Again she repeated that I must set an example for Naomi and give in to her every whim and wish. But mother's words were contradictory and didn't make sense. She wanted me to give Naomi everything but she also wanted her to be like me. I was tired of listening to the same words without understanding them, and I was scared of Naomi. I couldn't feel restful when she was inside our room but I was afraid to show her how scared I was because I already knew how mean she could be.

***

When I was still young I tried to understand the situation and make sense out of things. When everyone said that Naomi was smart, I didn't know what they meant because she always got into trouble with other kids. I knew her problems were somehow related to her mental state which was never discussed at home. The things that went on in our home were very different from those in other families. And they were always strange. Frightening and strange.

Only after growing up did I realize our family functioned like a seesaw, swaying up and down as per Naomi's moods. But it took me years to understand just how sick Naomi really was because I was too busy trying to survive the wild gallops of her manic depression, the terrifying out-of-control mountain train that fed on self hatred sowing vile and destruction along its way and ravaging everything in its path.

Over the years her warped sense of deprivation heightened and she vowed to avenge me, to avenge my very existence, making sure she sees me to my grave, as she told me years later.

I looked for ways to escape, run outdoors and wander the unpaved paths of our community in an effort to find logical explanations for the things that took place in our family. But I didn't always succeed.

My head was filled with questions that I couldn't ask mother or father who enabled Naomi to rule the family as she saw fit. I wanted to tell mother that I don't want to be forced to look after someone who's older than me; that Naomi is mean to me and that she pulls my curls and hits me. I wanted to ask why Naomi never washes her hands after spending hours in the bathroom and why the shower curtain remains dry after she showers. I wanted to know why Naomi carries bad smells and always wears black clothes and never smiles, and why I always feel so strange when she nears me.

"It's your fault!" was my mother's immediate response along with instructions that never changed, "You've got to let Naomi have anything she wants! Anything at all! It doesn't' matter what it is! If you'll do that, there won't be any fights and poor Naomi won't cry and you won't be punished! You need to be grateful that you don't suffer headaches and diarrhea like Naomi...which is why you need to be nice to her and give her anything she wants...anything! Absolutely anything! And again I'm warning you not to fight with Naomi. You need to set an example and give her everything she wants!"

Sometimes I'd hear the other kids.

"Look at that broom stick...it's trying to run."

When they'd point at Naomi my stomach would somersault.

Many years later after becoming a mother and returning to Israel,

I found the courage to ask my parents about my childhood and their leniency towards Naomi.

Dad, as usual, waited for mother's response, which she etched in black and white.

"We thought we should treat her gently and not anger her...poor Naomi...she always suffered from migraines and diarrhea ...it upset her so much... we wanted to prevent her from getting angry..."

"But it came at my expense ..."

"Oh, come on! You had a wonderful childhood! You had a warm loving home...and I always made sure you had plenty to eat! Dad and I did everything so you wouldn't have to suffer because of her migraines... we did absolutely everything... d'you really think you have good reason to complain?!"

"And why did I have to help dad hospitalize her?!"

"It only happened once...in Pardessiya, but I understand that you're unhappy with your childhood so I have nothing further to say!"

***

We were planted in a small community, light years away from the home in America where mother grew up nurtured and pampered by nannies. There was nothing said about it out loud, but rather a silenced air of disappointment that hovered within the four walls of our modest home filling the atmosphere with constant dissatisfaction and mother's deep sighs. She voiced complaints about dad's meager salary, the household chores, the stupid neighbors, school, the grocery store and the lack of her own free time.

We knew very little about dad's family, which was seldom mentioned and only when suited to mother's needs. Mother had a way of using sharpened words to scratch open old wounds. Dad reacted by withdrawing leaving mother to continue ridiculing his family.

My parents had met in the States shortly before World War II when mother returned to America to visit her family. She planned on staying for a couple of months but upon her arrival the war broke out and all traffic to and from the States was suspended. She was forced to remain with her aunt for seven years, during which time she'd met my father, whose parents had emigrated years earlier from Russia to Palestine and from there to America. After a short acquaintance my parents married. At the end of the war they returned to Palestine which was declared, two years later, as the independent State of Israel.

My parents insisted on speaking English with us and behaving politely, the American way, but unlike mother who didn't have a shred of a foreign accent, dad was forced to struggle with Hebrew until his last day. Naomi, who always excelled in curses, didn't have any problems in either language.

"Dumb head! Stupid shit!" she enjoyed spitting in my direction.

When people smiled and said I was prettier than her, she'd lose control, nail her mean eyes on me and explain.

"They're lying ...they're only saying it 'cause they want to suck up to you. Truth is... they feel sorry for you 'cause you're so dumb and stupid! Got it, idiot?! And don't even think you're pretty... 'cause you're not! They're only sucking up to you! So don't hold any illusions ... you stinking carcass!"

Over the years that stinking carcass became her favorite cuss word.

It seemed to match her natural hatred for animals.

***

The kitchen, defined as mother's kingdom, was where she proved her culinary talents as chef extraordinaire and supreme household manager; holding high her controlling wand, she dictated to us all where, when and how to execute her instructions.

While growing up I interpreted my father's silent acceptance of her constant nudges as a blind obedience to the love of his life, but when he was diagnosed with a brain tumor and lost all inhibitions, my understandings changed.

"I can't stand her voice," he called me at work one day, "and I don't know how much longer I can tolerate her. She doesn't stop complaining ...and constantly bosses me around. If she continues I intend leaving her...simply...I'll simply walk out the door!"

I was shocked. They'd been married, by then, nearly fifty years with father always being the one displaying his unwavering love to mother and declaring it out loud. But I guess things were different for mother's cold and dissatisfied heart. She fed on secrets and intrigues and enjoyed brewing complex situations by exercising her sharp brain and whiplashing tongue.

Sometimes, when we'd ask about the family in America, mother would reach inside the tall wooden chest next to the fire place, take out a big box and spread its contents on the living room rug. We'd rummage through a heap of old photographs, most of them taken during the seven years she'd spent with her family in the States, and get to hear about our aunts and uncles and the rest of our extended family. Mother would identify each one by name, add anecdotes and deride their weaknesses.

Naomi's imagination would immediately spark up. She enjoyed grinding into near ridicule the relatives she'd never met and even contributed her own wild elaborations. Together the two of them created a sniggering chorus sounding sarcastic remarks with wild shrieks.

Amongst the many photographs, one went unremarked by mother. Naomi also noticed it and never asked mother about the boyfriend she'd had before she'd met dad.

It made me wonder if mother had ever loved dad.

***

A week before Bilha's birth, Naomi and I contracted chickenpox. Aunt Abigail came to watch over us. Though a head taller than mother, she seemed shorter because of her near hidden face and stuttering gait; her eyes, glued to the floor, pulled at the emaciated shoulders and slightly humped back forming the shape of a drooping cowl. She moved with cautious trepidation taking one small step at a time, each leg making sure the other was close by. Her annoying habit of constantly winking while chewing tightly on both her lips, made her beautiful face look as though it'd been soaked in lemon juice.

"Tara...Naomi...Tara...? Naomi...? I'm here...here...where are you?" she mumbled as she toddled towards the house like a fragile parcel.

I ran to her with a big hug of a six year old. Aunt Abigail was my favorite Aunt.

After placing a big bag on the floor she sighed.

"It's so heavy...I didn't know what I should...I don't know...how long...they didn't ...they want me...but they only said..." her tight mouth released broken syllables.

I didn't quite understand who said what to whom. Naomi, who was hiding across the corridor behind the partially open bedroom door, nailed her black glaciered orbs on Aunt Abigail. Her wicked stare transformed her face into an ugly frozen sight.

I quickly moved my eyes away but then I peeked again and saw her. Aunt Abigail, immersed in her pure world of kindness void of any suspicions or evil doings, continued with her good intentions.

"Look Naomi...look...look at the books I brought you...I think you'll like them..." her eyes blinked like a damaged light bulb.

I shot Naomi another glance and saw her planning something really big with the patience of a hunter.

Aunt Abigail's face remained soft and kind despite the lips that kept chewing in and out of her mouth.

"...yes, the cover...so I thought maybe...it's very interesting...yes, why not?" she mumbled.

I again glanced in the direction of the corridor. Naomi had disappeared.

"And this...this if for you Tara..." she hugged me warmly.

"Thank you Aunt Abigail... thank you."

I didn't want to let go of her hug. Books were considered noble presents, a reflection of the person who'd chosen them. Excitedly, I opened the package she gave me, took out the card and read aloud the words she'd written in her beautifully precise tiny handwriting.

"Dearest Tara,
I hope you'll enjoy the present I got you.
You're a very special and talented girl.
I hope you'll continue painting beautiful
pictures and being kind to others.
I love you with all my heart,
Aunt Abigail."

"Thank you...thank you..." I hugged her tightly, shutting my eyes with the hope that her hug would stay with me forever.

"brrrrrrrrrrrrr!"

An awful roar sounded.

Naomi appeared from nowhere, bare-footed with face and head covered in tattered rags, her hands strangling a broomstick squeezed between her thighs. Like a whirlwind gone mad, she flew across the living room with her frizzled albino hair, gazillions of steel wool threads that dizzied themselves around her as she cackled and screeched and flung herself against walls, hitting ornaments and embroideries and tearing curtains from windows.

"I'll slice you .... I'll shred you into tiny pieces! Brrrrr....I'll rip out your heart and feed it to the dogs! Just wait 'till I catch you! Brrrr... look at you...you shriveled old bones!"

Aunt Abigail let out a heavy sigh and fell to the floor.

Naomi continued with her wild galloping then at once cut through the corridor and disappeared.

Fearful, I waited for her famous encore but when nothing happened I bent over Aunt Abigail. Her eyes remained shut. I ran to the kitchen and returned with a glass of water then tapped some lightly on her cheek to make sure she was still alive. I tapped again on her other cheek and forehead and lips, and in between I dried my own eyes. When I finally saw Aunt Abigail open her eyes I was so happy that I didn't care anymore about anything. I put my arm under her head.

"I love you Aunt Abigail...I love you..."

I loved Aunt Abigail for her kindness of heart and gentleness and for the fact that she truly loved me and cared about me. But only in her later years, when she became ill and required my mother's assistance, only then did I fully understand the complexity and sensitivity of her personality.

To this day, Aunt Abigail's memory with her kind heartedness and frailty ignites in me an inexplicable sense of remorse and sadness that remind me of the missed opportunities I'd encountered throughout the various crossroads of my own life. I can still see her standing with her left hand flattening her dress and tightening the belt around her ascetic waistline. Aunt Abigail never quite recovered from the ordeal. Every time she'd see Naomi, her eyes would flicker like mad and her mouth would chew wildly. She'd then hug me and whisper in my ears:

"Remember...do you remember what she did? I'll never forget..." and she never did.

I don't remember how long it took dad to reach the house and revive Aunt Abigail, but I do remember standing at the edge of the corridor trying to listen to the words that passed between him and Naomi.

Dad's voice remained, as always, calm and quiet and his words were few. He had a way of silencing Naomi all at once and keeping her hushed over long days.

Naomi never shed a tear.

I miss dad more than ever and keep thinking of his eyes. Though he never made mention of it, the incident with Aunt Abigail made him realize just how sick and twisted Naomi's soul really was, a realization that left a sad little indent at the base of his eyes.

***

Naomi who was born with a swift brain, a sharp tongue and a stick in hand, loved more than anything to exercise control until it became her choice of drug. It took me years to understand her inability to control its usage and the longer she used it the more she consumed it in insane quantities.

When Bilha was born, Naomi took her under her wing and turned her into her pet.

"She's mine! She's mine! And don't you dare get near her!" she roared and demanded her all to herself even after Bilha and I had already left home.

Naomi couldn't stand to see her talking to me and manipulated her at every opportunity.

"Bilha, say please and I'll tell you a joke."

"Please," little Bilha repeats.

"Let's start with a dumb joke."

"Okay." Bilha smiles, her small face shining tiny dimples.

"Tara!" Naomi bursts out laughing.

I open my mouth but Naomi is faster.

"Are you trying to assert your own dumbness?!" she holds her tummy releasing wild shrieks.

If I keep silent.

"Her brain is dead!"

Any response works against me so I only think of all the bad words which best suite Naomi and keep them locked inside.

***

Naomi's fluctuating moods dictated the atmosphere of our Saturday luncheons. We'd all squeeze around the oblong shaped wooden table set in the room that served as a kitchen, dining room and pantry. I always preferred to sit at the edge next to the window, in case things got out of hand and I could stare outside at the bushes and trees in the back yard.

My imagination helped me escape, run away to faraway places saving me from Naomi's hysterical presence. Running, eventually, turned into my passion. I could cover long distances and keep it up for a long time, until it became second nature to me, exchanged, over the years, by stormy walks pounding away my aches and frustrations.

Our crowded Saturday lunches resembled a cautious walk through a mine field, toned down by dad who was always funny joking around and making all of us laugh. It felt nice and cozy until Naomi would lock her crooked eyes on me clarifying she's hungry for a fight.

"Don't even try saying that you understood the joke!"

Dad, mother and little Bilha wait for something smart to leap out of my mouth.

"You're not the only one..."

"You're way out of your league when it comes to smarts so zip it, idiot!" Naomi spits in my direction at top speed as her eyes turn monstrously huge.

"You're mean!" my eyes are wet.

"Slut!"

Mother shuts her eyes and covers her ears with both hands.

"Stop! I can't take it anymore!"

"She started it..." I burst out crying.

"Piece of sh...I won't even waste my time over it!" Naomi clenches her teeth and spits out fifty-seven words at insane speeds and finishes as only she knows how to finish, "She's got a brain the size of a pea! No wonder she doesn't get the jokes!"

Naomi goes on and I only want mother to hug me and say that it's not my fault that Naomi says nasty things; and I want dad to tell me that I'm not as dumb as Naomi says, but when they don't say a thing I know that Naomi is right and there's no one to defend me. I look at Naomi's mouth and I see rot.

"Are you happy now that you've upset your mother?!" dad asks as everyone leaves the table.

I'm left alone, all by myself, listening to dad's angry words and all I can do is bite my lips. I don't want to cry but my mouth fills with heat and the fire inside my throat swallows my tears. There are so many words that I want to say to dad, many more than to mother, because dad's heart is softer; but now even dad can't help me. Nothing can. I always get the jokes and I know I can laugh but I don't always want to.

When Naomi trills her voice like a ladder and does whatever she wants with it, I know she's brewing something nasty. But mother and father always smile at Naomi, even when there's nothing to smile about. If I tell them Naomi is mean to me it only creates problems and I'm blamed so I don't tell them anything. I already know I'm dumb and stupid and now I'm also ugly so I don't have any reason to smile or laugh.

***

When looking at her from the back, mother resembled a teenager with a slender figure and narrow hips that moved swiftly. She usually wore shorts with a cotton T-shirt that sat to perfection over her bountiful front. I'd look at her with envy hoping one day to have breasts like hers. On the rare occasions when she'd wear a dress with high-heeled shoes, I'd smile and enjoy her beauty.

Mother always busied herself with new creations, knitting or sewing or painting or any other thing that could compensate for the little there was. She embroidered an ocean full of colorful fish on an old sheet and hung it as drapes in our bedroom and used thin yarns to crochet tiny cap shades for our night lamps. Sometimes she'd gather flowers and tender branches and hang them upside down to dry in the back porch. Then she'd add an assortment of leaves, twigs, a colorful feather or a misshapen shell and glue them all on canvas or ply wood to create a dazzling nature scene.

I sensed that she constantly searched for things with which to fill up her world, but I was never able to ask her about the emptiness she stored within and the reasons that made her so stormy. We were simply never that close. She was reserved by nature but also sharp tongued and melodramatic. Words came out of her mouth without any effort or emotion. Mother was very frugal and stingy when it came to hugging or touching us and rarely expressed any form of affection. My father was the one who used hugs and soft kisses to fill up the gaps of her frozen deprivations.

My parents seldom went out anywhere, spending their evenings in the living room with mother seated on her tall rocking chair and dad sprawled below at her feet on the carpet she'd woven by hand. Her chair made out of thick matted wood was placed next to the bay window overlooking the sea. Given its shape and size, the chair turned into a formidable entity all by itself, taking over the entire north-west corner of the room, with countless wooden book shelves added, over the years, behind its back and on both its sides. Clinging to its right was a tall reading lamp, its round head shaded with macramé crocheted by mother next to a small three legged wobbly wooden table, with only two legs identical in height. A thick slice of wood covered with wild eyes, made up the table's surface and served as space for mother's ashtray and the large tea mug, served to her with quivering respect by dad, at the end of each evening.

No one dared sit on mother's chair. Not even Naomi.

Seated in her chair, mother projected strength fortified with confidence, tantalizing the world around her with her amazingly creative hands that seemed detached from the rest of her. I couldn't figure out how she was able to smoke and read and knit all at the same time. Every so often she'd flip the book upside down on her lap, take a quick glance at the knitting needles and make any necessary adjustments. After taking a deep puff into her lungs, she'd place the cigarette in the ashtray, turn over the book and continue reading and knitting. I tried imitating her movements and began knitting but it never came out as evenly as hers.

Mother's back was mean, a rotten trunk that always caused her pain even when she walked, baked, cooked and sewed. I'd see her cover her face with her hands and sigh.

"My back is killing me."

I lived in constant fear that one day it would simply snap.

Mother couldn't go down on four and scrub the tiled floors or carry heavy loads of laundry so Bat-Sheva came to help.

"She's old and she can't hear well...don't be scared of her shrieks," mother warned us.

Bat-Sheva looked like a heap of used clothes, a colorful mess of layered throw downs, her body bent in half with a flowery kerchief rolled on top of her head. Her shrilly voice sliced the air even before the first light of dawn, when only a thin shy ribbon appeared in the bluing horizon.

"Rachel! Rachel!" she hollered like a chicken being slaughtered.

The birds hushed.

I jumped out of bed and joined mother, looking through the kitchen window at the wrinkled face.

"Bat-Sheva," mother said, "why at four thirty in the morning?"

"After is hot." She answered in a thick Yemenite accent.
She had good intentions but she always scared me.
At eleven she demanded lunch.

"Rachel!!!"

"What's wrong?"

"Me hungry!"

The pickles and pickled herrings appeared from nowhere. Each jar contained two fish a total of four per family each month.

"First Bat-Sheva will choose. She'll take as many pieces as she wants and then you can take some."

I knew how little we had and mother explained that Bat-Sheva has even less but I always hoped she'd leave me more than just the tail ends.

Life at home was never easy, especially during the austerity period and budgeted food. Mother did her best but despite all her efforts none of us could escape the little there was, not even Naomi. We all tried to make do with what we had; Naomi simply took from others to ensure her own share, she couldn't stand not having all she wanted.

Mother excelled in finding original solutions for the greasy lump of meat portioned out to each of us once a week and even managed to change its smell by adding a few onions from the small garden we grew in the back yard. She'd fry them with the fatty lump, adding an occasional carrot or a green pepper, a sweet potato, if she was lucky, or any other vegetable she could find and sprinkle lots of spices on it to blur the taste. Then she'd place it in front of us and tell us to eat it, or else...!

"Swallow Tara! Swallow everything that's in your mouth!"

My mouth is stuffed with meat balls in tomato sauce, a repulsive gooey lump that never ends. I bounce it from side to side hoping that, somehow, it'll disappear. My eyes are half shut as my mouth goes up and down with small venting openings at both ends hoping to rid myself of the smell.

"You'll swallow it if it's the last thing you'll do!"

Dad is angry. I know he remains seated only to watch my mouth.

"Swallow! Swallow already!" he's agitated, "I can't sit here a whole day. You need to be grateful...there're so many hungry children in China that are starving right now... they'd do anything to have what's on your plate. Anything!"

I sigh.

"D'you want to end up with raisins instead of boobs?!"

I shake my head.

"So you better feed your body!"

"I need to use the bathroom."

"First swallow!"

Dad knows all the tricks but I manage to drag it on long enough that he finally says.

"I'm going to the bathroom and when I come back I want to see that you've swallowed it! And don't try any tricks!"

I've got exactly thirty seconds to take care of the dead thing sitting in my mouth. I spit it into the palm of my hand, shape it into a tiny ball and hide the awful thing deep inside the panty then I quickly wash my hands, rinse my mouth, gargle and spit out the leftovers.

Dad amasses long hours gawking at me while I learn the value of patience.

Nothing extraordinary happens until mother discovers the stinking leftovers inside the pantry.

"Don't ever do this again!" she warns me, "Look at it! A cemetery full of half eaten meat balls... and those ants... a live procession in the kitchen!"

I nod my head but inside I'm laughing because I can't believe everyone loves meat balls in tomato sauce even if mother says so.

Food was the only thing that Naomi and I didn't fight about. She hated fish and I couldn't stomach meat. Naomi was never really

34

bothered by bad smells or tastes. She ate incessantly, every bite heaped with self hatred.

"Rachel, why is Naomi so..." grandma Pearle would whisper behind Naomi's back, twisting her nose in disgust and moving her arms up and down behind Naomi's anorexic body.

Mother, true to her habit, would roll her eyes and stretch both arms to the ceiling.

"Why?!"

***

We both studied piano with Doovid, the eighty-four-year-old teacher who lived near the cemetery. He reeked of garlic and cigars and lacked all patience for slowness of mind and body. I couldn't read the music notes as fast as Naomi and mother said she could only pay for one lesson so I continued with ballet and Naomi stayed with Doovid and the piano and the magic her fingers produced. It was so different from everything else that grew under her greasy fingers. When she'd get into the right mood she'd make the keys dance in amazing ways.

"She's good. She's talented. She needs the music conservatory!" Doovid kept saying but for some reason Naomi refused.

When Doovid turned senile at age eighty seven, Naomi quit her music.

There was only one more thing that I could do by myself. Draw.

I drew and drew until I turned eight.

Night time. There's only one street lamp on the narrow path leading from our house to that of grandma and grandpa's eight houses away. When it's so dark, the trail seems longer with big, creepy shadows on both sides. I'm terrified but my hunger to paint is stronger than my fear. The darkened pathway is marked on both sides with Cyprus trees, blackened now and enormously tall creating weird shapes and sounds with crickets that drill in my ears. I run fast 'till I reach the gate, open it wide, enter the front yard then carefully cross the small wooden bridge set over the pond that serves as home for the gold fish.

The split pond resembles a huge pair of eye glasses connected by a short nosed bridge. The cool air is saturated with humidity and a strong scent, a mixture of algae with jasmine and wide awakened night flowers. Beyond the wooden bridge is a short stony path that leads all the way to grandpa's house and the studio behind it. I'm scared of the pitch black that engulfs me. My fingers flutter over the velvety plumeria flowers and the elongated leaves of the giant mango tree next to the anona and its neighboring fejoya. I keep walking until I reach the outside wall of the studio and feel for the key with my hand. I'm the only one allowed into grandpa's studio when he's not there.

When the door opens I find myself inside a large room with grandpa's paintings. A strong smell of oil paints mixed with turpentine floods the place making me feel good and safe.

Grandpa tells me I'm smart and sometimes he even takes my drawings and hangs them up next to his own in the gallery down town but then Naomi gets angry. She stands to the side with that sour face of hers and complains about a headache so we have to hurry back home.

I love grandpa's special studio because it's the only place where I can hide from Naomi. I check again just to make sure, and when I know it's absolutely safe I quickly repeat all the words that I'm not allowed to bring home, those that mother and father don't want me to say to Naomi.

"Witch, liar, mean person, walking stench, ugly fingers, sour mouth, evil eyes, why won't you be my friend?!"

Inside grandpa's studio I feel strong but not strong enough to stop fearing Naomi. When her anger jumps out of nowhere and latches onto one of her weird moods, Naomi loses control and there's no guessing what she might do and that's the scariest part in her.

I stare at the shelves bursting with large white drawing sheets, brushes, empty jars, tiny bottles and tubes filled with paints, smudged pieces of cloth and other materials that hold a permanent place inside the studio and I try to understand why things are so different in our home. My friends also have brothers and sisters but I never see them hide or run away from each other. I'm only six but I feel much older and I want to have a sister-friend the way Deborah and Ruty are sisters and friends at the same time.

Grandpa has long white hair with thick, black eyebrows. I love playing with his silky hair, pinning it all over or clasping together bunches of little braids. His slanted eyes are kaki colored, a special tint that takes a long time to mix on the paint slab.

When I'm in his studio I don't have a reason to think about the future or even imagine that twenty six years later the color of my son's eyes will be identical to those of grandpa's. Mother has grandpa's long fingers and I have them too, with a big moon on each of my nails. Mother says it's a sign of good luck so I shut my eyes and make a wish but it never comes true and Naomi remains the same.

Grandpa's hands and finger nails are clean except for leftovers of oil paints and turpentine that make him smell the same. Mother's hands and nails stink like cigarettes.

Sometimes grandpa comes to our front yard in his red pickup truck and honks.

"Tara...'wanna come paint?"

I'm happiest when grandpa calls me but I only smile. I can't really show my happiness because then Naomi will cry and run to mother. Grandpa drives in the direction of the railroad tracks and looks for a shady place. I'm not sure he really knows how to drive because he always gets stuck and then he talks to the dash board.

"Oy vey...oy vey...the needle is again hot."

The car coughs. Grandpa deadens the engine and the truck slides on its own. When it comes to a stop grandpa removes from the back seat two easels, a silver box with oil paints, some jars and turpentine. He carries with him a large bag with a bottle of water, drawing sheets, a slew of torn cloths and leftovers for cleaning and drying brushes and another bag full of fruits. He looks around and chooses a firm place for the easels then attaches drawing papers to them using wooden clothes pins.

"And now to work!"

And all at once I'm in another world.

Grandpa makes me feel grown up and smart and other good things because I'm the only one he takes with him and when I'm with grandpa I feel like a butterfly. But the good feeling doesn't last forever and only seldom does grandpa come by.

At age eight I stop painting altogether fading into a colorless silenced world. I keep hoping that Naomi's evil attacks would stop, but she continues relentlessly and not only with me. She sucks my parents' strength dry and squeezes out of them any remnants of joy.

***

There was another way of escaping Naomi. Spending time with Yankel the shoemaker.

I loved sitting inside his small wooden cabin and watch him repair shoes. His cabin, shaded from above by the carob tree's elongated branches, was clouded with a thick layer of cigarette smoke that forced Yankel's eyes to squint. He'd blink, pick up a shoe and study the rotten heel through spiraling gray curlicues. He'd spend long minutes thinking about it, moving his head this way and that way, his thinly lined eyes bouncing between the heal and the leathered sheet until he'd make up his mind, pick up his knife and slice it like cheese. When the tail end of his cigarette threatened to burn his lips, he'd fish a thin piece of paper out of a small silver case, sprinkle some tobacco on it then lick its end, glue it and light up the fresh cigarette with the leftover butt.

His small work table was heaped with weird things that didn't occupy permanent places, tidbits shuffled around with his black fingers, small rusty tined cans, knives and files, leftover pieces of leather, piles of nails buried under mountains of ashes, dirty cloths, laces and cans with oil, glue and shoe polish. After he'd finish cutting the leather, he'd get up and return the sheet to its permanent place at the back of the small shack where I sat silently watching his every move.

Only once did I ask him about leathers. He snorted and spat then placed a finer on the side of his nose and blew out quickly. After clearing his other nostril I understood that he didn't wish to speak with anyone. Everyone knew Yankel had a blue number tattooed on the inside of his left arm but he always kept it hidden under long sleeved khaki shirts. His tiny shack smelled peculiar but not so bad that I couldn't sit and enjoy the way he'd make old shoes look like new. His warped fingers fished out the thinnest of nails, black lines which he'd stuff into his mouth and wait for the right moment to feed them to his hammer, one by one, and nail them to death.

Unlike the rest of the school children who annoyed him and were chased out, I was always allowed inside his tiny cubicle, sitting quietly on the low stool and listening to his silences. Yankel's silent world enabled me to relax from the frenzied atmosphere of our home.

Sometimes I'd simply roam dirt paths that led to nowhere and dream of faraway places.

***

An avid reader, dad never missed an opportunity when it came to reading. He'd let us choose any book from the hundreds that were piled and scattered on long wooden shelves in every room throughout the house. We got to hear about dusty fairies, tall Greek monsters, golden fleeces, exotic underworlds, and he even let us choose to believe it or not. Dad took us to foreign lands and remote places and shared with us the brilliance of his mind.

Mother declined adventures and busied her mind and hands with odd shaped stones and branches, sea shells or any unusual flowers which she'd dry and shape into animals or twisted faces, cramming our living room with her extraordinary handmade crafts. Her incredible hands birthed amazing creations, burying every window and shelf under artistic creation, ornaments of sorts, too many to count, some dangling others nailed firmly to the wall with countless particles collected outdoors and turned into some form of art. Her stitching and knitting and weaving covered every snippet of wall in the living room and gazed at her high chair until the day her eyesight began deteriorating and she was forced to let go of her creations.

Dad invested his entire energy in us. With him we went on long walks, trying out every alleyway, trail, barrier, and thoroughfare. He knew every roadway track and bypass, whether dusty or muddy, and he'd take us for the sake of a rare cloverleaf, a lost bird or the simple pleasure of nature.

I loved walking next to him and feel my hand inside his huge one. His curious eyes checked every bug and snake skin found along our way. Sometimes we'd just follow a swarm of insects or lie silently next to a hidden burrow waiting for a rare glimpse of something interesting.

I shared dad's love for the outdoors and for nature and I couldn't understand Naomi. Walking, for her, was as bad as eating fish. Dad always suggested we go out with him on walks. I guess it had something to do with mother's free time but when Naomi refused a walk, both of us were forced to stay home.

It's a beautiful wintry day in January, a perfect mixture of fresh, feathery wind with a touch of warm sun. We've spent the past three days indoors hiding from the rain but today I'm eager to go outside.

The air is buzzing with flies and bees and grasshoppers celebrating the sudden burst of warmth. A lazy blue sky rests above our heads, its divine monotony broken only by aimless white fluffs that slide along dreamily.

Dad suggests we go on a hike to the fishponds and look at the blooming daffodils that carry my favorite perfume. I'm all excited thinking about the white heads with their tiny yellow faces.

Naomi doesn't even flinch. I look at her face and I know it'll cost me but I don't care. My insides are screaming for the freshness of the outdoors so I make a quick offer before she opens her mouth and demands even more.

"I'll give you a napkin if you'll come on a walk!"

We both collect paper napkins, the thin single-ply kind printed in a variety of colors and designs and used by grandma for her guests. Now that austerity is over and food is no longer rationed out we can sneak into her pantry and dig inside the special jar that's always filled with candies and chocolates in beautiful silver wrappings and add the shiny wrappers to our collection. But we must be careful not to trash them as we smooth out their wrinkles with the back side of a tablespoon.

Naomi stands with both hands on her waist-less waistline. She makes a sour face and declares.

"Ha! No less than two napkins and a silver wrapper!"

I hiss an okay though I know it's not okay, and we're on our way.

Naomi drags her feet and complains of pains but dad tells her she needs to go on. We're both wearing our new red boots and I can hardly wait to see all the things dad promised us. I enjoy looking at every tree and leaf and I can tell dad enjoys it too because when I squeeze his hand he squeezes mine in return.

Again Naomi complains.

"My legs hurt. You need to carry me."

"I'll give you a piggy ride on the way back."

Naomi cries and moans and I'm hoping dad will disregard her

and tell us more about the trees and the bees and the interesting bugs along the way.

"See over there...see the blue?" dad picks us up, one under each arm, and points with his chin in the general direction, "That's where we're heading!"

"I'm tired and my legs are also tired," Naomi whimpers.

"You can do it," dad says "I know you can."

"No! I can't move another step! I want to go home!"

Dad looks at me and at once I'm cold.

My eyes bounce quickly from dad to Naomi and back and I can tell there's laughter behind those tears of hers. She wants to see how quickly she can change dad's mind and I can't figure out how she does it but she always does.

Dad's eyes are sad when he bends down to my height gives me a kiss and promises to take me out to see the daffodils another time.

My eyes burn. I know I'll never see the honeycomb or the small nest hanging from the crab-apple tree and I don't know if I can ever trust dad again.

Moments later we're back home.

"So soon?!" mother looks at my red eyes. "What happened?! Oh... you probably had a fight with Naomi!"

I burst out crying and feel terribly alone. As soon as I enter the room Naomi demands payment.

I lie on my bed and hug my collections album.

"I'm not giving you a thing!"

"Don't even try it!"

"No! Don't you even try it!" I hiss back.

"Mom! She's bothering me!" Naomi shrieks and smiles at the same time.

Nothing helps. Not my explanations, not my tears, threats or screams. Naomi gets what she wants and I count thirty-one paper napkins and eighteen silver candy wrappers still left in my album. I swear to get them back.

A week goes by and I'm still thinking about my dwindling collection but I can't touch Naomi's because I'm afraid of being caught. She counts her paper napkins and silver wrappers everyday so I decide to wait. I already know I'm strong when it comes to patience and Naomi knows it too so she's nervous.

Two weeks later the torrential rains return. Dad switches on the hot water boiler which means that we need to be quick with our showers and follow each other in a fast row. I'm in the room when mother calls out.

"Naomi is in the shower. Get ready, Tara, you're next!"

That's my chance.

I scout the room with my eyes and try to understand what I'm looking at. Naomi has a way of hoarding hidden treasures, scrambled heaps in black and gray. I see skirts and crumpled shirts all thrown together with gray and black knee-high socks, somber looking sweaters, some dirty laundry, a shoe or two next to a hair brush with a piece of candy stuck to it, all muddled and scattered in confusion and scrunched together inside bags thrown under her bed.

Then they're the other things, the real important ones that make up secrets which Naomi keeps elsewhere, those hidden in dark corners or shoved behind fat lumps that reek of weird assortments and never change shape.

I peek behind the closet but the macramé bag looks soft and flabby. I work fast feeling through the smelly piles and at once I'm part of the sour smell. When I shut my eyes and try to think like Naomi, my legs lead me to the heavy mattress on her bed. I search under it with my hands, feel the album, pluck out two paper napkins and one silver wrapper and return it to its silent place before Naomi is out of the shower. My heartbeats are loud and my hands can't stop shaking but as I hold the treasures in my hand, I know my victory won't count until the loot is glued into my own album. I look around for a good hiding place but then I hear the key turn and Naomi's feet shuffle in the direction of the room so I shove everything under my sweater and rush to the bathroom. Behind the locked door I feel safe and hide my treasures under a large stack of towels.

Late at night when everyone's asleep I tiptoe back to the bathroom and without switching on the light paste my catch in the album then return to our room and place it under my pillow.

Naomi never notices the pillage.

***

Sometimes when the sun isn't too harsh and mother doesn't mind the outdoors and dad can spare time from work and Naomi is in the right mood and baby Bilha is all bouncy and healthy, we go on a trip.

All's quiet outside but I can tell it's already morning because of the birds and the hesitant light. I tiptoe into the kitchen, stand next to the window facing east and look at the back yard. It's large with tall eucalyptus trees and wild brooms marking its square borders.

The sun reveals itself slowly, releasing shy radiant stripes with gentle touches and at once exposes its heart and excites the universe. At four-thirty in the morning everything looks like a dream and I like dreaming.

A small handle rotates the kitchen window. I pull it inwardly, brush off its frame, erase the dust and fingerprints and move it slowly, turning the glass into a mirror to reflect the guava and pomegranate trees outside, now seemingly nearby. When I move the glass pane all the way to the side I'm able to see the wild bushes that grow around the tall clothes-line where the laundry hangs. The world reflected in the glass looks very different, a clean and pretty place, but then Naomi jumps into my head and all at once the window moves real fast and all the flowers and branches turn ugly and distorted.

I keep looking at the first light that winks in the horizon and pretend that our home is different from what it really is. Ours is not a sad home, Naomi is my friend and I'm not afraid of her. But within minutes there's a thrust of yellow accompanied by a dazzling light that turns wild chasing away the soft blueness. The magic is gone and the sun is blinding so I quit the game and step out to the front yard.

The grass looks fresh with the carissa bushes outlining its borders next to the citrus trees with the plums and peaches. All is calm and peaceful. The pitango is no longer a bush. It grew in height and width and by now it's a proud tree that refuses to bear fruits so we use it as a live umbrella.

It's already the end of winter and I'm thinking of the nearby cliffs cloaked in their graying moss. Soon they'll redress in freshly green outfits adorned with millions of golden primrose smiles.

I'm excited. We're going to Tiberius. Dad promised us a dip in the Sea of Galilee and I'm just waiting for mother to get up and pack the food. Bilha is still asleep. Everything is very quiet and very calm.

I shut my eyes and gulp in the fresh breeze and listen to the bird chirps and I want to stay ten forever.

By six the house is noisy. Mother is busy in the kitchen, dad runs in and out of the car, Naomi is her usual self and baby Bilha is already four years old. The car is ready and we're on our way. I'm excited but at the same time I fear Naomi's acrobatic moods. Mother keeps feeding her salami sandwiches and I'm nauseated by the smell but when I roll down the window Naomi says she's cold so the window goes up again and I retch.

We reach an observation post above the city of Tiberius. The sea below is more than just plain blue: bathed in royal hues, its waters magnetize with their arresting beauty. Turquoise follicles adorned with greening sparks flicker against the sun silvering its liquid body to resemble sharpened spears.

I refuse to allow Naomi's bad words to spoil the beautiful sight. The car begins its steep descend into the city and as always, Naomi gets a sudden stomachache and baby Bilha cries and mother is rattled and nervous.

"I don't need this!" she waves her hands in the direction of the back seat.

Dad is quiet.

He parks the car at the water front and Naomi goes to shit. Dad takes hold of Baby Bilha's hand and both dip in the water. Mother, as usual, lights a cigarette and looks for shells. I follow her and at once spot a sparkling turquoise.

"It's a real ancient piece of mosaic... from the Roman period... what an interesting color..." Mother is impressed.

I know precisely what she means; we've already found such special stones in the past scattered in various places, ancient souvenirs that make their finders a hero.

My blue finding irritates Naomi so she develops one of her headaches and we're forced to return home and once again Naomi gets her way.

Mother places my finding in the living room on the marbled slab fronting the bay window and that's an honor all by itself. I feel proud knowing she'll tell everyone who walks into our house that I'm its finder and no one, not even Naomi, will be able to take my finding away from me.

Naomi stares at it and I can smell bad intentions. She reaches down and grabs my finding. Her face turns crooked. I already know what's coming but I can't help myself and walk right into the trap and grab her hand. Naomi sends me to the floor with a kick. Her lips turn into a knife blade stretched across the width of her face in an evil smile. She screams forcing mother and dad to fly instantly to her aid and just like a reset switch, she bursts out crying, gulping breaths and forcing herself to gag as she tells them whatever she feels like telling.

"Punish her! Punish her! She kicked me over here!" she points to her stomach.

Mother throws me an angry look and takes hold of my finding.

"It's confiscated until you learn how to behave!"

"She's lying! I didn't kick her!"

"You're lying!" Naomi sobs and wails.

"I'm not lying!"

"Enough!" mother roars, "You know Naomi mustn't get upset! Do you want her to stop breathing?!"

Dad only shakes his head and I know I've lost my finding though it'll always remain mine.

As soon as mother and dad leave the room Naomi whispers.

"And now I'm 'gonna hold my breath and they'll think you killed me!" her face all twisted.

"Snake! It's not 'gonna help you! Mom and dad aren't stupid!"

"But I can make them believe anything I want!"

"Not this time!"

"'Wanna bet?!"

Naomi holds her breath long enough to turn her face into a balloon on the verge of explosion. Mother and dad hold a three person meeting in our bedroom and for the millionth time clarify that Naomi is to be treated differently and all her wishes obeyed.

Naomi is crowned as winner and my finding is confiscated. Nothing helps, not even when I tell mother and dad how Naomi forced herself to stop breathing.

And by now I know how little my birthright counts, sandwiched to a dot between Naomi and Bilha who continue sharing similar laughs and secrets.

**

It's now past lunch time. Mother's gone to rest for an hour so we must be quiet. When the noon sun threatens to scorch, we're not allowed to go outside so we sit on the large rug in the living room and play board games.

Naomi makes up new rules as she goes along, but there's nothing else to do so I throw the dice. I know I can never win a game with Naomi and I know I'm going to lose this one, too.

My eyes catch a glimpse of a bloated agama inside the empty fireplace. Naomi has her back to it. She leans forward and throws the dice.

"There goes your other soldier!" she flings it off the board and releases a nasty laugh.

The agama's square head resemble that of an iguana. It creeps out of the fireplace then stops in its tracks. I stare at the tiny feet with the horrid scaly skin and long tail. The creature blinks and moves towards us. Then it stops again, stares and shoots out a snaky tongue and runs towards Naomi.

I let out a shriek.

"Agama! Agama!"

Naomi doesn't waste a second and climbs up on the coffee table.

I burst out laughing. Naomi shoots me one of her deadly looks.

My face changes and within a split second resembles that of the silent Buddha sitting cross-legged on the mantelpiece.

***

The sea, cloaked in magical gowns of oscillating blueness with its eternal presence fronting the arched horizon, was seared onto the pupils of our eyes rooting within us an unwavering sense of existential permanence.

Fluctuating with the flow of tides and seasons, the azure waters relented then slid again, unleashing richly iodized waves that crashed against the soft sand, dancing back and forth until swallowed by the darkness of night. Our morning eyes blinked at the majestic brilliance and its sprinkled air, a fragrant breeze saturated with salt that filled our mouths with a grainy feel and imprinted oily stickiness on the tips of our fingers.

The long limbed summers crawled at a slow pace, chaperoned at times by unbearable steamy waves of heat. Nights were heavy with stilted dead air that made us dream of imaginary fans. Winters were shorter but just as extreme, with little heating to keep out the frost from biting us. Only the mellower seasons, those calm and tenderly soft times, were barely noticeable inside our stormy home rushing in and out in a hurry.

It's now winter. We're all in the living room, the single heated room in the house.

The wind howls and the rain whips threatening to break the windows. Mother is in her chair reading while her fingers knit by themselves. I try to keep track of the woolen string twisted around her pinky and pointer, enjoy watching their ups and downs to the beat of the clicking needles. Every so often she stops, reaches for her cigarette and inhales deeply. Bilha is on the carpet playing with her building blocks and small dolls. Dad is sprawled next to her reading a book and chewing relentlessly on what's left of his finger nails. Once in a while he gets up, pokes the wood in the fireplace and sparks up the embers. Naomi is glued to the piano. Her eyes are weird, dreaming into a faraway distance known only to her.

I'm sitting on the carpet in front of the fireplace both arms wrapped around my knees and listen to the silence. The smallest word or movement can ignite Naomi and change the bewitching air. I watch the flames as they dance in blues and greens and twirl with the reds and the fiery yellows well aware of the fragility of the momentary magic.

Naomi moves her head, stares at the piano and touches its keys. We're all tuned in. The music is so soft and beautiful. I keep looking at the fire wondering how such hands can be so mean, two opposing sides to each palm. The sounds that fill the room make me want to cry but no one says a word and I don't want to spoil the magic.

Only a small tail of wood is now left inside the fireplace. Dad rushes outside and within minutes he's back, his face soaked in sweat. The carpet is pushed to the side and the huge trunk lands thunderously on the tiles. Dad's hands are tightly locked around the beast's heavy body; he forces its wet head into the open mouth, smashing it forcefully against the back wall and igniting a storm of fireworks. The room fills with the small crackling sounds of a bonfire, tiny sparks that make the air tremble accompanied by a thin trail of smoke that's sucked up into the chimney.

The hesitant fire sprouts golden tongues in bright yellows snapping tendrils and twigs that try to escape the inferno. The wet log releases hissing sounds to the tune of sprigs and chips that break and snap. When the dead limbs and boughs separate from the block, sparks shoot in all directions applauded by little popping sounds, background rhapsodies to the spectacular sights in rainbow colors.

Strong winter odors come to life carrying with them an enchanted universe composed of nature's tiniest crumbs all glued to the dampened wood. I'm mesmerized by the miraculous granules that fill the air with their strong odors creating a bewitching coziness. The wet trunk is sprawled heavily across the room. Dark chunks of earth hide within shredded pieces of green moss and lichen, tiny oases that are velvety to the touch and richly soiled to lure the bugs and worms as they wiggle their way through the decomposing decay. The tail end of the trunk, sawed off to an uneven roundness, begins to warm up forcing its cold wet insides to stir. The hisses are initially delicate much like porridge on the verge of boiling, but as the noises increase so does the thickening frothing saliva that oozes out of its crevices. Dotted with mysterious particles of nature and a slew of bugs, the foam bubbles and covers the entire face of the wood and sparks it back to life. The smoke sucked into the chimney leaves behind an ancient odor, a trail of a warm cave with a scent that ignites within me a yearning for the family warmth that I seldom knew.

I look at the torn skin on dad's hands. Like Naomi's, they too are stamped with two faces but both of his are good. One is of enormous strength and the other too gentle to hurt a bug or a small child's heart. Dad's face is a sea of perspiration forcing the thick glasses off the edge of his fat nose. He twitches and they bounce up again then slide back down.

"How about some fruits?" he asks mother.

"Yeah…I wouldn't mind…."

Seconds later dad is out again with a big bucket. I'm sad and feel sorry for dad. He always tries so hard to please mother and get her to smile and I want her to do the same and make dad happy because he's always so good to us and we see how much he loves her.

The wind continues to cry and howl and the lights flicker and I know dad must be cold outside in the blackness of night. A terrifying spark shatters the air painting the room in cyanide blue followed by thunderous roars and beating rains. Dad storms back into the room with a bucketful of fresh oranges and pummelos. He leans down and kisses mother on her forehead. She shudders.

"Come on Rachel…honestly… give me a tiny kiss…even half a kiss is enough…don't I deserve it?" he smiles at her, trying to squeeze a drop of warmth out of her.

"Yuck!" again mother shivers and shies away from him and I try to understand if she really feels the way she acts or if she only wants to impress Bilha and Naomi, the only two who are laughing.

We gorge ourselves on fruits in front of the open fire, throw inside curlicued peels and watch them dance in excitement. The air is heavy with intoxicating odors of peeled citrus fruits and the mesmerizing sight of sensuous flames. We're all huddled around the fire and I feel a tingly sense of warmth and belonging even if Naomi is sitting just a few steps away from me. When her mouth is stuffed with food she behaves like everyone else. I'm crouched into a tiny ball but I can tell Naomi is happy now that her mouth is stuffed with fruits. It means that she won't bother me tonight.

***

Grandma Pearle always relied on mother when it came to baking and cooking.

Someone had to cater to the endless beehives of artists, bohemians and politicians who congregated inside the spacious living room with its walls practically erased under crowded paintings.

Grandpa enjoyed the hubbub and laughter of friends and acquaintances who sought his company, his sharp humor and wit and the fun filled atmosphere of their home. But mostly they were inspired by his endless devotion and hard work for the sake of fulfilling the Zionist dream.

Grandpa loved everyone and everything, people, tumult, dogs, geese, chickens, noise and laughter and they all loved him in return, but as far as family matters were concerned, my grandparents were less successful. They simply saved the smallest space left in their hearts for the family, since nothing could possibly compare in its importance to the realization of their dream and the establishment of the new Jewish state.

"Rachel, the Canadian delegation is coming next week so I'll need you to prepare at least three lemon pies and an assortment of cookies... we'll also serve small sandwiches with salami and pickles..."

"What day exactly? I need to know..."

"It doesn't matter...you'll have to help me regardless... so you might as well not make any plans."

Mother never made any plans except those directly connected with grandpa and grandma and the frequent events that took place in their large front yard. Our small kitchen turned into an improvised bakery gone restaurant, with cakes, cookies, and sandwiches spread on all shelves and cabinet tops. I remember mother in the kitchen, frantic with all the baking and cooking for grandma's guests, and realizing that she now has even less time than her usual shortage.

It's already late and both of us are in our room. Naomi whispers as she starts undressing but I know mother can't hear us because she's in the kitchen baking.

"I'll tear out your eye if you dare look and mom won't even notice you have a missing eye!"

I'm in bed with both hands covering my face just as Naomi instructed me, but then I move my fingers like I always do when I watch a scary movie and I see her standing in her new white brassiere sewn by the seamstress and I want so much to have one too. Naomi switches off the light and all I can think about are the things that I don't have. My heart is crammed with words about sacrifice and austerity. Any hints of wants or self-indulgence are considered shameful so I know that I mustn't even think of wanting anything.

Our clothes are never new. They come in brown carton boxes shipped to us from America by our relatives.

"There's a package...let's open it."

I hear mother's announcement and I'm scared because there's no telling what we might find inside. Naomi turns real mean if there's something in the heap that she wants for herself but given her weird shape it doesn't fit her. Mother digs inside and fishes out a purple item covered with pink flowers.

"Here's your dress, Tara!" She holds it out.

"It's ugly."

"This is what they sent us! You should be grateful! Other girls don't have such caring relatives!"

My eyes burn.

"But I don't like purple..."

"You're simply ungrateful!"

Mother storms out of the room and I burst out crying.

"Trash!" Naomi hisses in my direction.

On Passover night mother forces me to wear the hideous cloth. Naomi wears hers, an identical flowery eyesore.

Passover is next week. Grandma takes me to the kitchen and

shows me the box with the special silverware. I'm excited. It's considered an honor to shine them. I carry the heavy box to the front yard, empty the knives, forks and spoons along with other silvered dishes used only on Passover and plant each one in the moist soil under the mango tree. After they're well covered in mud, I pluck them out again, brushing each one thoroughly with a sliced lemon and place them on the side to dry. When they're all dried up and heavily smeared with a grainy mixture of mud and lemon juice, I polish each one with a special cloth that makes them glitter like new. Late in the afternoon I return them all to grandma.

The day before Passover we all congregate inside my grandparents' living room and help attach the tables. We cover them with freshly starched table cloths to create a gleaming white train that stretches across the entire room from the fireplace all the way to the corridor. To its right is my grandparents' bedroom with a large desk and two small alcoves that serve as closets. On the left is the dining room with the small kitchen and pantry where Grandma stores jars filled with special sweets and cookies.

The Passover table is stunningly beautiful with forty-two smiling guests that admire the splendorous setting. Naomi cringes when she hears a good word about the shiny silverware. We're ten cousins all excited over the Afikoman. Naomi is the eldest, I'm next then Bilha. Aunt Abigail has four daughters and Uncle Mordechai two daughters and a son but within a few years our family ties will be totally unraveled and their memory erased thanks to my mother's talent as a seasoned accountant who knew how to tally grudges. Whenever she'd get angry with her sister or brother or one of her nieces or nephews, she'd make sure to note it in her head and demand a painfully stinging compensation. If her demands were not met, she'd simply blot out and erase that person's very existence.

When it's time to hide the Afikoman, Naomi gives us precise instructions. We all know it's useless to argue, so we scramble under the tables, reach grandpa's feet and hide behind his chair. When

Naomi tilts her head from across the room, we reach out with our small hands, grab the Afikoman and bring it to her immediately.

At the end of the Seder, Naomi speaks on our behalf, bargaining and negotiating the present she wants. Grandpa laughs and the guests enjoy it. We stand on the side in utter silence as Naomi makes grandpa promise to give us the present of our choice, though we all know that he won't keep his promise because he's way too busy to take us to the zoo.

***

I envied my girlfriends, those who always played with their sisters. They'd spend the hot hours together under a shady tree talking and lacing necklaces made out of seashells or castor oil seeds. Naomi never did any of that. She'd go off on a tangent and scream or simply hit whatever stood in her way. There was no such thing as a simple conversation or a playful time with her.

When I was very young and still believed mother's every word, I'd get real tense when I'd hear her say.

"Everything is so expensive...we can't afford it...we simply don't have the money."

I was scared of having even less than what we had and worried about it from an early age. Sometimes I'd try to imagine what it's like having so much money so as not to have to think about it all the time.

"Where do rich people live?" I asked dad.

His answer took me to faraway places I didn't even know existed.

"Are we poor?" I asked Naomi.

"Twit! Can't you figure it out for yourself?!"

No. I really couldn't. Maybe because Naomi knew how to work wonders with her screeches, always getting what she wanted.

My parents spoiled Bilha and kept her wrapped up in moth balls.

"Bilha doesn't understand...she's simply too young ... you shouldn't bother her..."

Bilha remained A Baby long after she'd left home. I'm not sure how much exposure she had to Naomi's delusional world or if she really understood anything, but by the time I tried to find out it was too late and there was no one to ask: Bilha sustained a severe head injury with memory loss while travelling in Italy and tripping on the steps of a church. All her childhood memories were erased.

It seems that fate saw to it that all imprints of Naomi's sick world be erased from her mind and replaced by odd shaped nostalgia.

***

"Naomi is all brain. Tara only has the looks and Bilha has it all."

That was the unspoken mantra at home. It must have loomed in the background for a very long time, because throughout my growing-up years I believed it to be true. I'd go on long walks and watch silent ants and fresh blooms wondering how to appraise my worth.

Naomi who was in the habit of taking Baby Bilha to the side and whispering secrets into her small ears, kept it up even when Baby Bilha wasn't a baby anymore and even after we'd already moved to England.

I'm eleven when Dad comes home one day and whispers into mother's ear and the next thing I know we're moving to London. As per British tradition, five year old Bilha is sent to the local church school, while Naomi and I are placed in a strict private school with twelve hundred other girls all dressed up in gray and purple uniforms.

And now I'm glued to Naomi.

The first snowy winter is exciting accompanied by freezing temperatures. Getting to school isn't simple, walking fifteen minutes to the train station followed by a twenty minute train ride then another walk from the train station to school. It's nice only when the sky is dry.

Our mornings begin in the large auditorium. All of us are crouched on the well polished hardwood floor, squeezed together at the foot of the stage as Miss Hog, the headmistress, stands on the podium preaching moral values intended to ameliorate our behavior to perfection.

At the end of her sermon we tune in to a short classical piece played on the gramophone followed, twenty minutes later, by a silent dismissal to the various rooms where our prayers are held.

"The Jewish girls are requested to join Miss Weisman and the rest must join ....." the headmistress notes the specific religious groups with the names of each of the teachers. Most girls belong to the Anglican Church and remain in the auditorium for their prayers.

At ten thirty we're summoned outdoors to the large yard and required to drink a cold bottle of milk. Two hours later we're again in the auditorium that's been transformed by now into a dining room with long rows of tables and chairs spread across its width. One long queuing line, silent and obedient, forms at the entrance to the auditorium. The food, at times, is strange and indefinable but once we've made our choice we're obliged to finish up everything that's on our plate.

Some of the older students chosen as supervisors stare at our every move, ensuring our backs are straight, legs properly crossed, and our elbows don't touch the table. With daring eyes they scrutinize our every move, gawking at the way we hold our fork and knife making sure we take small bites and chew with our mouths closed.

A deadly silence rules the auditorium during lunch.

We all do our best to adhere to the rules at school and avoid Miss Hog's ruler. Even Naomi knows what's best for her, which is why she makes an effort. At least within the school setting. Everything around me is new and I don't have any friends or a sense of belonging. The other girls speak fast with an accent I seldom understand and can barely make out what they're saying.

Three months into the school year we're handed our first report cards. The teachers write that my English has vastly improved and my behavior is good and that I'm very smart. I'm totally overwhelmed and confused because it's not how I feel. Not at all. Nothing's changed on the inside and I can still hear the silent mantra, even though our home is now in London.

Spring shows up for the first time and marks the beginning of my womanhood. It feels strange. Mother never spoke to me about such matters and I don't feel comfortable telling her about it so I figure things out and use sanitary napkins until they're all gone and I have no choice but to tell her.

It's night. Bilha and Naomi are already in bed. I go and stand outside mother's bedroom for a long time but I'm scared and I don't even know why. After much hesitation I tiptoe in and tell her my biggest secret.

"Why didn't you tell me sooner?!"

Mother is angry.

My face burns. I lower my head and walk out the room.

***

When we return home from school in the afternoon, mother is always there. She hates the cold, the depressing sky and doesn't stop complaining about the constant drizzle, the gray air, gray buildings, gray people, gray life and anything else she defines as gray.

As always, she and dad seldom go out anywhere, but one afternoon the three of us find ourselves alone at home.

Naomi pulls Bilha towards her, leans into her ear and shouts in my direction.

"You can't hear this secret!"

"But I also want to hear it!"

The look in her eyes is frightful. She nears me, moves awfully close, her eyes glued onto mine so I can actually read her thoughts all the way through.

"Never!"

I jump back just in case even though I know she's not really a witch but I'm not sure Bilha understands. I stare at the strange things she's doing and the way Bilha is looking at her and it's clear she's confused and doesn't understand Naomi's intentions.

Naomi looks at Bilha and shrieks.

"Catch!"

The small pillow flies in my direction. I duck and Bilha catches it with both hands.

"I caught it!"

Again Naomi shrieks.

"Move!"

Bilha steps to the side.

"Watch this!"

Naomi flings a pair of scissors. Again I duck, cornered behind a desk. Naomi moves closer, leans over the desk and stares at me and I can tell she really means every word that comes out of her mouth. It's because of her eyes, they're suddenly different.

"I hate you!" her voice sizzles.

She picks up a wooden clog and slams it forcefully into my face.

My right eye disappears. I put my hand over it and feel a huge lump all wet and sticky. The pain is so awful it takes my voice away and when the scream is finally released Bilha bursts out crying.

Naomi is scared and says that I bumped my head against the desk and they should move to another room. I don't dare move and remain under the desk until mother and dad return. They look at me with worried eyes.

"Why did you do it?" they ask Naomi in a calm tone.

"She started it!"

Billa's head moves from me to Naomi then back again her small face all wrinkled with worry.

"You'll just have to go to school with a blue mark," mother turns to me.

I'm ashamed of the blue. I keep thinking it'll soon fade out but it just stays and stays until I'm convinced it'll stay forever.

Naomi too stays the same along with her long list of threats.

"If you won't give me what I want, I'll give you another blue one!"

And just like Naomi, I too don't know how not to stay the same.

"You're mean! And you stink!" is all I say, even though by now I know Naomi is out of her mind, really crazy but I can't bring myself to say it.

"Idiot! Can't even find original curses!" Naomi hisses back.

And mother too stays the same even though we're now in London.

"Naomi needs perfect silence!" mother whispers while tiptoeing around.

"Why?"

"She has a headache...but The Baby doesn't need to know..."

I once imitated mother and did the ballerina walk for three days.

***

Now that we're back in Israel I'm scared of attending the same high school as Naomi. Our school is located in the nearby city forcing us to travel on the same bus both ways. The mere thought frightens me. Naomi is now in tenth grade but when I look at her from a distance I see an old woman. I wonder if that's the reason why the boys look at me and not at her. They ask me questions and stare at me in a way that makes me blush. The neighbors also whisper.

"The younger one is real pretty ... and she's nice..."

I decide to implore my parents.

"I want to study drama!"

I had it all figured out. There's only one drama school located in Tel Aviv, an hour-long bus ride away to the central station followed by a brisk twenty-minute walk to school.

The highway to Tel Aviv is in its early stages of construction, allowing for a narrow single lane in each direction. The ride is windy, following the seacoast as it swerves left and right on the freshly paved asphalt. Hugging the course on both sides are untamed hilly dunes with tall, wide shouldered acacia bushes, their branches dotted with yellow pea-sized blossoms. The tiny buds are velvety to the touch and very slow to open up. They remain tightly clenched until the time is ripe and they're ready to unravel themselves. Millions of tiny dots burst into golden blossoms, delicate hair-like plumes that release sensuous aromas at the wee hours of the morning when the sun is barely out and just before it dives into the sea. As the perfumed yellows expose their scents, Nature joins Sea sparking up powerful odors that fill the air with salts and iodine to create a potent fusion. The universe loses control turning into a state of utter drunkenness and there's nothing more exciting or enjoyable than breathing in the intoxicating air twice a day.

"Have you lost your mind?! A drama school?! In Tel Aviv?!" mother shrieks.

Grandpa says.

"Absolutely not! Tara must concentrate on her academics! Theater is for the winds and birds."

I'm confused. I can't understand how someone who walks around with long hair wearing strange clothes and always smelling of paints and turpentine can say such things.

Mother says.

"It's a long and expensive bus ride...you'll have to get up very early ..."

"I don't mind."

"We'll have to think about it."

Dad bites his nails.

I'm anxious to hear their decision but I can't imagine another year with Naomi.

I find myself worrying not only about school but also about the fact that Naomi's illness is the biggest secret in our family. I can't discuss it with mother or dad and surely not with Baby Bilha. My thoughts are wrapped around Naomi like gauze on a festering sore.

I'm already clear about certain facts and I know I'm not as ugly as the ugliest girl in class. The ugliest girl in class is simply one huge lump, but my own nose is straight and I have high cheekbones and when I gather my hair into a ponytail I'm left with a large forehead. I'm five feet seven and my legs are long and I've got mother's tiny waist and full bust. But there's something else going on, strange things that have to do with my friends and I can't understand why they're happening.

Eli is taller than me. He has green eyes and a blond forelock and he's the envy of all the girls. He asks me to meet him after supper.

I'm on the front porch when Eli comes riding his bike.

"'Wanna ride?" he releases casually in my direction

I can barely breathe. The crossbar cuts into my thighs but I don't complain. All I feel is Eli's breath on my long hair and it makes me dizzy. Eli is shy and so am I and there're many silent moments that pass between us. On the way back home Eli helps me settle on the crossbar and our hands meet again. I shut my eyes and all I can think about is a kiss.

We're silent all the way home except for my noisy heart.

"'Wanna ride again on Friday?" Eli asks.

"Sure," I smile shyly and run into the house.

Mother, as usual, is in the living room.

"What's wrong?" she asks.

"Nothing!" I say, but I can't hide my smile.

"Where've you been?"

"I went bike riding with Eli."

Naomi's eyes pierce into me. I feel hot all over. I know she's capable of picking my brain so I turn my back on her and move away.

On Friday evening I'm on the porch again.

"Where are you going?" mother asks.

"Eli is coming."

I wait outside but Eli never shows up.

Later on, at night, when we're already in bed, Naomi's words are convincing.

"You're just one big failure! Your face is repulsive, your eyes are mean and everyone knows how dumb you are. Even your friends have you figured out by now! That's why they don't return!"

And at once I realize that I'm ugly and my reddish hair is a mess and my breasts are too big and my brain's the size of a small pea just like Naomi always says.

My head droops even lower when my wishes are denied and I'm sent to the same high school as Naomi. I have no choice but to force my parents into changing their mind.

I stand in front of the two-storied building staring at the locked gate with its chipped green paint and I see a jail house. I try to convince myself that it's only a school but I know there are forty-four students neatly packed in each class, seven classes tightly sealed in each grade-level and the sheer thought of how tight things will be over the next four years makes me feel all choked up and panicky. I'm sure I won't survive the year so I work on a plan of my own.

I wait a few weeks and get acquainted with the routine. The teachers are so busy they rarely check the attendance list so I give it a try, one day, and simply walk out the gate. Ten minutes later I'm on the beach crouched under a cliff. After making sure no one followed me, I shut my eyes and surrender to the gentle sun.

It's October and the air is fresh and lovely and the beach is flooded with sea shells. Some are rigged others flat-faced, no two identical in color or pattern. I sift through them and stash an occasional odd one inside my bag. The sea releases into the air spicy aromas that add flavor to my sandwich. I listen to the rolling waves and join their games. They visit my feet and tickle me so I smile and they run back then hide behind stronger ones. My feet skirmish playfully with the white sand, gentle sandpaper that allows for a soft grainy feel.

Around noon I head back home. The thought of being caught scares me but when I reach home no one says a word. Not a word. And the following day I realize that I wasn't missed at school, either. But my sense of euphoria is soon replaced by that of disappointment. The really bad students, those who skip school regularly are chased and reprimanded by the teachers but no one mentions my absence. I don't complain because I'm enjoying my once-a-week-regular-day-off-from-school that soon turns into two with an additional one or more in between.

My special days of freedom are splashed with golds and blues and by now a month has gone by and it's a glorious November with tender warm air. The weather cooperates and the gentle brass holds all the way into the month of December. When the teachers inquire, every so often, about a missed class or two, I fake stomachaches, leg aches, earaches or any other made-up ache and I even try some of Naomi's pains until the lies come out easily.

Even the teachers seem to enjoy my excuses. They laugh and say I'm original and smart but they'd like me to take school more seriously. But their kind considerations only work against my plan.

The first report card at the end of the semester still reflects my previous days of glory and the grades I received at the school in London.

"It's a new school setting... very different from the one in London... she needs time to adjust..." they add in handwriting on the side.

I'm scared of being stuck in that school so I work diligently on my days of absence. Each new day fills me with excitement in anticipation of something which is neither definable nor expected, an inexplicable sense of freedom and care-free self indulgence that only spurs me to continue with my plan.

As I sit on the grainy sand, my feet flirting with the gentle waves, I try to figure out the system that enables someone like me to get away with what I'm doing. I never do homework, I don't read books and I disregard all given instructions.

And now that the school year is coming to an end I fear the outcome of my actions yet hoping for its success. I'm on my way home with the report card in my hand, smiling outwardly but storming from within. Stirring inside of me are shame and pride that quarrel with each other over the thirteen "Fail" grades in my report card and the one "Excellent" in physical education.

Nearing our front yard I see Dr. Nate's car, my parents' friend whom they refer to as 'Yes!Sir!' given the way in which he shares his eyes with the air above while using his voice to make the people around him feel worthlessly small. His face, smeared with a permanent forgiving smile, only reinforces the sense of arrogance and contempt he radiates. When asked a question, his head tilts backwards pushing his chin sideways and up some. His clinic, overflowing with patients too fearful to complain, reeks of chlorine and other disinfectants.

I try to guess why he's here.

The front door is wide open with only a screen to guard against insects. I can smell mother's chicken in the oven with the usual weekly baked cookies that fill the large jar in the pantry.

Dr. Nate's words sound above the music and the daily news blaring from the radio.

"You asked for my opinion, Rachel. I think that Tara is mentally disabled and her overall abilities are quite limited! She's incapable of handling academics! She needs a special training school so that she can learn how to earn a living and survive independently. And the sooner you accept this fact the better off she'll be!"

Mother is silent. She doesn't release a single word.

I turn around and head for my usual hide out.

The castor oil plants grow in various places, but I prefer the large bushes just past the eucalyptus trees in the direction of the dunes and the wadi below. I sit quietly and let my fingers sift through the soft sand as I replay the conversation I'd had with my teacher.

"There's no way you're 'gonna pass into tenth grade with such a report card! And wipe that smile off your face! It's shameful! Really shameful!"

I return home after dark.

"Where have you been?" mother asks.

"Outside!"

My throat is swollen with anger but no one seems to care. I tell her I'm not hungry and mother resumes her knitting. Bilha is sprawled on the rug next to dad who continues reading. Naomi's face is her usual permanent smirk. I want to be by myself so I go into the bedroom but Naomi trails me and I'm forced back into the crowded living room and I don't know how to rid myself of the awful anger that's inside of me. Mother's thunderous silence, much like Dr. Nate's words, continue to echo inside my head.

Two days later mother and dad are summoned urgently to the school. When they return I'm asked into the kitchen for a serious talk.

"We've decided to give you another chance," mother speaks while dad just sits there, "You can study drama but only if you promise to repeat the year and try to do better next year!"

I don't say a word but now I know mother and dad aren't as smart as I thought they were. I don't mind repeating ninth grade as long as I don't have to watch Naomi's face all day.

Once again I'm in ninth grade at the new school still haunted by Dr. Nate's whipping words and mother's awful silence.

The ‵Renanim‵ school, located in Neve Tzedek in the southern part of Tel Aviv, was set on the grounds of a privately owned large villa belonging to an art lover and a philanthropist who donated his house to the municipality on the condition that it be used as a school for the arts. The municipality accepted the gracious donation and arranged for old buses to be converted into classrooms scattering them randomly throughout the back yard. Most teachers were famed artists who went out of their way to expose us to the studies of the classics enriching our outlook on the arts and contributing from their own personal experiences. In later years, several of its graduates went on to become Israel's prominent actors, play writers and novelists.

It doesn't take long for me to recalculate my worth within the frame setting of school, concluding that I am at least equal to my classmates. By the end of the first year my grades are as boring as Naomi's but when mother and dad don't comment on my sudden metamorphosis, their silence only reaffirms Naomi's words.

"Don't even try to compare your grades with mine!"

"But I also got straight ..."

"But your so called A's are worth only half of mine! Your school is designed for defective creatures like yourself!"

Her mouth spits venom and hate. But her words only ignite within me a spiteful determination to prove her wrong.

From the distance of age and time I realize that I've always had a stubborn fragment planted within me but I didn't always identify its positive sides, nor did I know how to use it effectively.

***

There are six of us sitting on the hot beach licking popsicles and enjoying the waves. We race each other into the water with the swiftness of young teenagers then splash and dip and at once I feel the force of dark smiley eyes. I return the smile and when Zvika asks to meet him on Friday I agree.

We stroll along familiar paths and settle under the tall mulberry tree in the school yard. Zvika puts his arm casually on my shoulders and when his lips touch mine I'm convinced I've met the love of my life.

"Can I see you again next week?" Zvika holds my hand.

I'm dizzy, smiling outwardly and exploding with excitement and happiness from within.

Zvika sees me home and kisses me once more in the entrance

of our front yard. When we part I feel drunk, carrying with me the memory of the first lips that ever touched mine, bursting with a crazed energy and the excitement of a first young love.

Everything around me seems magical and beautiful as I count every hour of every day replaying the feel of Zvika's kiss and I can barely wait to see him again.

On Friday night I stand on the porch with a stomach full of aches and knots but by ten o'clock I realize Zvika isn't coming.

I'm all alone in our room. Naomi is out studying with a classmate and there's no one that can hear my cries. The pain is so fierce that I swear to shy away from boys.

***

Summer's warm rays stroke the trees the blooms and the industrious ants. The evening hours are lighter with fresh sea breezes and smells of tanned young bodies and hearts. We're all excited at the start of the summer vacation and congregate in the old school yard that still holds its nostalgic magic for us and exchange anecdotes from the different high schools. Naomi is home, enjoying her books and encyclopedias and conversing with the walls while spitting nasty remarks at the rest of the world.

The atmosphere at home is bad, even more so than usual. Naomi doesn't quit arguing and picking fights with everyone. She screams and shouts and mother and dad don't know what to do. I hear them whisper but nothing happens until Naomi loses control.

It's nearing dusk and Bilha is out front playing with her girl friends.

"I want blue eyes! I hate my black ones!"Naomi roars again.

"But you can't change the color of your eyes," mother tries logic which only exacerbates the situation.

"Of course you can! I want contact lenses! I want blue contact lenses!"

Mother and dad exchange glances.

"I wish I could have given you blue eyes," dad forces a smile.

"You could have given me gray ones! Like your own!"

I'm sitting on the side listening to the crazed words that bounce back and forth and feel that something awful is about to happen. It's the waiting part that's scariest.

"If I don't get blue lenses I'm 'gonna jump off the tallest building in Tel Aviv! I can't stand my eyes! I can't stand them!"

"You mustn't even think of doing such an awful thing!" mother's voice is faint.

"I'll think about whatever I want to think!"

"Enough!" mother whimpers, "Enough!"

"Stop telling me what to do!"

I move slowly out of the living room and into our bedroom.

"We're only trying to help you...we don't want anything bad to happen to you..."

"It's enough that you bore me! You don't need more than that!" her voice is way up the ladder.

"But..."

"Shut up! Just shut your mouth!"' she spits in mother's direction, "I either get blue eyes or I jump!"

"Do you even have an idea how much contact lenses cost?! And I'm not even talking about colored ones...it's a brand new thing...I don't even know if they have them over here..."

"I'm not interested in your excuses! I don't want these black ugly ones like yours **dear mother! I hate my eyes! I hate them!**"

Naomi doesn't quit until her throat is dry.

I'm sprawled on the bed listening to mother's cries. Dad is quiet.

After spending long hours screaming and hollering and filling the house with lunacy, Naomi picks herself up and storms out slamming the door behind her.

Four days later Naomi gets her contact lenses.

I can't even imagine how much they cost. I try to understand how my parents were able to afford them, because the only thing I kept hearing at home were mother's constant complains about not having enough money.

I'm scared of meeting Naomi's new eyes so I get early into bed. Naomi shuts the light but I can feel madness wandering inside the room.

"Ah!"

Naomi pokes my hand. I jump out of bed.

"What's wrong?!"

I have no idea what time it is.

Naomi releases a wild laughter. She shines a flashlight on her blue ones and opens wide a stenchy mouth. I shriek and run out the room.

Mother says I should sleep in the living room. On the carpet. Naomi is dangerous and I'm scared. The only thing separating the living room from our room is a thin glassed door. Naomi leaves a slit open and I can hear her raging all night long, swearing angrily and talking to herself. I can't fall asleep.

The following day mother gives Naomi's condition a name and adds hesitantly.

"You've got to understand... it's not that Naomi's really mean ... on the contrary... she has a good heart... it's just that ...she has some personality issues... she wants to do harm...but only to herself... she's destructive...but only towards herself..."

I'm not sure mother understands the words that come out of her own mouth and I don't really care what Naomi's condition is called. She scares me and I never know what I should or shouldn't do when she's around. Mother and dad also don't know what to do but that's never discussed at home. Not ever. Not in our home.

***

70

The new school year has just began but all I want to do is run away and escape the madness at home, the crazed after school hours when Naomi returns home draped in her moodiness dragging along stenches with cusses and wicked words.

The New Year holiday of Rosh Hashana is two weeks away and I'm already dreading the long school vacation that follows.

Today is one of those moody days. Naomi is angry but in addition she also hits everything that stands in her way. In the evening she enters the room, shuts the blinds, draws the curtains, refuses to take a shower or open a window or switch on the light. Wrapped up in her madness, she buries herself under the blankets and remains there for four solid months.

She stays inside the room. She doesn't go to school. She doesn't talk. We don't even see her. I move into the extra room that serves as mother's tiny workroom and squeeze into Billa's old bed which barely fits along the short wall.

Our hushed house threatens to explode under the weight of whispers and careful tiptoeing. No one is allowed to mention Naomi who is deeply tangled within her madness.

"Everything's going to be okay Bilha...it'll be okay...Naomi only needs some rest."

Mother, as usual, tries to iron out every wrinkle.

Bilha listens but I have no idea what she's thinking about or how much she really understands.

Bilha has lots of friends that constantly buzz around her. They ride bikes together, bead necklaces out of castor seeds, go to the public pool, listen to music, laugh and fool around like other eleven year olds.

I escape to Maya's house or just roam around and go on long walks that allow me to think quietly.

Mother and dad are worried. They don't want Bilha to know about Naomi's illness afraid it might make her sad or infect her with similar aches and pains.

I hear mother whisper to dad.

"Tara always knows how to take care of herself...we don't need to worry about her...she's okay..."

My mouth is bursting from all the words that I'm not allowed to release into the air, painful words that sit at the tip of my tongue and threaten to bury me under their heavy weight. I try to find a way to tell mother that I'm scared and confused and that I don't know what to do with all the secrets we're not allowed to discuss.

When we're alone mother repeats.

"Shshshshsh...don't say a word....the neighbors might hear..."

But I know the neighbors are too far and they can't hear us.

***

Spring transforms our yard into a breathtaking carpet of brilliant colors. The air threatens to explode with intoxicating fragrances of citrus blooms mixed with jasmine and magnolia, creating an air of debauchery orchestrated by bees, flies, grasshoppers and nature's miniatures of sorts.

There's a party on Friday night.

Mother says.

"Let's go into town and get you a new dress."

It sounds like a dream.

Mother takes me on the bus, only the two of us, and tells me I can choose a new dress but I'm not sure what she means because I've never bought new clothes before. We visit all the stores and I get confused with too many beautiful things.

I'm thirsty so mother buys me a glass of plain soda water. There's only one more store left near the market.

I look in the window and see a beautiful dress but mother says I have expensive taste so I need to choose a different one. I don't understand what she means but the white one stays in the window and I get to choose an orange one and when I try it on I feel like a queen.

"I'm happy!" I tell mother on the way home but I don't hug or kiss her. It's not something we do at home.

On Friday night I put on the new dress but when I look at myself in the mirror I know Naomi won't like what I'm seeing. She's in the living room by the piano, so I quickly cross the room and hurry out the door.

Maya's house is a five minute walk from mine. The gramophone sounds Paul Anka followed by the Platters. My heart beats fast. Eli approaches me with a smile and asks to dance. My face blushes but I can't refuse him. As he wraps his arms around my waist I try not to show him how I feel because I still carry with me the bitter taste of my hurt pride.

When the party is over Eli says he has something important to tell me.

I stride alongside of him and listen.

"It happened two days after our first date... I was playing soccer in the schoolyard with my friends and we stayed there until it got dark. When we reached the school gate Naomi was there. She said she has an urgent message for me so I thought you'd sent her. I asked her about the message but she said she'd tell me once we reached the old cypress trees behind the art room. It was already pitch dark. She put a finger over her mouth and let out a 'shshshshs' then grabbed my arm and told me to be quiet. When we reached the small wooden clearing she began limping. I asked her what's wrong but she simply leaned on me...kind of hovered over me and pushed us both to the ground and then...then she loosened her hair. She told me to move closer so she could deliver the message. When I moved ...she lowered her head and pushed herself on top of me.... she just... pushed herself... later on she warned me never to go near you again. I'm so sorry Tara...I didn't mean to...I'd like ..."

"I'm not interested!"

"But I didn't mean to..."

A million things buzz all at once through my mind, connecting the strange incidences of the past two years. I'm angry and hurt and my eyes sting and all I want to do is punch Naomi.

When I'm back home all curled up in bed, I start thinking clearly about Eli and Zvika and all the others who vanished abruptly. As faces and events flash by, new fears spark up and gnaw at my realization that Naomi might never quit.

***

It starts early on a Friday morning. Bilha has already left the house on her way to school and I'm about to leave, too, but mother puts a finger to her mouth and gives me the sign.

So I wait.

"Don't touch me! Don't you dare touch me!"

Naomi kicks and screams. She cusses and spits and flaps her arms in dad's direction.

"What's going on?" mother asks.

"You piece of shit!" Naomi is in mother's face, **"You're shit! A piece of Shit! Fucking mother! I hate you! I'll show you what fucking means! You're sick! You're all sick! Look what you brought into this world! I didn't ask to be born!"** Her voice screeches.

Naomi goes on screaming and mother doesn't stop crying.

"Where did I go wrong?! Tell me where?!" she howls.

"Look in the mirror! Look!"

Naomi is in the living room, slumped down on a low wooden bench facing the empty fireplace. Mother and dad converse with her back. Naomi's cusses continue, spitting obscenities in between my parents' back-and-forth's.

I step into the corridor, crouch on the floor and wait. As the minutes pass my fears grow.

Naomi again stands on her feet, kicking and screaming and trying to shove her fingers into mother's face then turns to dad.

"If you don't calm down we'll have to hospitalize you!" mother shouts above the din.

"You ugly thing! You don't deserve to be called a mother! You're loathsome! A loathsome creature!"

"Tara!" Mother screams, "Come quickly! Grab her hands!"

I help dad hold Naomi down and by the time she's all bundled up and squashed in a corner mother is wet with tears. Dad takes me to the side and asks that I join him.

I see his eyes and I don't ask any questions.

"I'll stay home and wait for the Child..." mother's voice keeps breaking.

The car is bursting with one long aching silence. Dad and I are on the way to the psychiatric hospital in Pardessiya, a remote place with only scarce houses along the way. It takes us nearly an hour to reach the row of gray buildings huddled together and fenced behind barbed wires.

Dad parks the car on a sand trail that leads to a large and partially open gate stained by rust and peeling paint. Two men and a woman head in our direction. The men are wearing filthy underwear. The woman has on torn nylon stockings and loose shorts. Nothing else. They move aimlessly and pass us by. Their hollowed eyes stare in the direction of the fence where the garbage oozes out of rusty barrels next to the gate.

We cross the gate and enter the hospital grounds. All around us are frightful looking barbed wires. Dad holds my hand as we squeeze together on the narrow path.

A barefooted emaciated looking man wearing dirty light blue pants approaches us. I squeeze dad's hand. The man leans towards me and begs.

"Cigarettes...cigarettes..."

Dad squeezes my hand and whispers.

"Just keep on walking."

I wipe my eyes.

We near the first building. A toothless woman leans into me and mumbles. Her yellowing fingers hold the burnt tip of a cigarette.

A small sign appears in front of us: "Chief Psychiatrist."

I cling even more into dad until we reach the office.

"Wait here... outside."

Dad disappears behind a door that refuses to shut. Only a small slit is left open. I don't dare move. All around are strange looking people. They move oddly in slow motion and keep asking me for cigarettes. I can hear the psychiatrist repeat his words and I can understand what he's saying but I can't hear dad's voice.

A tall lean man with both lips sealed inside his mouth nears the door. He pushes it slightly with his finger then looks at me and bursts into a crazed roar, backs up and pushes it again releasing a hideous laughter.

I can now hear dad through the open crack.

"But my wife can't cope... and we have another young daughter at home... we're afraid ...what she might do....yes, also to others... ....."

"I'm sorry but I can't help you. It's Friday and the Sabbath is in shortly... I'm the only one here on duty ... I simply can't take in a new patient... you'll have to return on Sunday and then we can have her evaluated ..."

Dad wipes his eyes and the psychiatrist adds.

"But if things are as bad as you say...you can request an emergency order from the court ... have her forcefully hospitalized ..."

The door opens and dad walks out slowly. He again coughs and wipes his eyes with the back of his hand. I wipe my own and dad takes my hand in his and once more we're on the narrow pavement walking silently towards the gate. I try to keep myself as thin as possible and I don't dare look sideways but the touches on both sides make me feel dirty.

Dad is silent and I can tell he's at a loss.

When we reach the car dad says that the psychiatrist doesn't think Naomi is posing a physical threat. Not yet, at least. I don't understand what they're waiting for because Naomi's already hurt me so many times in the past and if that's not a physical threat I don't know what else needs to happen before they institutionalize her. I'm already old enough to understand the hidden secrets that mother and dad refuse to discuss but I only wish they'd stop whispering and playing games.

Dad is silent all the way to the police station. We go in and stand in line surrounded by handcuffed bodies that cuss and spit and push and shove. They don't quit so we move to the side and wait our turn. When the officer calls us, dad bursts out crying, he can't get a word out and returns to the bench. I try to explain the situation but the officer only stares at me and doesn't say a word. I apologize for dad's crying and beg him to help us. His eyes bounce between me and dad then back again.

He raises his eyebrows.

"How old are you?"

I'm nearing sixteen but I'm scared of talking to the officer. I try to explain the situation with Naomi but I'm not sure how or what to tell him. The officer listens. When he asks questions he looks at dad who's sitting on the bench all crouched up in his sorrow. I know Naomi needs to be hospitalized but the officer says it requires a special court order.

I look at dad's face and I want to cry. The officer can't help us.

"It's already late today. You'll have to wait until Sunday."

We return home empty handed. Mother's face is grim.

"D'you want to tell me that you couldn't even find **one** person to help you?! Not even **one**?!" She lashes out at dad.

Naomi fills the house with shrieks and the three of us watch over her throughout the night and following day.

I have no idea of Bilha's whereabouts.

Early on Sunday morning Naomi is forced into an ambulance and hospitalized in a closed psychiatric ward at Tel Hashomer hospital.

Mother and dad continue with their daily routines and just as before they don't discuss the situation.

Once a week they go visit her and return home sadder than before. And only on occasion, when the three of us are alone at home, they mention drugs, medications, electric shocks and other forms of treatments. It scares me.

Mother cries and says that she can't understand Naomi's complaints.

"Why does she keep blaming me and dad for all her problems? We don't deserve it. We were always such good parents...she should appreciate everything we're doing for her..."

Several silenced weeks go by before I'm summoned to the kitchen.

"It's important!" they say.

The three of us are seated around the table. Mother and dad exchange glances until mother says.

"Naomi told the doctors that you're to blame for all her problems ...you're the cause of it all...so they want you to come and talk to them..."

I feel blood coloring my face. I have no intention of being sucked into Naomi's sick world. Dad doesn't utter a word. I think he understands Naomi's condition better than mother who tries to convince me that it can only improve the overall situation at home.

"It'll help all of us!" she says.

"No!"

"Just talk to them...they won't hurt you... they only want to talk to you... get to know you..."

I refuse to say another word.

Two months later the three of us are on our way to visit Naomi. The air inside the car is tense with endless instructions.

"Remember not to ask her about it... or about what the doctors said...and don't say things that might aggravate her...also don't mention any of her treatments or medications ... just listen to what she has to say...but don't ask her why...and in general don't ask too much... just let her be. Show her that you're interested and let her tell you only what she wants to tell..."

I don't understand mother's insistence that I come with them.

The hospital grounds are comprised of small pavilions, low structures that are scattered in total disarray and form a dilapidated gray view on the verge of collapse. A bitter taste fills my mouth. Dad says there're plans to enlarge the place and turn it into a big modern hospital. A twisted sidewalk leads us from the sandy trail where dad parked the car to the entrance of the psychiatric ward. Fearful and hesitant I follow behind.

The door opens. A strong stench slaps my nose, a nauseating mixture of mold and urine dipped in rust and disinfectants. All around us are people who resemble shadows moving in frightfully slow motion. I turn my head in the direction of the corridor, an endless linoleum path dotted with brown spots. Mother and dad are already familiar with the place and continue without hesitation until they reach the kitchen where Naomi is sitting on a chair looking like one big sore. Her body is bloated from anger and medications and her filthy hair resembles overused steel wool. She doesn't react. She stares at us through murky looking eyes that don't see a thing and continues to mumble senseless words.

Mother wipes her tears. Dad is in a lost, sad world. There's nowhere to hide or run to. My back is against the kitchen wall forcing my eyes on Naomi. I don't dare look away, even when she picks herself slowly off the chair, staggers on her slippered feet and drags her bloated body into the corridor where she settles into another chair with her back to us. It's the waiting that's hardest, one long trail of meaningless time. We continue to stand and wait. Long minutes pass before mother and dad decide to leave but the hospital smell with Naomi's eyes are relentless and haunt me for years to come.

Eight months later, when Naomi returns home, it's as though she'd never left. Everything seems as usual, though she's even more emaciated than before and her black and gray skirts are narrower pinching her thighs to the point where she can barely move. The shirts she wears resemble a second layer of skin forcing her breasts to look enormous and when she puts on her black nylon stockings with the line going all the way up and steps into her high heeled shoes, Naomi resembles grandma's broom, the one made of twigs with which she sweeps the back porch.

I'm glad we don't look like sisters.

***

Springtime practices its seasonal zigzags. It's fun lounging on the sandy beach with friends enjoying the soft warmth of the sun.

I keep thinking of Naomi. No one knew where she'd been these past two weeks until her dramatic reappearance two nights ago, when the door flung open at four in the morning and the familiar voices woke us up.

Mother keeps mumbling.

"If only the army would have agreed to take her..."

But I'm not surprised that it hadn't and I dread to think what will happen when my turn comes.

Naomi's disappearances are as unpredictable as Naomi herself. Mother doesn't stop crying and Dad's silences echo the melancholy atmosphere at home. I try not to think about Naomi all the time but I never know what to expect when I open the front door. Strange things happen in our family and they're always connected, in one way or another, to Naomi.

It's my seventeenth birthday but I don't expect any surprises. Naomi develops one of her headaches and mother is quick to explain.

"I'm sorry Tara...you'll get your birthday cake another time... when Naomi feels better..."

I'm sick and tired of the excuses. If I'll ask mother to explain the correlation between Naomi's headache and my birthday cake she'll say I'm egotistic, and that my questions are only meant to aggravate her, and dad will ask why I'm upsetting mother with my questions, and I'll argue back and mother will cry and dad will say that I'm selfish and he hopes that one day I'll understand what they're going through.

I'm not interested in what they're going through. I'm too busy trying to survive Naomi and all I want is to be left alone.

It's evening and I'm glad to find the room we now share again, empty. I open wide the large French window that overlooks the front yard and get into bed.

A light wind breezes through the window flooding the room with softness and the whispers of night. The air flutters taking on rounded shapes inspired by crickets, frogs and the moon's silent whispers and its glittering light.

I'm sprawled in bed, my head next to the window with eyes lingering on the front yard. A velvety light embraces the universe spilling its magical hues gently over petals and foliage turning the front lawn into a shimmering blanket of magic. I shut my eyes and tune to nature's soft strokes and soothing melodies.

Strange noises awaken me. I jump out of bed stand by the window and gawk at the silvery radiance that glows over leaves and grass. Tiny geranium buds salute the beauty of the mesmerizing light. Staring at them from their tallness are the citrus trees stretching their elongated arms and dancing like fairies to the beat of the percolating air. A cat releases threatening yowling. It springs out of the bushes, its tail swaying to the rhythm of the moans coming from the left side of the lawn. I turn my head and see Naomi's bare back with the long loose hair wiggling and slapping her nakedness. Her legs are elsewhere twisted around another silhouette while her frame wallows grotesquely forming an inseparable shape of hands and legs.

She groans.

"Did you enjoy it, Zvika?"

The wind is gentle sending small touches to my wet face. I move away from the window and feel my heart turn into ice.

***

Seasons changed and years went by but our home remained the same.

After the army rejected her military service, Naomi turned into loathsome chaos, a muddled mass that sought to control everyone. I could barely wait to be drafted to the army at the end of the Six Day War.

I'm on night duty at the base. There are five of us manning the phones. The job is interesting and sensitive requiring immediate response in case of any activity. Things are casual tonight with ample time for jokes and small talk. The three guys are busy exchanging notes about a certain slut they've all shared in different places on various occasions. They don't mind the two of us sitting on the side listening to the smallest of details. It makes my face burn. I can't believe anyone is capable of doing such things, even if she's a slut.

A sudden activity makes us all jump into action. One of the guys spits out a last word.

"She's one of a kind that screwy Naomi from Bo-AchaYam! You should have seen what she did in Eilat..."

And my breath stops.

When I try to sharpen my recollections and figure things out from the distance of time, I'm faced with remembrances stamped by Naomi's oddities and bizarre events, dark nights that are deeply rooted inside my head. It's not just one night. There's an entire trail of delusional nights.

It's two in the morning. Mother picks up the phone on the first ring.

"Oh...oh no...oh ...yes, of course...we're on our way..."

Dad's voice is muffled. He coughs and his voice is choky.

"He said an hour...we have an hour to get there otherwise he's calling the police..."

I'm already used to it. I jump out of bed and get dressed.

Dad appears in the doorway with watery eyes.

"Naomi is in Tel Aviv. We'll leave within two minutes, okay?"

It's not the first time that someone complains about Naomi in the middle of the night. The complaints are always about the riots she creates with the shrieks and mad behavior, but worst of all is the fear of the unknown that's always there.

Mother cries.

"I'll stay here with the Child."

Bilha is fourteen but she still calls her a child and uses her as an excuse for her dysfunction as a mother.

Dad and I are in the car.

"I'll stop by Moti's house just in case there's a need..."

We both know that when it comes to Naomi the need is always there.

After a short ride dad stops the car, runs out and knocks on his best friend's door. Seconds later the three of us are in the car. We only have a short hour to reach Naomi before the police get her.

Dad reaches the main road to Tel Aviv. Despite its long years of construction, the narrow course is still incomplete forming a single swerving lane that makes for a mere alternative route. The car is filled with scary silences we each hold within. There's no telling how it might end up this time.

The silence is broken only when dad coughs and dries his eyes.

"What time is it?" he again asks in the entrance to Tel Aviv.

"We still have ten minutes."

"Remember, Moti... she's in his apartment threatening to jump out the window. We should try and talk to her..." dad explains adding instructions I've heard more than once.

He again coughs. Moti places a hand on his shoulder.

"It's 'gonna be okay, Ariel...everything's 'gonna be okay..."

I wipe my eyes for the umpteenth time. It's never okay where Naomi is concerned and as always, the situation only repeats itself and even worsens.

The car stops in front of the building. Naomi's obscene shrieks cut through the silenced night. Dad parks the car close to the pavement and asks that I take his place at the wheel.

"Make sure you're ready, Tara... as soon as we bring her out start the engine."

The entrance to the building is flooded with neighbors, most of them wearing pajamas. Dad and Moti hurry inside the building. I'm in the car. Waiting.

"She threatened him," someone says.

"He told me..." the man lowers his voice and the entire group bursts out laughing. My face burns.

Soon the voices change and the neighbors turn angry.

"Enough! I'm sick and tired of her! They should get that lunatic out of here... get her the hell out!"

"Yeah! We don't want her here in the building!"

"They should institutionalize her! That's all! She needs to get the hell out!"

The neighbors continue long after dad and Moti disappear up the stairwell.

When Naomi screams the neighbors turn silent then regroup.

Ten minutes go by. Again they tune into every word then burst out giggling. Every so often someone laughs out loud. I stare ahead through the front window and imagine things that will never happen. My thoughts go wild and at once are lost. I again dry my tears.

Naomi doesn't quit. She continues hollering and wailing giving the neighbors more reasons for laughter and ridicule. When her screams get louder I know the hard part is about to begin. I'm scared. Naomi cusses and foams. She spits and bites and her wailings, like the stairwell, go up and down and I know she'll soon cross the entrance and reach the car. I can see her in my left side mirror being dragged. She's wearing a loose singlet and underwear. Dad and Moti support both her sides with their strong arms trying to get her forcefully into the car. She fights them all the way but when she reaches the car, her ugly head with its wild straw-like hair, is stuck next to mine.

"You stinking bitch! I'll make you pay for this!" she spits into my face, "I'll kill you for this! I hope someone fucks the hell out of you! You're the reason for all my problems! I want you dead! **Dead!"**

I wipe away the spit with the tears and concentrate on the road ahead.

"And you!" her evil eyes are on dad, "You'll be sorry you ever bore me! You son of a bitch!" she spits on him a mouthful of foul saliva.

The following day Naomi is institutionalized for four months.

DARIEN

At the end of my military service Naomi is released from the psychiatric ward and returns home laden with the usual problems. Mother and dad are sad but as always, they don't discuss the situation.

Mother places a finger on her lips and whispers.

"Hushshshshshsh, we don't want The Child to know..."

I find myself lacking any wants or wishes and try to understand what I should do next but I haven't the faintest clue. Maya, my closest friend, is self absorbed in her own troubled world and I'm afraid of being sucked into a similar apathy.

I decide to try my luck and apply to the Hebrew University of Jerusalem, a three hour drive from home.

My enormous insecurity is stashed under a long mane of shiny reddish hair that reaches below my shoulders. I have long legs with feminine curves and when guys look straight at me, my eyes quickly escape to the floor and my fingers jump to the top button of my shirt, scared they might find out that Naomi's my sister.

When I get accepted to the university mother lets out a sigh of relief. Dad says.

"But it won't make you any smarter."

They keep reminding me how little we have and I know I can't ask for any help so I find a position as a receptionist in a hotel and when things get tight I babysit my neighbor's spoiled kids or write addresses on thousands of envelopes with my neat handwriting.

Juggling between my various jobs and my studies keeps me busy from six in the morning until midnight. I'm very careful how I spend my money ensuring I have enough to pay for food and board and cover my tuition. The bus ticket is expensive forcing me to spend lonely weekends in the tiny dorm room.

On Friday nights I use the public phone downstairs to call home and end up listening to mother's complaints.

"You're lucky not to be here...or see what Naomi's putting us through...stay in Jerusalem for as long as you'd like..."

But I don't feel lucky and I wish I didn't have a reason to stay away from home.

Weekends in the dorm room ache with loneliness. Three buildings serve as student dorms but they all empty on Thursday and fill up again on Saturday night. Among those who stay behind are a handful of foreign students and those studying medicine who are forever glued to their chairs.

Sometimes there are dances or gatherings downstairs inside the large TV room that we all share. Occasionally we go hiking as a group and visit the market place in the Old City of Jerusalem. When guys ask me out I accept their invitation for the sake of feeling wanted but I don't really understand what love is about or how to build a loving relationship. I prefer to choose situations that are free of risks or emotional commitment.

***

My three years as a student come to an end. I pack up my few belongings in two large bags and return home.

"I'm done!" I tell mother and dad, "Except for one more exam in two week's time..."

If there was a reaction it didn't register in my mind.

Over dinner mother asks.

"So what are you 'gonna do with your degrees?"

English literature and theater studies enabled me to dream and not have to face questions about my future, but something else has caught my interest.

"I'd like to go on studying but... something that really interests me."

Mother, dad and Naomi look up from their plates. Bilha is already out of the house, serving in the army.

"Dentistry!"

"Idiot!" Naomi spits out.

"What for?!" Mother asks.

Dad raises his eyebrows.

The days that follow remind me of why I'd left home in the first place.

"D'you really want to study dentistry?" Dad asks.

"Very much so! I've already applied and I have a good chance of getting accepted."

Dad's hand goes up and down like a fly swatter and within a split second my dream is crushed and the bit of confidence I've managed to accumulate is vanished.

The mood at home resembles a puddle with murky waters and I know things will forever stay that way. There's a part in me that wants to chase my dream and prove them all wrong but I'm scared of failing, especially after dad's swatting hand.

I never got a chance to ask him about his hand. I guess I feared his reply.

Two weeks later I'm on my way to Jerusalem for my final exam.

It's a Friday and I'm glad to have a reason to leave home.

The air is exceptionally hot and sticky. I pack up a small bag with books and clothes to last me four days and catch a bus that takes me through the noisy streets of Tel-Aviv and continues on its slow crawl up the snaky road to Jerusalem. Along the path are heat stricken oaks and pines that follow the twisting asphalt with exhaustion. The hilly ride is slow. I move an imaginary finger over the hilltops, their soft domes curled up like skullcaps next to stony trails, and wonder about the meaning of joy and happiness. Tall cypress trees draw a mountain range that stretches well beyond the horizon. I shut my eyes immersed in my own thoughts and try to imagine myself elsewhere.

The bus strains noisily emitting black clouds of smoke. I'm nauseous but when I open the window the stench only intensifies. The man sitting next to me is asleep. I feel trapped squeezed into my corner trying to avoid his heavy body from pressing into mine. I lean my head against the window, shut my eyes and see myself ten years ahead trapped in a grim cloud of a wretched life. I know Naomi will stay the same and so will mother and dad and baby Bilha. And our home, too, will remain as always, joyless and full of madness. Dad's good humor and laughs will be gone and with them all joys of life and whenever the demons get hold of Naomi's head, I'll be called to help and that's not what I want.

What I want is to get away from it all, run as fast as I can and keep running until I'm out of breath and out of reach. I'd like to have my own place, clean and tidy and void of any secrets and lies and mother's dramatic stories which she kneads with her talented hands. Her pliable words are suited to her needs and used as an excuse to treat the three of us differently; she injects them into each of our ears, separately, adding secrets to create triangulations and erect heavy-weight walls that serve her purpose of isolating each of us. The weight of those walls equals the gravity of my thoughts and is as threatening as the boulders that mark the path into the city. My head is filled with words I've absorbed throughout my childhood, axioms that paint life in black and white.

And so, long before the bus ever reaches Jerusalem and without my being conscious of it, a decision roots itself in my mind and I know I must latch onto the first opportunity that comes my way.

The city is noisy and crowded with people preparing for the Sabbath. The man in the grocery store knows me. For the past three years I've been buying my food from him.

"Would you like the usual?"

"I wish I could afford something other than the usual...I'm already sick of the chicken with the tomato, pickle and chips!"

My words swipe the smile off his face.

Within minutes I'm inside the small dorm room, staring through the window at the stony hill tops as they melt into the white skies. Clouds dressed as feathers glide silently through valleys of blue. The sun is busy dazzling the air with its majestic golds weaving a thousand and one legends. I force myself to ignore the arresting beauty of the universe and sit down to study. The evening hours ignite a wild fire in the sky: the pinks go wild, goofing around with stripes of daring blues and purples teasing the hot reds that refuse to let go as they all rub against each other in shameless lust. My eyes are on the magnetizing sky.

***

The next day I spend a few hours studying before going out on a long walk. I reach the hotel that served as my workplace up until a month ago. The lobby is noisy, bustling with businessmen and tourists. I enter the jewelry shop looking for my friend and find her occupied with a tourist who's looking at pendants. I step to the side trying to guess his accent.

"What do you think?" he turns to me abruptly. When I hesitate he quickly adds, "Sorry... do you speak English?"

I smile and within minutes we're chatting about the golden pendant in his hand.

"Are you from Germany?"

"Yes. My name is Darien."

"I'm Tara."

We exchange more words with some light laughter.

I notice the ease with which he moves and speaks and the time he takes to try on different chains and pendants. He keeps asking for more colors and designs and I can tell he's used to plush hotels like this one, but without understanding the reason, now that I'm next to him in the splendorous hotel, I feel the meagerness of my life.

My friend goes out of her way to appease him. She answers all his questions patiently, shows him rings and cuff links and smiles at him even when he tells her he has no intention of purchasing anything but a pendant. He finally settles on the golden Chai which he wears on his neck as he exits the shop.

"Would you like to join me for coffee?" he asks.

I smile in agreement.

There's something in his heavy accent that reminds me of faraway places and at once I recall sitting on dad's lap and asking him.

"Dad, where do rich people live?"

And now the guy I'm sitting with reminds me of those very same places and I just want to stay there and never come back.

"I was born in Germany but I've lived in Belgium for the past several years."

I get to hear about his love for Israel, and especially for Jerusalem, about the places he's toured, and I sense that he likes me. He goes on with his white smiles and takes me to small hotels throughout Europe and they all smell of fresh flowers and heavy perfumes with tasty foods and the strong aroma of red wines.

As I look into his eyes, honey colored and somewhat sad, I'm overtaken by sweet thoughts hoping his thoughts are similar to mine.

He inquires politely about my studies and future plans.

"I have one more exam on Monday and then I'm off to America."

"Why America?"

"I just want to air myself before resuming my studies."

"What do you want to study?"

"I'm thinking about dentistry…"

"That takes so long!"

"Yes, but that's really what interests me."

"Where do you live?"

"In the coastal area. Have you been there?"

"No, not yet."

I again mention my upcoming exam on Monday ending the conversation politely.

"Well… our house is close to the beach so if you ever feel like visiting the area…" I give him my phone number.

I'm back home, counting three weeks until my flight. Every so often I look at the plane ticket I've managed to purchase on my own with money saved over the past three years.

***

A letter arrives from the university detailing the graduation ceremony.

Mother is quick to ask.

"You don't seriously intend going there just to receive a piece of paper, do you?!"

All eyes are on me.

"Of course not!"

I feel defeated but fail to internalize the significance of my feeble conduct.

I make sure not to mention my own piece of paper in order to avoid any mention of Naomi's paper, the one she never received from high school, and request that my diploma be posted to me.

"Poor Naomi… she really should have studied medicine… she could have been a brilliant surgeon…it's all because of her headaches… you have no idea what she's going through… with her diarrheas…"

I know Naomi didn't graduate from high school but I can't understand why I don't feel proud of my own achievements.

Darien surprises me. He calls and asks if the invitation is still open and arrives the following day. I move into mother's small work room and Darien gets Bilha's room. In the evening he joins me and gets to meet some of my former class mates who remained in the community. The following day Darien stays close to dad; he follows him everywhere, helps him carry heavy bags from the open market and returns home with a gleaming face.

"It was great fun!"

He jokes around with everyone, calls mother by a nickname and hands her a gift.

On Friday night he puts on a Kippa and tucks a Siddur and a Talit under his arm.

"Would you like to join me to Schull?"

"No way! The only one that still goes to the Synagogue is grand-ma Pearle."

"Do you think she'll want to join me?"

"I'm sure she will."

When she returns from the Synagogue grandma Pearle is full of smiles. She whispers in my ear.

"Darien is crazy about you."

My face reddens and I have no idea if she's serious.

We spend the next several days roaming beaches and visiting nearby sites and I'm starting to feel that perhaps grandma is right. But when I look into his eyes I see sadness.

Darien's been with us for over a week now. Naomi goes out of her way to spice her jokes and make him laugh her way. They both sharpen their words while sparring and outwitting each other like two butchers. When we're seated around the table Darien releases a wink in my direction and creates a tiny secret that remains between us.

The atmosphere surrounding the Saturday meal is filled with smiles. Dad jokes and tells funny stories; Darien adds his own, joined by Bilha who has a way of sparking laughter with words.

Naomi fixes her black ones on me.

"I've got a joke about black colors."

I disregard her.

"Don't you have something to say?!"

Her eyes are glued onto me like a leech readying for a suck.

She knows how I feel about her jokes, the ugly ones she targets at anyone whose color and origin differ from hers.

Darien teams up with her.

"I wouldn't mind hearing black jokes as long as they don't stain me."

They both crack up laughing hysterically.

"Enough," mother's voice is weak.

Dad's face is grim.

I get up and leave the roaring table but the laughter follows me into the small room where my stomach gets all tangled with knots.

Darien joins me.

"I'm sorry..." his head tilted slightly sideways, "I didn't want you to leave the table."

I choose to believe him though deep down I know he truly enjoyed Naomi's jokes.

Darien sparks within me an unfamiliar sense, a kind of silent promise hinged on a tacit precondition that if I become his, I'll never have to worry about a thing.

I succumb to the new thrill much like an icicle under a blazing sun and give in to the sense of laxity that engulfs me. My low self esteem decides on my behalf and orders me to pacify the man who wants me to accept his invitation to visit him in Europe. I look into his eyes and select the things I wish to see; I imagine a worry-free life without complications or hardships, and choose to disregard the hefty tag price attached.

Darien decides we should fly together to Belgium and from there I'll continue on my own to America.

We have four more days left to pack up. I try to cram the two pairs of shoes, four pairs of pants and few shirts that are spread on my bed into my small suitcase.

Darien is next to me in the room.

"Need any help?" he smiles.

"What's the weather like in Belgium?"

His eyes roam my clothes.

"Unpredictable...there's really no telling...do you have anything else? Something nice for going out?"

When I don't respond he adds.

"I mean... evening clothes... you know...for going out at night. I'd like us to go to some fancy night clubs..." releasing a white smile in my direction.

His sharp eyes scout the meager heap of clothes with the two pairs of shoes. He clears his throat, taps his carved nose lightly with his pointer and at once I feel poor.

"I'm sure you can buy something nice in Belgium..."

I'm ashamed to tell him that I've spent all the money I had on the clothes spread in front of him.

"What's this?" His finger fishes a black shirt, "You don't really mean to wear this thing...do you?!"

"No...it's here by mistake."

My face burns. I feel totally miserable.

It's our last night in Bo-Acha Yam. We stroll through the quiet streets of the community and the words flutter but they don't really touch. Darien talks about city life, nightclubs, and his real estate business with little mention of friends. His responses are short, touching lightly on the boarding school he attended with few words about his childhood and the fact that his parents still reside in Germany.

As we sit under the mulberry tree in the school yard his hand reaches for mine. He adds amusing anecdotes from his former life as a student and when it's my turn I give a falsified version of my fun-filled student life. I don't have a sick sister and my parents are very supportive of me and I know my worth which is why I have so many guys chasing me.

I know I've said the right words because Darien holds up my chin and kisses me lightly on my lips.

***

The following day we fly to Belgium and spend four days in Ostend, a beach town located along the shores of the North Sea.

We both suffer from blindness and insecurity, acting in falsehood and masquerading under pretentious masks in an effort to aggrandize ourselves in front of each other.

Darien's strong body and good looks are cobweb trappings that dazzle and lure me into a fallacious puddle reflecting the sights I choose to see. There's something amazingly captivating in the way Darien uses his deep voice. He never asks for things; they simply float his way. I listen to the tone of his voice and I can't rid myself of the fear, knowing there's something lurking deep inside.

Come evening, Darien again fumbles through my meager clothing.

"Why don't you put on something else? Actually...don't even bother! It's a waste of time!" he slams shut the suitcase, "Let's go shopping! I need to find you something nice for a change. You should have left all this crap in Israel," he points to the suitcase.

The boutique is exquisitely beautiful with so many delicate items that I'm scared of touching them. Darien negotiates his demands in French and hands me an elegantly wrapped box, insisting I untangle each ribbon separately.

"I love you," his strong hands hold both sides of my head, "And from now on you'll be dressed like a queen. You're mine and you'll never have to wear crap again!"

He seals his promise on my lips.

"I'll go on working here a few more years ... then we'll move to Israel..."

And I choose to believe him for all the wrong reasons.

The two of us are standing in front of a window overlooking the North Sea with its dreary waters and endless beaches that stretch as far as the eye can see. The sea gulls screech as they circle the air in a wild frenzy then dive again into the gushing waves and resurface balancing themselves until swallowed by the darkened waters.

I cling to Darien's body, sensing his hands over my shoulders yearning for my budding nipples and nakedness and at once I feel wanted and desired.

I shut my eyes and lean back. Our heads touch each other in a newly awakened urgency as I give in to his manhood against the small arch of my back.

"I love you Tara," he again whispers and leads me towards the bed.

"Say it...say it, Tara...tell me you love me too..." his heavy breathing is hurried.

"I want you..." I whisper and move my legs to meet his.

Around noon we walk along the windy pier, struggling against the stormy air and laughing ourselves silly using small touches reserved for new lovers

The foggy air is thick and heavy with salt turning my ears into icicles.

"I'm freeeeeeeeeeezing!"

We stand on the pier as one silhouette drunk with hunger and lust.

"Let's go to Adelinje," Darien pulls me into his chest.

The mussels and oysters are served in large bowels accompanied by white wine, and mark our togetherness with small giggles, a smile, a brief touch of hand on thigh, long stares and gesturing eyes that hold reminiscences of love making.

We then return to the room for our last night together.

The following morning is a Friday the thirteenth of the month.

We both chuckle at the coincidence without my realizing that providence is laughing at me from the distance of years to come.

We're at the airport.

"Promise me...promise you'll be back..." Darien chokes back his tears.

I wipe my own then wrap my arms around his neck.

"I promise."

We vow to write to each other and keep our promises of love.

The plane takes off on time with only few passengers on board.

***

I spend the next few months in New York working as girl Friday while reading Darien's daily letters.

"Please Tara...please come back...I love you ...I don't want to lose you...I'm counting the hours...the minutes..."

It feels good and safe knowing someone's found me worthy of his love.

My insecurity grows, nourished by loneliness and voices from my past. Every letter from home pushes me further down the slope of painful remembrances, channeling all my desires and dreams to nowhere. I find myself in a familiar state of passivity, a burned out wick void of any wishes to conquer the world or continue my studies.

Dear Tara,
"We were glad to get your latest letter and read about the job you found..."

Mother asks for additional details then goes on.

"I think you should be practical and quit dreaming about med school ... it takes too long and you won't have time for anything else. It's really not practical.

You're lucky not to be here right now. Poor Naomi...my heart breaks to see her this way...with her diarrheas and headaches...it's killing us ... there are no words to describe her suffering...she's such a wonderful girl and she's suffering so much... Now that you're away, you should enjoy yourself and not have to worry about what we're going through... it's absolute hell... poor Naomi..." a detailed description of her last hospitalization sums up the letter.

Darien makes all decisions on our behalf and manages our togetherness as he sees fit and as per his instructions, I leave New York and join him in Belgium.

***

Our apartment is located in an old brick building set in the heart of Brussels, just a block away from the posh Avenue Louis with its exuberant boutiques and refined clientele. The morning air bustles with sounds in French intermingled with Flemish as high-heeled ladies coquettishly parade the sidewalks next to men wearing three-piece suits. Everyone carries an umbrella. The weather is persistently unpredictable. At any given moment it lashes at the gray sky with a blinding light to create ominous overcasts. Tall-glassed towers, freshly washed by the near constant drizzle, stand isolated, interspersed among old, gray and unimpressive heavy structures. Streets and pavements are wide with cars swooping by at high speeds alongside trams that zigzag intermittently throughout the city. Small quaint patisserie shops are everywhere bursting with strong aromas of freshly brewed coffees, wines and beers, alongside a wealth of baked pies, cookies, biscuits and breads with pralines and sweet creams and thick butter heavily smeared on newly baked croissants and baguettes freshly out of the ovens.

Darien mentions friends but I don't see any. We spend time with his parents who come to visit the big city and at once I'm exposed to another world.

The meeting is conducted ceremoniously. Stella, his mother, kisses me thrice on my cheeks followed by his father Helmut with his icy blue eyes. It's my first meeting with his parents but within minutes I find myself in a familiar environment, a family tapestry I recognize from my past.

Over the weekend I join Stella to a plush boutique.

"Do you all go to the same synagogue?"

"What do you mean?" her honey colored eyes stare at me.

"To the same synagogue as Darien...the one he attends on Rosh Hashana and Yom Kippur...do you and Helmut go there too?"

"We're not Jewish, eh? We're humanists. I know that Darien goes there... but don't say anything to Helmut about it, eh?"

I'm silent, overwhelmed by the shocking lie.

At dinner I'm unable to swallow a thing.

"What's wrong?" Darien whispers.

I refuse to meet his eyes.

Later, in his room, he again asks.

"What's wrong?!"

"You told me you were Jewish. Why did you lie to me?"

"I didn't say I was Jewish and you didn't ask!"

"But you took grandma Pearle with you to the synagogue when you visited us!"

"So what?! I just felt like going there! That doesn't make me a Jew, does it?!"

"And what about the Chai necklace you bought? And the Kippa?"

"Enough! What exactly don't you understand?!"

The lie refuses to let go, but when I write to mother about it she writes back.

"What difference does it make if he's Jewish or not?!"

And nothing really matters after that.

The bedroom is spacious and contains, among other things, a wooden chest with two draws where Darien keeps the things that really matter to him. He asks that I don't look inside or ask him about his childhood. I already know it's where he hides his Kippa with his Talit and Sidur so I try to explain that I only want to get to know him better and share my own secretes with him, but he smiles and says that he doesn't remember any.

"And besides...who the hell cares about what happened in childhood?!"

I'd like to be like him and not have to drag along my own remembrances of Naomi.

It's the weekend and Darien announces.

"Surprise... I have a surprise for you! Go put on something nice!"

"Where are we going?"

Darien smiles and wraps me in a tight hug.

We've just finished one of Stella's fanciful breakfasts with freshly squeezed juices and brewed coffee and an assortment of eggs and cheeses next to tiny butter rolls and croissants purchased from the nearby bakery.

Darien grabs hold of my long, thick hair and I know he's holding the nicest part of me though he pretends not to like it.

"It's like grass...you need to mow it from time to time..."

"Mow your own grass!"

He laughs.

"So tell me", I ask again when we're in the car, "where are we going?"

Darien only smiles but by the time we reach Alexandra's I already understand.

Darien kisses her thrice on her cheeks and announces in French.

"Bonjour Madame! I know my fiancée is in the best of hands! "

He pecks me lightly on my forehead and disappears.

"Coffee? Tea?" Madam asks me with a smile.

I look anxiously at the huge scissors Madam Alexandra is holding in her hand.

"Mademoiselle, you lof him verri moch, yes? zis air... is very booti-ful..." she moves her hands over my thick reddish strands.

My tears mix with the warm rinse following the aftermath.

Madam Alexandra seems to understand.

The curly short hair looks short and curly and my smiles are gone forever.

***

Darien's voice is heavy and commanding.

"Why did you nudge me about the garbage if you did it yourself?!"

He slaps me with his roaring words.

"Because you didn't respond when I needed your..."

"So stop asking me! Enough! I don't 'wanna hear you!"

I hug him and try a quiet tone.

"Let's not fight..."

"Shut up!" his mouth whips, "shut your trap!"

I escape into the bedroom and lie on the bed and by now it feels as though I've made a full circle and returned to the place from which I'd escaped.

Within minutes Darien joins me, his eyes soft with regret.

"I'm sorry...I didn't mean..."

He washes me with hugs and kisses but his stormy voice remains with me long after he's asleep.

***

When he's with his parents, Darien is never at ease. He extends a hand and a cheek ceremoniously, the French way, but there is no love in it, much like the lack of love in our home. Helmut, as usual, hollers and shrieks and argues with everyone; Stella's smile is white

103

and pearly. She's always perfumed, her blond hair is always perfect and her nail polish is never chipped and I don't know how she does it.

"Looks are everything, eh?" she says.

"That's why I married her!" Helmut releases the words into the air with a smile that skips his eyes.

Stella asks that I join her in the kitchen and says she wants to show me something but I must promise to keep it a secret.

"Don't tell Helmut. He doesn't like to remember..." she holds out an old photo.

"This is Helmut's grandfather, eh? He has ... how do you say that?"

"Side locks?!"

"Yes, side locks. He was a rabbi, eh?"

"But why is it a secret?"

"Like that, eh?"

She eyes me, adding her senseless 'like that' to the other secrets she's already entrusted to my ears.

***

Darien suggests we spend the weekend alone. He's had his fill with his parents and wants us to create a mold of our own, erect a new world for us both, but I make the mistake of repeating all the excuses I've heard at home, words about family loyalty.

"You're their only son... they miss you...you need to respect them..."

"You're right...we should go visit them."

We've been together now for nearly a year but we exist in separate worlds. There's no true friendship between us and we're always arguing and quarrelling. Darien's thoughts are as cold as the black waves of the North Sea, a tall man with a white smile that resembles foamy ornaments that ride on stormy waters; a powerful man, who carries his chest in front of him to announce his wide shoulders. His slightly elevated chin looks angled and somewhat sideways, with hands hidden inside his pockets like an exchanger counting secrets.

I, too, carry ugly secrets, and my thoughts are filaments of sunshine threaded with reds and the glumness of my childhood. I'm convinced of my lowly worth, but retain the rules of my early ballet lessons and hold my posture firmly upright. We are two polarized entities prevented from meeting each other. At the first attempt to create a dialogue, a spark ignites within each of us, a defense mechanism as a reminder of our own childhood. It flares up and causes monstrous storms.

Autumn is cold and rainy with a near constant fogginess that paints the world in a depressing grayness. Darien travels most of the time and I work as an English teacher in various schools scattered around the city. Our togetherness is familiar with predicted arguments seasoned with stinging words that we each carry with us from home. There's a deep unsettling sense within me, a strange sensation of a familiar past and sometimes I wonder if I even had another life before we'd met. Naomi's crazed roarings around the dinner table have now been replaced by terrifying silences, with constant arguments and angry tones accompanied by verbal abuse.

"Shut your trap, woman! And don't tell me what to do!" Darien explodes into my face.

I jump back. His eyes are swollen with anger.

"Got it?!"

I burst out crying and run to the bedroom. Seconds later Darien joins me with teary eyes.

"I'm sorry Tara...I won't do it again...I'm so sorry...my father always did it... so I think I've learned it from him..."

We could have caught the moment and tried to change things, made an effort to create new love steps replacing those we each carried with us from our own past. But neither of us recognized that precious moment. We conducted ourselves like two blind children trampling on each other's toes.

My inner voice signals that it's not too late and that I must leave, but I feel like I have nowhere to go back to. Naomi is in and out of hospitals and Bilha consumes the rest of my parents' time and strength.

We hug each other through tearful eyes that blind our thoughts and drug our souls refusing to see the truth.

"I love you Tara...I love you so much...I'm sorry..."

Darien hands me a red rose, and as always following a painful incident, his eyes are flooded. Whenever I find myself in threatening situations, all beaten up and frustrated with no way out, I turn silent captivated by passivity that churns my emotions into bitterness.

When we make up, we both cry with tears of shame and humiliation for having agreed to compromise on a miserable life together. Immature and lacking self confidence, we latch onto defense mechanisms that have no power to defend.

Darien's outbursts become a way of life followed by apologies and tokens of forgiveness in the form of presents. I know there'll always be another explosion and another apology and it only causes me to be angry at myself for lacking the strength to get up and walk away. And as my insecurity shrinks, my shame grows, forcing me to cling tighter onto Darien, creating a self entangled loop without head or tail. Convinced of my worthlessness, I'm unable to fathom the notion of escaping the sick situation, the only way of life I've known since childhood.

Life without Darien simply doesn't present itself as an option.

On Saturday night, following a five coursed dinner, Stella and I move into the kitchen. It's nearing midnight. Helmut and Darien are in the living room reading newspapers and sharing a silence. I ask her about Helmut because I want to understand why he's always angry and how she can live with it. She responds that the situation now is by far better than it had been before.

As soon as she utters these words I'm sorry I've asked because I'm already carrying a load of secrets related to the man I live with and their weight lays heavily on me.

I release a burdensome secret of my own and share with her Darien's outbursts. Stella nods her head and says that he probably learned it from his father. I feel sorry for the long years she'd suffered with Helmut but I don't realize I should guard myself from a similar fate. She adds that she's happy, now that Darien is with me, because maybe I'll be able to change him. And I'm foolish enough to believe her.

When Darien isn't angry and doesn't shout like his father, I like him. I really like him.

***

It's my second year in Belgium and by now I'm obedient and submissive and my hair is short. There are moments that give me cause to believe that Darien is the best thing that ever happened to me, but sometimes, when I catch him day dreaming I can tell he's hiding secrets. His sad eyes are remote as though requesting a pause before opening up and exposing the horrors of his childhood. But many more seasons will pass before he'll dare voice his remembrances. Much like a mollusk shell with its camouflaged cooing sounds, Darien too excels in disguising his pains by using vast amounts of wine and chivas spiced with humor and charisma for the sake of anyone who comes his way.

Life is full of surprises with gastronomical weekends spent in small hotels in the Belgian Ardennes and in Luxembourg. Sometimes we visit neighboring France with its vast lush farmlands splashed in green hues that change with the windfalls of seasons.

Darien likes surprises.

"Let's go somewhere. I feel like having a good meal."

I'm exposed to an abundance of new tastes and get acquainted with fresh flavors and smells; I learn about new tangs and smacks of the savory and of the pungent and sample spicy steaks in buttery textures accompanied by tantalizing sauces. There are countless shades of wines in delicately varied hues, tints and tones and smells, a richness of tastes brilliantly fashioned to boggle the mind and drug all pains. We stay in small hotels and sample typical regional foods while enjoying their special preparations.

Shortly before Darien's twenty-ninth birthday we venture on a long summer vacation.

"Let's go to Switzerland and from there on to Italy. That way we can meet Aunt Maggie on my birthday."

I hear stories about Aunt Maggie who married a German tycoon but when I ask Helmut he says he never cared for his sister and goes on reading his newspaper.

Darien is excited.

"It'll take us a few days to get there and back but we'll still have plenty of time to tour around."

We cross the flat lands of Belgium and reach the twisted Alpine passes in their blinding whites and icy colorings. Colossal glaciers with mummified glares and slick fossilized bodies anointed in bottle greens, shriek in silence as they stare from their terrifying heights. We pass fairy-taled sights with tiny waterfalls next to wooden houses and gardens dressed up as colorful postcards. Razor sharp ridges with harsh looking eyes flood the vast surroundings shared by evergreen trees able to stand the violent winds. But even the arresting beauty all around can't change the atmosphere inside the car.

We near the Italian border. The weather is stormy with winds and rains; there's no chance of sitting outside with cheeses and a bottle of wine. It's three in the afternoon and all I want is to have a small snack. Darien is busy navigating as he studies the map spread over his lap.

"We'll drive this way...there's a beautiful observation post here right next to the border...then we'll follow this road..." his finger trails over small paths meant to connect us to our final destination.

He folds up the map into a small square, plants a kiss on my forehead and concentrates on the wet road. Thunders with lightening burst into the air adding to the heavy curtain of rain that blinds the windshield and slows us to a near halt.

"Why can't we eat something ... it doesn't matter what, anything..."

"Because I want us to enjoy the view!"

"But look at the rain... as it is we won't be able to see any..."

"Stop nudging!"

An hour passes.

"Please Darien... let's get a sandwich or something...even a plain baguette will do... I don't feel well..."

"Suck your fingers!"

Twenty minutes later a sign appears:

"Border ahead. Prepare to stop."

And at once we're in Italy.

"Godverdomme! We couldn't have missed the observation post! Let me check again!"

He again studies the map then drives in silence past the officer who waves his hand.

"See the houses on this side? They're a bit run down... more like the ones you'd see in Italy than in Switzerland. And the people..." A lengthy lecture about the various European races and cultures follows.

A sign appears: 'Trattoria'. It's already four thirty in the afternoon.

"Wait here. I'll get something."

Within minutes he's back with a brown bag.

"Idiot! His store is empty! There was nothing left except for a baguette with some stinking cheese. We'll eat this now and stop later for something decent."

"I've got to eat something...I don't feel well..."

"Wait...wait a bit longer...I'm sure this place is not too far...we'll be able to see the entire abyss from there... let's eat there."

"I feel sick Darien...please..."

"Wait... just a few more minutes..."

Several more minutes go by before the observation post is found, and by now it's a mere post without a view.

"You see? All you need is a bit of patience! The view is amazing! Okay, let's eat."

The rain by now is totally blinding, no longer just a pestering annoyance. Darien hands me the bag. I put my hand inside, grab the first thing I touch and shove it into my mouth. Darien is busy with his. When I turn my head sideways, I notice a black dot where Darien is readying himself for a bite. My mouth is stuffed with bread and cheese and the only thing I can do is point to his sandwich.

"What?! What are you trying to say?!" he prepares for a large bite and now I can clearly recognize the dung fly with its bluish-green colors tinted with purple and turquoise.

"What?! What's so funny?!"

I point with my finger but I can't open my mouth.

"Mmm...Mmm..."

"Stop making those stupid noises!"

He opens his mouth wide clamping on the baguette, cheese and fly with its radiant wings. I'm choking with laughter. Darien is busy chewing. Once his mouth is free he roars.

"Are you out of your mind?! Quit that stupid laugh of yours!"

"You ...you..." I start several times.

"Enough already! You either tell me what's so funny or I'll open the door and make you walk the rest of the way! That'll cool you!"

"You swallowed a fly," I spit out quickly.

"What?!"

And all at once it's no longer funny.

"What did you say?!"

"I said you swallowed a fly."

"Where?"

"With your sandwich."

"What are you talking about?!"

"There was a huge dung fly on your sandwich... that's why I laughed... I tried to warn you."

"You're sick! You're sick in the head!"

Later that night, in bed, after the soft words and touches, he asks.

"Was there really a fly on my bread?"

"Yes."

"No...it's not true... please tell me it's not true...please..."

And now it's me that's laughing. At least for a short while.

***

We've been together for three years and by now all my dreams are buried and gone. What remains is a bitter lump lodged somewhere between my heart and my stomach. I cling blindly to Darien taking comfort in knowing that I'll soon become his wife though there's no excitement or great joy in it.

The civil ceremony is conducted by the city clerk of Brussels.

A few days later, Darien moves to a new workplace in The Netherlands.

The spacious house spread over three floors is located in a small Dutch village east of Amsterdam, hidden among thick elm forests and reddish heather bushes. Along the way and as far as the eye can see are pastures spotted with grazing cows and windmills overlooking gray wet bicycle paths.

The drizzly rain is constant bursting out of a gray misty air that perpetuates the dullness of the sky. The village is swamped with flowers and gardens. Next to each house is a rectangular shaped lawn, seemingly greener than its neighbor's, though all gardens are identical with a neat and well tapered path that twists around the house ending by the entrance door. Klompjes, heavy wooden shoes painted in bold colors, serve for garden work and stand like sentinels outside the door.

Darien is never around. He travels during the week and returns home over the weekend. I'm curled up in bed counting my twenty-nine years overwhelmed by a sense of emotional vacuum. I don't know a soul in the village, feeling choked as though drowning in a familiar sense of hopelessness that takes me back to the place from which I fled. I try to escape loneliness by calling Stella, speaking with Helmut, writing long letters to mother and dad and reading the usual stories about Naomi.

> *"Dear Tara,*
> *How are you and how is Darien managing with his travels? It's*
> *probably hard on him, every few days in another country. And*
> *what's the weather like? There's nothing new over here except for*
> *the apartment we've recently purchased for Naomi. We decided to*
> *help her and make sure that she has a permanent place. We don't*
> *want her to have to depend on anyone. It's a small place but it's*
> *enough for a single person. Poor thing, she suffers so much. She's*
> *home right now but she's not well. I don't need to tell you what*
> *that's like. We have to whisper and we can't make any noise... but*
> *maybe the apartment in Tel Aviv will do her some good. We paid*
> *twenty thousand pounds for it which is a lot of money, but I told*
> *dad that we don't have a choice and we need to do it, otherwise*
> *who knows what might happen when we're no longer around. So*
> *now we're in debts and every penny can help... but I don't want*
> *Darien to know about it because it can really anger him, but if*
> *you can help we'll keep it between us..."*

Mother adds that Naomi hasn't changed a bit and I already know what that means but I overlook the main point. Many more years will pass before I grasp the full depth of her point and detach myself from my family's diseased core.

Life with Darien is never dull despite the fact that my entire existence amounts to fulfilling his needs. He's always somewhere, travelling and homing in on the next acquisition and the next target while I shrivel inside and become smaller and smaller. Nearly erased. All that's left for me to do is adhere to his dictations and applaud him.

When he recognizes loneliness and sadness in my eyes he becomes angry.

"Go to museums! Visit interesting places!"

I visit every known corner. Once again I tour Amsterdam, return to places I've already been to and visit new ones, stop in coffee shops, taste new foods, go to exhibitions, museums and open markets, try tiny meat balls dipped in mustard and wipe with a glass of beer or try more coffee, but nothing can compensate for the loneliness and sense of void that amasses within each of us. Darien is always busy. He doesn't have the time to sit and talk about the togetherness of our lives, and even if he could he wouldn't know what pains him or where. I remain dormant, enclosed within my inner world, unable to define myself or my wants.

***

One evening Darien returns home early.

"I need to be at the police station tomorrow... something about taxes...but I want you to go instead and see a certain van Druk."

"But ...I don't feel comfortable ... I prefer that you go."

"I can't. I'm seeing an important client."

Darien demands that I take care of the mundane and insignificant things in life, the daily annoyances that threaten to consume his precious time, and without realizing it I find myself in a familiar role gathering leftovers and sweeping up messes. Throughout my younger years I've had to collect the trash left behind by my older sister on her dubious trails of life. Darien too knows how to realize his demands, but prefers to do so by using elegance and the whiteness of his smile.

He's not clear about the details but insists that I go.

"It's only to fill out some forms..."

The following morning I'm at the police station.

"Mrs. Schmidt," a tall, blond-haired police officer extends a strong hand, "My name is Officer van Druk and I am in charge of the investigation. Please..." he points to a chair fronting his desk.

A warm wave hits me. Darien didn't mention an investigation; he only instructed me to play dumb.

"You won't even have to rehearse for the part!" he added with a wink and a bear hug.

Officer van Druk gets up from behind his large desk and walks past a second officer seated to my left. He hands me a sheet of paper in Dutch. At the bottom of the page I see Darien's undecipherable signature next to mine.

"Mrs. Schmidt, did you sign this?"

I have no recollection of the specifics. Darien would routinely present me with an assortment of documents to sign.

"It's those dumb tax forms," he'd say and shove a pile in front of me.

"But I'd like to know what I'm signing..."

"You don't need to worry about it. The tax advisor at the office gave these out to everyone. Just sign here...next to my signature."

"It looks like my signature," I answer officer van Druk.

"Do you understand what it says?"

"Well... I'm an American and my Dutch isn't that good... I'm sure my husband explained it to me at the time... but I really can't remember..."

"Then I'll remind you," van Druk returns to his seat and picks up a pair of glasses. "It says here that you have money from your husband's job, but that you don't have any more...how do you say it?...income...yes, I forget the word."

He smiles but his eyes remain cold. "And we have here another document where it says your money, a lot of it, is in Luxembourg."

Officer van Druk details his findings. My face is hot.

"I don't know anything about it. Maybe it's a mistake..."

Officer van Druk snickers.

"But I see his signature on it and also yours." He holds his glasses in one hand and the letter in the other.

"Look officer van Druk... you seem to imply certain misdeeds so why don't you ask my husband?"

"Oh! Because your husband is resident of America... and we cannot do that...at least not right now."

I try to understand how Darien was able to register himself as an American resident and suspect that he took advantage of my American citizenship. The large amounts of money that are supposedly in Luxembourg also sound odd. Darien had never mentioned them and as far as I know we're living strictly off his plumpish salary. Not that I've ever seen the actual amounts; they're deposited automatically into his bank account, one of those subjects that aren't open for discussion.

I can tell Officer van Druk enjoys his job and even more so practicing his English because he keeps me in his office for over three hours.

As soon as I return home I find out Darien is in Germany.

"How could you send me to van Druk?! And why?! You knew..."

"Oh come on! He's just a stupid Dutch! What can you expect from a Boer like him?!"

"And how come you're registered as an American resident?!"

"It wasn't difficult after our marriage... and you don't have to make such a big fuss over it. I go there once a year, don't I?!"

"What are you talking about?"

"I'm registered under the address you had in the States."

"The address from five years ago?!"

"What's the problem?!"

"And what about all the money that's stashed in Luxembourg?"

"I see van Druk perked up your curiosity so why don't you ask him for answers!"

The line is cut off.

I'm left to wonder about the slick way in which Darien made use of my former address.

Two days later Darien parks the black Mercedes in front of the house carrying an enormous bouquet of flowers.

"Don't say a word. Just give me a kiss. Happy birthday Tara...I love you..." His arms close around my waist drawing me nearer and fending off any questions.

That evening we dine in a gourmet restaurant and eat a special meal ordered in advance by Darien and prepared by the head chef. There's candlelight and a rare bottle of wine and as usual Darien hands me a small velvety box. From Tiffany's.

The exquisite diamond ring sooths momentarily my raw pain and muddles my sense of self-abasement.

***

When they're with us over the weekend, Helmut tries not to anger others or get angry himself and Stella becomes Dutch.

"How come you change your Flemish accent whenever you speak with the neighbors?" I ask her.

"Well... because... like that, eh?"

I look at Stella and I think of a chameleon. Darien also changes his Flemish to sound Dutch and when in France his accent turns Parisian. Both have a knack for trapping their wishes by changing costumes and sounds.

Darien loves entertaining his clients at home, the European way, and brags about the dinnerware and trappings that come with it.

My fingers flutter over the handcrafted tray specially designed for him and purchased in Germany meant to serve shrimps, a swirl of heads and tails with no beginning and no end chasing each other on the slippery crystal surface. I count thirty-one endings that match my years and liken to our stormy vacuous lives but I can't tell whether the shrimps are coming or going and if I'm confused because I'm thinking about children or because I'm scared of having a little Helmut.

Darien tends to every small detail.

"Keep the shirt buttoned all the way up! You're my wife and you need to look the part!"

I'm as passive as a chrysalis. I don't object anymore to any of the clothes Darien chooses for me. I lack self definition convinced that I can't survive without him.

He charms his guest with his mannerisms while taking pride in handling the drinks and salting them with witty jokes. It keeps everyone roaring and I feel lucky to have someone like Darien, want someone like me.

When I become overwhelmed with longings Darien shouts.

"Stop it with that sad face of yours! Whom exactly do you miss?! Naomi?! Your parents?! Let them come and visit us over here! And besides...you know things have a way of working out for the best."

Now I'm crying because I want to understand what exactly is meant to work out for us. And how. And when.

"I'd like to talk about us...I feel..."

He rolls his eyes towards the ceiling and spits out.

"I'm not interested in how you feel! I already told you and I don't want to have to repeat it: it's all in your head! If you won't look for problems, we won't have any!"

The following day Darien brings me another small box wrapped with strings and says he's sorry. He's already given me so many small boxes yet he always repeats himself lashing out and hurting me. When I threaten to leave he applies silent pressure with lopsided logic forcing me to reshuffle my sentiments like a deck of cards.

"I need you here with me...if you go, I won't be able to function..." he whispers.

I'm paralyzed. And I stay.

***

On Friday night Darien returns home with news that the company is moving us to the States. The following week our three years in Holland come to an end and we're relocated to Illinois.

The direct flight lands us in the heart of Chicago on a frosty October day with eleven suitcases containing clothes suitable for all seasons. While waiting for the shipping container with our household goods, we're placed in a two-room convenience suite with a small kitchenette and an option for daily meals at Cricket's, one of Chicago's best.

It's all very different from the small Dutch village we'd left behind. Over the weekends we tour the various suburbs of Chicago in an effort to find a permanent place of our liking and meet with the realtor chosen by Darien.

"She's got the reputation," he tells me, "So make sure you leave a good impression on her!"

"Oh hi... hi Mrs. Schmidt, I'm Laura Kirk."

Laura is all smiles. When she sees Darien her smiles widen.

"Mr. Schmidt... I'm so glad to finally meet you ...we've spoken so many times on the phone..." her voice is like butter on a warm pan.

"The pleasure is all mine."

"Well, folks, if you're ready..."

We sail in Laura's car to look at the ins and outs of the most fashionable properties. Laura is very informative and flowery and sleek with her words and smiles. She knows the gossips and the latests and the musts and the no-nos.

And then we reach Lake Forest.

"Well folks... we're now entering the northern suburb of Chicago. It's also the most ...well...the most prestigious..." her words are carefully measured as she takes a deep breath.

"I guess it's safe saying this to you folks..." her blue eyes stare at us through the rear view mirror. "I'm pretty sure I'm safe saying this... as you'll understand..."

I notice her perfect nose. It does a tiny twitch before she continues.

"You see...I wouldn't say this to all my out of town clients...but ... the company really wants me to give you the best service...and I know it's safe saying this to you..." she again gives us that glance and I know she's measuring us.

"Well...Lake Forest is THE place for folks like yourselves..." her blues move to rest on my brown ones. "You see... up until a few years ago, we couldn't even show properties to people who were...well... unlike yourselves...you know..."

"Of course, not everyone can afford to live here...that's for sure!" Darien loosens his tie and relaxes.

"Oh... no... that's not what I meant...it's just that...well... the folks over here always preferred... certain types of people...church going people... you know what I mean?...well ... they've always been people who wouldn't sell their properties to anyone who didn't belong to... you know...a church..."

"Like to Jews?" I stare into the mirror and meet her pinking cheeks.

"Exactly! I knew it would be safe saying this to folks like you! In the past we couldn't even show properties to blacks or Jews...the city ordinance wouldn't allow it..." Laura provides us with additional details chiming tiny syllables accompanied by her dazzling whites.

Darien takes my hand in his and winks at me.

Laura keeps driving around showing us breath taking mansions and private beaches.

When we're back at the hotel Darien explains.

"Laura's just a stupid cow. Disregard her stupidity! But you've got to admit that the houses she showed us are gorgeous!"

Darien is captivated and settles on a large colonial house in Lake Forest amidst an affluent community with very old trees and equally aged money. He continues to spend long hours at the office leaving me with the task of caring for the house.

The drive from Chicago to Lake Forest follows a serpentine route next to Lake Michigan. Sapphire hues paint its waters in spectacular metallic blues from every conceivable angle, tones that constantly change under the impetuous sun and gusty winds. Silvery ripples quiver in the freezing waters of the lake, swaying one way then another flaunting their electrifying beauty. An hour later I'm in Lake Forest with its lush parks and mansions that remind me of children's fairy tales surrounded by magnificent gardens and matching fences.

The town centre is lined with luxury shops and Rolls Royces that sail slowly creating a laidback atmosphere. The shoppers are just as lax, most of them in casual blue denims and T-shirts worn under heavy minks, sables and chinchilla furs adding to the relaxed air. Across the shopping center is a quaint train station with direct service to Chicago's down town. The trains are equipped with silver trays and extra services for their unique clientele.

"Yes, of course, Mr. Shmidt... you can order any drink you'd like, Mr. Shmidt... and choose any newspaper ...certainly Mr. Shmidt, we can bill you in the mail once a month, Mr. Schmidt..."

An arched parking frames the front yard of the large brick house with its wooden paneled bay windows. The weather is vicious with hounding black skies that open up without warning and whip down torrential rains. I rush into the house, then cross the spacious entrance, climb up to the second floor, roam the three bedrooms with their attached vast sized walk-in closets and bathrooms and then enter the fourth and largest room. The window opens wide and I find myself surrounded by a small forest with very tall ever-green bushes and naked trees waiting for the first seasonal snow. I smile at the future that awaits me and imagine a house full of laughter and noisy children and at once I'm in love.

I spend the next two hours cleaning the upstairs until a sudden ring forces me downstairs. When I open the door two police officers tilt their hats in my direction.

"Welcome to our community, Mrs. Schmidt, we just stopped by to welcome you. We understand Mr. Schmidt works downtown...so if there's anything you need, we're here to help and serve."

Again they tip their hats and leave.

***

We're still at the hotel waiting for our container that's due to arrive within a week.

My flue worsens so I go to see the doctor.

"How long have you had these symptoms?"

"About two weeks."

"The blood test shows you're pregnant."

I don't respond.

"Are you okay? Are you happy with the pregnancy?"

"Of course...of course..." I smile, too overwhelmed to react.

I feel like in a dream. I cry and laugh but then I think of Darien and at once my thoughts get all muddled and confused. I'm not sure how to tell him about the pregnancy because every time I feel a spark of happiness things change and turn sad.

It's evening by the time Darien returns to the hotel, gives me a small peck on my cheek and asks routinely how my day went.

"I saw Dr. Brook."

"And?" he pours himself a drink.

"I'm pregnant."

The silence is loud.

"Aren't you happy?"

"Tcha"

"I thought you wanted children..."

"You should have told me ahead of time..."

"What do you mean? You were there all along!"

"Tcha"

"Can you say something besides tcha?"

"I'll have to work longer hours from now on ..."

"Don't you want to know when the baby is due?"

"Tcha"

"Why aren't you happy?!" my eyes sting.

Darien retains his silence. He moves his hand picks up the paper and continues reading and I'm left with the awful emptiness that defines our dialogues, off-beat dances that cause each of us to step over the other's toes.

"It's your fucking timing! You never know when to move your feet!"

And now when I'm facing him, I understand that we never actually managed a dance.

He goes on reading his newspaper and I watch TV and that's how we spend our first evening together when we both know we're expecting our first child.

A week prior to the due date mother arrives with two heavy suitcases. She spreads their contents on the large bed creating a colorful prairie of tiny clothes she'd knitted with her own hands. She picks up a pair of doll sized pants with a matching jacket and sweater and miniature hats and gloves and I can't stop smiling.

I tell her it's a boy, for sure, because that's what I'd like, a tiny Darien but without the parts that belong to Helmut though I know that's impossible.

It's Sunday eight in the morning. I wake up with a strange feeling. Dr. Brook checks me but can't find a thing.

"You should take it easy. After all, you were due five days ago...so today might be your lucky day..."

Again I'm in my baby's room staring at the small embroideries hanging on its walls all hand-stitched by me. The colorful lamp sounds a nocturnal melody next to the new bassinet and the chest of drawers loaded with tiny clothes, diapers, blankets, creams and powders and I can barely wait for my little baby to come.

By eight, that evening, the contractions are stronger. Dr. Brook decides to hospitalize me.

The following morning, Monday, Darien stops by to visit me.

"I'm on my way to the office. Let me know when it starts."

The nurse interrupts.

"You might not make it on time, Mr. Schmidt!"

"Oh... it only takes an hour or so by train. That's okay with you, isn't it Tara?" His eyes dart from me to the nurse and back, "I mean... just sitting here and waiting is a waste of time."

He gets up and leaves.

The nurse sees my tears and understands the situation. I'm thirty two and I still believe that a baby will solve our problems.

It's eight in the evening by the time Darien returns to the hospital wearing a three piece suit and exchanges words with Dr. Brook. For the past twenty four hours I've had strong contractions. The obstetrician again checks me.

"We'll give it another three hours and if nothing happens we'll do a caesarean..."

The nurse peers from the door.

"There's an urgent phone call for you."

"I'll be right back. Don't run away." Dr. Brook smiles and quickly leaves the room.

Darien is sitting outside the room reading a newspaper.

A strong contraction paralyzes me. I push the emergency button and at once the room is filled with hustle and bustle and nurses who wheel me wildly into the delivery room.

"Hold on Tara... hold on...don't push... don't push yet... we're almost there..."

The white ceiling with its blinding neon lights and countless water sprinklers moves fast.

"Okay! We're in the delivery room! You can push now. We're ready..."

A deafening stillness fills the room. Staring at me is a white wall with a mirror and above it is a round shaped clock. My eyes are glued to its long arm that seems to be in a hurry, flicking from one line to the next skipping over the numbers. All's quiet. There are no cries. And no sounds. Only silence.

"Is everything okay?"

"Just a minute Tara... just a minute..." the obstetrician replies and at once I catch a glimpse of a tiny grayish-purple body. The room is heavy with whispers and movements but all's so maddeningly quiet and slow. And the arm continues on its own, running like amok skipping one more line and one more digit and by now it nearly completed an entire circle around the white face. All in silence. In utter silence.

I already understand but I'm still hopeful.

A sudden loud cry breaks the silence. I smile through teary eyes.

"Congratulations! You've got a beautiful baby boy!" Dr. Brook says, "Just a second... we need to clean him up..."

The nurse places the tiny baby in my arms and I feel that my heart is bursting with happiness and tears. My face is wet when Darien leans over and whispers.

"Thank you... thank you, Tara... thank you...I'm so happy it's a boy... I wanted a boy so much...thank you..."

I look at my tiny baby and my breath stops. It's the first time that I see his bright, slanted eyes staring back at me. His black hair is thick and shiny. The tiny mouth yawns and fills each of his cheeks with a piercing dimple and now I'm crying and laughing and drowning in happiness that fills my soul.

Later on, after Dr. Brook checks me again and the nurses tend to my aching body, I'm wheeled into the recovery room where Dr. Brook explains that it was a case of meconimum, the baby's first stool that's released while the baby is still inside the womb and causes problems.

"It's only a question of time, Tara, we need to wait and see if and how it affects him. There's no way to predict these things... some babies inhale or swallow it which worsens the situation... we'll just have to see how it'll affect his development..."

It's two in the morning. A gentle touch awakens me. My blurry eyes refuse to open. I see a white coat hovering above me. Another white coat wheels an elevated tray in my direction.

"We're here with your baby...he's not doing very well...we need to transfer him to another hospital and place him in intensive care ... but we didn't want to take him without letting you say goodbye to him..."

I don't understand what they're saying. I look at the doctors and glance at the tray. I see a tiny baby connected to threads and pumps but I don't really grasp that I'm looking at my own sweet baby. His five-hour-old dimples are buried deep under tapes that connect to what looks like, electrical wirings over his face and small body. I reach out with my hand and feel glass.

"He's only five hours old."

I don't know how to say goodbye to such a tiny baby that arrived only five hours ago.

"I promise... we'll take good care of him...you need to say goodbye now..."

I cry. I only cry. I don't know how to say goodbye to a five-hour-old baby.

It's Tuesday morning and the sun is shining through the window facing me. A sudden panic washes over me. I can't remember my baby's face and I'm not even sure it was really him on that tiny tray.

"Good morning, I'm Dr. Flank," the young physician is full of smiles.

"Where's my baby?"

"Oh...he's beautiful, isn't he?"

"You... have you seen him?!"

"Oh sure! I've seen them all. Girls and boys. Now I need to see the Mamas. Can I check your incision?"

"No! I'm Dr. Brook's patient."

I'm glad it's all a mistake. Dr. Brook will soon be here and I don't need to worry about my baby because Dr. Flank says he'd seen him, which means that what happened a few hours ago was just a dream. A nightmare of a dream.

"Dr. Brook is sick...yes, he came down with a sudden fever... so I'm the one checking his patients. You don't mind, Hon, do you?" he chuckles.

I don't answer.

Dr. Flank checks me and announces all's well.

"What's wrong with you? You should be happy with that beautiful baby of yours. Sometimes things go wrong. Some Mamas don't even get a baby after the delivery. You should be happy."

"But they took my baby away."

"Took him where?"

"To Evanston Hospital...he's not doing so well...last night he ..." the tears choke me.

Dr. Flank quickly checks the stack of papers he's carrying. I watch his face because I want to see his eyes when he tells me he'd made a mistake.

"I'm sorry Hon...I really am," he says after a brief moment, "I didn't have time to read the report. I also have a cousin in my family...yes, with the same problem...he's retarded, of course, but you

never know...each case is so different that I don't want to upset you...
nothing is predictable with meconium ... you really can't tell but my
little cousin... well, he's in his mid twenties by now...he's always
been a source of pain to my aunt and uncle ...really ... a real sadness
and all that, you know...but you never know...like I said, you just
never can tell for sure..."

At noon I receive a white cake from the hospital.

"Congratulations!" it says in blue letters.

My stomach is filled with a sickening emptiness. I cover my face
with both hands trying to hold onto the miniature image of my baby
but it keeps drifting away and by now all that's left are two tiny dimples that smile at me.

It's five in the afternoon. The nurse enters the room, asks how I'm
doing and tells me I need to get out of bed.

"You need to get up, Tara, and move some...you need to get
stronger..."

I'm in the corridor with other women heading in the same direction. When I reach its end I see the nursery. All around me are new
mothers gleaming with happiness. They laugh and smile at each
other. I move to the side and stand alone trying to stop the trem-
bling. My cheeks are burning. The door to the nursery opens again
and a fresh mother steps out and now they're all holding little bun-
dles. One by one I watch them cuddle their tiny babies and I can't
stop crying.

That evening I'm released from the hospital empty handed.

The following morning we're on our way to see our baby and
Darien says that I don't need to cry.

"You'll soon see him..."

I keep seeing those slanted eyes with the two dimples and I realize that we haven't even named our baby.

The sky is cloudy and everything is blurry.

Only thirty-six hours passed since the delivery.

Two white doors with red directives front the Special Infant Care Unit located within Evanston Hospital north of Chicago. Beyond them is a passageway with several large sinks where we scrub our hands and arms thoroughly with sanitizers and put on long gowns. We step forward through two additional doors that swing open and at once we're in a large sized noisy room filled with blinking lights. All around us are ticking machines and monitors that beep continuously and sound alarms. It's hard to tell what I'm looking at because from where I'm standing I can only see small trays filled with birds. Only when I get closer do I realize that I'm looking at wires hooked onto doll sized bodies.

Darien holds my hand.

"This way," he leads me gently.

My stomach is heavy with fear and I can't stop the tears. We move slowly crossing the room to its far corner, and there, inside the last incubator is a tiny baby.

I turn around. Darien stops me.

"You've got to see him... and touch him," he forces me back to the small dish.

"I can't... I can't..."

"Yes you can! You can! You've got to! He needs you...please..."

I'm scared.

One of the physicians joins us and extends a hand.

"I'm Dr. Shane."

We stand around the tiny container watching it. Carol, the nurse in charge joins as Dr. Shane points to the various monitors and details their functions. There are so many tubes in various shapes and sizes that form tiny mazes around my baby's body and they're all taped to his soft skin. I'm standing close, so close that I can almost hear his breathing and all I want is to pick up my baby and cuddle him.

Time passes quickly and it's time to leave but I don't know how I can leave my baby.

"You can come here every day... anytime..."

I feel sick and my head spins. Darien holds my arm and walks me out.

The drive home is long and silent.

When we're home Darien is quick to update his boss.

"Hi Doug...congratulations are in order...yes, of course! I made sure it's a boy...I'll bring the cigars as soon as I'm back at the office..."

I hear Darien's laughter and listen to his chatters and feel hatred brewing within me.

I can't tolerate the loudness of his laughter with which he tries to over-simplify the situation and smooth things over.

"Sure... sure...she's okay...it's only a matter of getting used to the new situation."

Darien plants a kiss on my forehead.

"I need to run some errands. Feel like joining?"

I want to tell him that I don't have a reason to smile or joke or be happy and that I'm not interested in running errands because I'm thinking about our baby and about Dr. Shane's words.

"The next four days are critical ...we need to wait and see if he'll make it ... "

My head is swooning with millions of frightening what-ifs and all I want is to share them with Darien who's too busy to sit and talk.

"We need to fill the house with some decent Champagne...and wine ...people will want to stop by and visit."

"Why would anyone want to stop by? Our baby is hospitalized in critical condition!" I shout because I want Darien to hear me.

Darien plays with the car keys bouncing them between his hands totally oblivious to my words so I shout louder. It's the third time today that he's gone out to run errands.

When the phone rings he's quick to pick it up.

"Hi Pam ...yes, of course...of course she'll be happy to speak with you..."

I don't want to talk to anyone, especially not to Pam but Darien shoves the receiver into my face.

"Hi Pam."

"So tell me... tell me... how did you manage it first time around? Darien tells me it's a boy and a handsome one..."

I don't have the patience for her even if she's Doug's wife.

I don't answer but Pam is a relentless type.

"So how much does he weigh? And can he already count money like his dad?"

I bite my lip.

"So when can I come over and see...eh...what are you naming him?"

"He's in the hospital, Pam, and we don't know if he's going to make it."

"Oh ...I'm sorry to hear... that wasn't planned, was it? I mean... Darien didn't mention it. So what do the doctors say... and how did it happen? And why exactly?"

Darien is sitting across from me making sure I say the right things. Pam refuses to let go.

"What do you mean by ...tremors? Maybe it's seizures...? I'm sure you realize, Tara, that both are caused by malfunction of the brain ..."

"I know Pam! They've already explained..."

"Don't interrupt her!" Darien hisses.

"Well... I don't get what you're saying, Tara. Is your son...well...is he...brain damaged?"

I throw the receiver into Darien's lap. His face reddens but he carries on in his casual tone.

"No...no Pam... it's not you at all Pam... not at all...I apologize again... she's not feeling so well... "

The conversation ends only when Pam is satisfied.

"Don't ever do this again!" he shouts into my face, "Pam is Doug's wife and if she wants to speak to you..."

"I don't want to speak to her!" I shriek into his face and storm out of the room.

***

The following morning we're in the hospital again.

"Dr. Shane," I try to catch his eyes through a curtain of tears, "I need to know if... if my baby ...if he's brain damaged..."

Dr. Shane lowers his head.

"Right now we don't know anything for certain. Last night one of his lungs collapsed and he's not doing so well...we don't even know if... we can't tell at this point...it's too early... we need time to follow up..."

I feel dazed and don't have a clue as to how to deal with a blurry situation of ambiguities and perhaps. Mother has always painted life in blacks and whites without any shades of gray which are the true colors of life, and now when I'm desperate for grayness all I see is blackened black much like Naomi's words that echo from the distance of years.

"You're dumb and your children will be just as defective!"

I'm shrouded in childhood memories and can hear my mother's voice. She tells me that not everyone is like Naomi and that I need to accept myself as I am. I'm still too young to understand what she means but after repeating it so many times over so many years I understand that I'm lucky, because who needs Naomi's smartness when it comes wrapped up in her madness. When Dr. Shane says that he's not sure about my baby's future I want to tell him that it's okay, because I'm also not sure about who I am. The voices of my past keep echoing, convincing me that I'm just a dunce, a dull being that doesn't have within me what it takes to nurture a baby, especially not a damaged baby.

Darien, who'd practiced survival tactics throughout his life, thrives in ambiguous situations. I only know vaguely about his childhood, but from the little I know it's obvious that incertitude is his strongest side. When Dr. Shane says only time will tell Darien is relieved because now he doesn't have to worry about the frailty and uncertainty of the situation. He tells me to stop worrying and quit asking too many questions. I already know his parents well enough to recognize that he inherited that part from Stella. He calls her on Friday night and tells her there's no change.

"Tcha," she responds and at once all his worries are erased and he can, once again, sink comfortably into a state of emotional opacity.

The blackest and darkest of thoughts surface at night and I can only envy Darien's peaceful sleep.

In the morning he tells me.

"You should smile more ...go out shopping... get yourself some new clothes and start acting normal."

"But our baby was born only four days ago! I can't..."

"Listen! We need to start entertaining again. Why don't you ask Pam over?"

"Why not ask her yourself!"

Dr. Shane says we should wait a while longer but I'm scared that our baby might die before he's given a name.

"Oz," I tell Darien," I want to name him Oz."

I meet his smirk.

"Do you really believe that such a stupid name will save him?!"

"Oz means courage in Hebrew. He's fighting for his life. "

"Tcha!"

Dr. Shane repeats his words and says that only time will tell.

"I'm confused. If I have to wait until he's twenty to see whether or not he's damaged then it's going to be too late to help him. Right Dr. Shane?"

Dr. Shane says we need to follow the developmental milestones so I read three books about those stones but I still can't tell if Oz is damaged.

Dr. Shane fills Oz' tiny body with medications that make him drowsy most of the time but when he's awake he smiles and I get to feed him. I look into his eyes and wonder what's going on deep inside his brain.

"If he knows how to suck on a baby bottle nipple it means he's got a brain, right Dr. Shane?"

Dr. Shane has in-depth knowledge when it comes to theories, statistics and reflexes.

"We simply have to wait and see...there's no telling about the future."

Darien doesn't have the time nor the interest to wait and see. He's too busy entertaining his clients who aren't really interested in hearing about Oz. He doesn't have any friends so I wonder what he does with all the pain he carries with him but when he returns home reeking of alcohol I stop wondering.

He sneaks quietly into the bedroom, careful not to wake me up so that he doesn't have to meet my tears in the middle of the night. When he's next to me in bed I reach out and touch him. He turns to me and whispers.

"Tell me... tell me Tara... what's wrong?"

I burst out crying.

"It's okay... it's okay..." he whispers, "the baby will be okay ...you'll see..."

"How do you know?! Dr. Shane said there were complications with minimal brain damage...and we shouldn't expect too much... "

"shushshshshsh... it can't be all that bad...because genetically... and from my side, at least, he stands a good chance." He chuckles.

I'm overwhelmed by frustration and sadness. And all I want is for Darien to hug me and help me with my pain and let me hold his so that we can both get through this nightmare together. But Darien only repeats.

"Why worry?! You're so stubborn!"

And something within me ignites. I wonder if I might be able to put to use some of that stubbornness of mine and help my damaged baby instead of wasting it on self-pity. I realize I need to be strong and crawl out of my blackened misery in order to help Oz.

Dr. Nate's words echo from the distance of my childhood and fill me with a fiery defiance and that's the moment when I start to get to know myself.

Oz is three weeks old when Dr. Shane decides to release him. We're given bottles full of medications with precise instructions and warnings on how to treat his seizure disorder with a list of specialists and several dates for future follow-ups.

Dr. Brook, the obstetrician, circumcises him and says Mazel Tov and I shut my eyes with a silent plea.

"God... please give Oz a good life..."

When we're back home I sing to him all the songs that mother never sang to us. I cradle and kiss him and take in his baby smell and read him lots of stories from the many books that sit on the shelf in his room. I talk to him and move his tiny legs and arms and hear his cute gurgles but after forcing the pink liquid down his throat to prevent seizures, Oz' curious eyes fade and turn blank to the outside world. He tries to fight sleep and sometimes even succeeds but I can tell it's slowing down his awareness and reactions.

Dr. Shane says that some babies compensate for their poor beginning in life by eating and some sleep if off. Oz eats and by age three months he weighs ten kilos spread over sixty-five centimeters and the pediatrician says he's on his way to becoming a giant.

***

This is our third year in the big house in Lake Forest.

Winters in Illinois are longer than anywhere else stretching their gloom from October's head to April's tail. A sickening grayness lingers from above erasing any remnants of the horizon. The air is bleak and lifeless, spreading its shapeless yellowing-green rot over the naked vegetation to create a sense of death. The vast amounts of snow threaten to blind the eyes with temperatures averaging twenty five degrees Celsius below zero.

"The air smells like death!" Darien announces while his eyes scout the front yard buried under mountains of snow. He details his latest trip to Beverly Hills with all its opulence and splendor and the pampering he enjoyed at the Beverly Hills Hilton.

"Yes, it's really like death over here!" he repeats.

"Can we maybe go somewhere?" I ask, yearning to break the monotony and smell nature's fresh air.

"There's nothing to see over here. It's not like in California but... okay... I'll do you a favor."

We venture on an outing but within a short time the trip turns bitter and sour. It's nearly noon and Oz is crying with hunger. I ask Darien to stop for a few minutes.

"Oz will eat when I say it's time to eat!"

"But he's only seven months old...you can't ..."

"Well...he'll just have to adjust himself to our schedule! He'll eat when it's time to eat!"

Darien refuses to let go. He's glued to his principles like to oxygen and continues arguing. I respond and Oz screams and within an hour we're back home.

The big empty house with the constantly depressing weather, only intensify my sense of loneliness. Darien is never around except over the weekend. My tears are constant, even as I wrap Oz in several layers, bundle him with a thick quilt and place him carefully inside the sled. Both of us are out in the freezing air. The streets are deserted except for an occasional police car that passes slowly nearby. The officers already know me; they tip their hats in my direction and wish me a good day. There's no one else on the sidewalks or on the white streets, not even a dog a cat or a bird. They're all holed up inside their houses and I have no idea how they survive the long months with death smelling air.

I write long letters to mother and dad and share with them Oz' world. Darien is with his clients at all times, totally disinterested in hearing about his baby's poor health. Oz' seizures call for frequent hospitalizations and constant adjustments of his medications. Each one has different side effects that rely on statistics, much like the various responses I hear from the physicians regarding my baby's future.

I'm starting to notice a kind of strangeness in Oz, an inability to communicate with other toddlers his age and I understand that my baby is different.

My words anger Darien.

"Why d'you always look for problems?! Everything is okay with Oz!"

"But look how he..."

"It's in your head...all inside your head! I'll repeat! If you won't create problems, there won't be any problems!"

Stella calls and says that some people will do ANYTHING to get attention. ANYTHING at all. I ask her if she thinks that Oz is the one looking for attention or if it's me.

Stella gets all confused.

"Tell me Stella, do you think that the reason Oz doesn't recognize faces of people he's seen several times, is because he's looking for attention? And what about the strange noises he makes? And why do other toddlers his age shy away from him?"

Stella says I'm being sassy.

"I'm trying to understand, Stella, if Oz' eyes cross strangely while his head is tilted sideways... if he doesn't look into other people's eyes... and if he puts his hands on their head and bites them and then bites himself... and if he can't connect with other children his age...does that make me sassy?! And if I want Oz to be able to recognize me from a distance of ten feet... and be able to hold a small shovel and use it properly... and if I don't want other kids shying away from him 'cause they're frightened...do you think it's too much to expect of a two year old toddler?!"

She's convinced I'm insolent and intends proving it.

"J'ai une fable," she answers me in French, "It's a true story, eh? You can ask Darien, eh?"

I get to hear about six-year-old Darien who cut his leg falling off his bicycle.

"He screamed all the time to the clinic, you know? So I told him not to think about it so it not hurt him, eh? And even when the doctor stitched him and gave him pills for the pain, eh? He cried and cried all the way to home until I said enough, eh?! You must to stop the crying! This is not a theater, eh?!"

"So what happened, Stella?"

"He didn't want to stop so I told him to pretend so he then stopped, eh?"

"What are you trying to say? What's the moral of the fable, Stella?"

"Aloo? Aloo?"

"So what happened at the end?" I scream into the dead receiver.

But Stella stands her ground and says I'm being sassy because I didn't listen to her.

***

I get a letter from Naomi saying that she's jobless and desperate and her overall health is grave. She's nearly blind in one eye and the other is deteriorating, and her few remaining hairs are white and she doesn't even have enough money to color them. She needs my help and asks that I send her two hundred dollars each month so that she won't have to ask mother and dad for help.

I'm speechless and don't know how to react. I haven't kept in touch with her since I left home nine years ago but from the updates I get from mother I hear about her hospitalizations and the various jobs she finds from time to time. Mother writes about Naomi's back and forth's with Garry from New York and says that he's still interested in her even though she keeps holding him off.

Garry, a short, heavy set bald guy from New York met Naomi coincidently while touring Israel and fell madly in love with her. Several weeks later Naomi, who was in one of her emotionally declining moods, was institutionalized but kept tantalizing him through correspondence. While in the hospital she instructed me to write to Garry about her situation and let him know that she's not interested in ever seeing him again.

Shortly thereafter, Garry landed unexpectedly in Israel and went straight to the hospital to visit Naomi but she refused to see him. He returned to New York heartbroken and within two months married someone else but never got over Naomi. In between her hospitalizations and illnesses, Naomi kept in touch with Garry until she understood that her window of opportunities of meeting someone else was soon closing. She then urged him to divorce his wife and promised to marry him. Garry kept his part of the deal but Naomi went on with her games and has since kept him dangling on a sting.

After reading Naomi's letter Darien says.

"I'm not a charity box! Besides, your sister is a conniving liar! I don't believe a word she says! Not a word! I'll tell you something I've never told you before..."

To my astonishment I hear a story similar to those I've heard before. Darien describes how Naomi forced her way into his bed when he first visited me in Bo-Acha Yam and says he was physically repulsed by her.

"Nothing she does can ever surprise me! Nothing!"

Darien says he doesn't trust Naomi and we should simply ignore her letter.

Five months later Naomi calls me.

"I'm with Garry in New York. We're getting married on New Year's Eve."

"You're getting married next week?!"

"Yes!"

I try to find a flight ticket but none are available, not even in first class. Naomi says I shouldn't worry about flying in especially for the wedding because now that both of us are in the States, we can always get together. I shudder. I don't mind speaking to her on the phone but I don't want her near me.

She calls often, asks about Oz and voices medical opinions even when I don't ask for any. Her world, as always, resembles that of a parasite, meddling in foreign territories and nourishing on other people's lives while sucking the marrow out of their souls.

Several weeks later it's one of those stormy evenings at home and Darien shouts:

"It's all because of you! All the problems that Oz has are because of you! And you're to blame for all the other problems we have..."

Naomi happens to call that very same moment and I make the mistake of telling her about it. She immediately sides up with Darien and makes me feel even worse.

***

Darien refuses to take Oz to the park.

"I have better things to do than to waste my time in a stinking park with a bunch of stupid mothers!"

Oz has difficulties speaking, running and communicating with other two year olds and Darien avoids his company.

The doctors are lost for answers. They're unable to decipher what causes the high fevers that afflict him in cycles of three weeks apart and trigger a variety of seizures that force his hospitalization. I spend long nights next to his bed trying to cool off his small body and prevent the onset of seizures.

And by now I can feel my world distancing itself from that of Darien's.

I meet alone with the various doctors, experts and therapists and listen to the results of their evaluations. Darien refuses to join me even when Oz' condition continues into its second year. The opinions are varied backed up by theories that rely heavily on statistics but they all lack specific definitions and leave me frustrated.

"It's only a question of time, Mrs. Schmidt, only time...be patient, Mrs. Schmidt... only time will tell how Oz will develop...only time..."

Oz' illness is exhausting emphasizing the gaping space that exists between Darien and me, a vast universe of polarized views within our miserable relationship.

There are days when I wake up with strange thoughts and wonder what it would be like to have a healthy baby, one without gaps and gapes and angles but there's a long list of things I'm not allowed to discuss with Darien and dreams are amongst them.

"Do you think I should register Oz to the local kindergarten?" I ask him.

"Do whatever you think is right...you know what's best..."

"But I'd like your opinion..."

"I said ... you can do whatever you think!"

"But it's a difficult decision..."

"Come on Tara! Just make up your own mind!"

When the outcome proves good, Darien takes full credit for their success but when things sour he's quick to release.

"It's YOUR fault! It was YOUR decision and YOUR responsibility! Now fix it!"

Days and weeks drift by and I keep imagining a little girl and hope that this time I'll be lucky and she'll be healthy. One night nature's yearnings get the better of me and I find myself in an intimate dialogue with Darien. I switch off the lights to make him feel comfortable and when each of us is back in his respective corner of the large bed I smile and hope for a surprise, even though I know it's a planned one.

The following month Darien is off again. He calls me from somewhere.

"Tara?" the line keeps breaking, "I'm calling from the plane...is everything okay?"

"The results are back."

"What are you talking about?"

"The pregnancy test... remember?"

"Oh yes, yes...so?"

"I'm pregnant."

Silence.

"Darien? Are you there?"

I hear a small chuckle.

"Oh!"

"Aren't you happy?"

"Tcha."

Sevan comes into the world crying and screaming and kicking anything in her way, a bottle, a diaper, a warm sponge or a kiss and I get to learn about colicky babies. Oz is nearing three and he's proud of his baby sister. His eyes twinkle with happiness as he places his hand on her new head.

"Sevan... Sevan... Sevan..." his metallic sounding voice is slow, "She nice... she sweet..." he kisses her tiny hand and smiles.

Sevan is a funny baby with a permanent twinkle in her enormous dark eyes. She absorbs the world around her sharply and swiftly, staring at Oz and taking in his movements, his voice, watching his wobbly gait and staring at his angled eyes. She looks at books with amazing fascination and spends hours turning pages, putting together puzzles and playing with building blocks.

"She prefers books," Darien complains, "She doesn't want me near her. You put her up to it."

"She isn't used to seeing you. If you'd spend more time with her she'd get to know you."

He storms angrily out of the room.

Sevan is only a year old but she already uses complex sentences and I can't understand how she does it. The cashier lady at the supermarket hears the tiny voice and bursts out laughing.

"How old are you?" she asks her.

"Wike dis!" Sevan sticks out two tiny fingers.

I wink at her.

Darien is angry that I speak Hebrew with the kids.

"I don't want to hear that language when I'm around!"

I don't have an explanation for his sudden dislike of Hebrew or of anything else connected with Israel, but as always, luck is on his side. The speech therapist insists I switch languages and use only English with Oz.

"He's incapable of handing both languages. Even one language is a challenge for him..."

I make an exception for the word Ima and insist that he calls me by that name. When we're together in the yard and I show him a flower and repeat the word in English, it's as though he'd never seen a flower before. We move from flowers to leaves and now we're with trees and sidewalks and we start learning from scratch names of objects in English. There are so many old-new words that trigger his frustration. When he asks for water I insist that he say it in English and he bursts out crying. I hug him and hope that one day he'll understand.

***

Darien calls me from the office.

"Tara listen...Doug just told me we're moving to Dallas... yes, in Texas...we're moving there at the end of the summer..."

Within seconds I'm told that our five years in Illinois are coming to an end.

March marks the beginning of our summer plans. Darien's voice changes to match the spring and the summer ahead, using soft imploring tones of fresh green to get his way.

We're busy planning our yearly summer vacation intending to spend three weeks in Europe followed by a visit to Israel. Darien, as usual, refuses to accompany us. I've already stopped counting the number of years since his last visit there. He clarifies that at the end of the summer we'll be moving to our new house in Dallas.

Darien's summers are dedicated solely to the whims of his clients who supply him the oxygen he so desperately requires. When he's with them he gets into his chameleon mode, the way he'd always done in his youthful years and together they travel to exotic islands and visit famous opera houses and the chicest of restaurants.

But only when he's with us, at home, does he feel secure enough to unveil his disguise and become a full blown Helmut.

When Darien calls me from the office I can hear papers being shuffled in the background.

"I've only got a second... I want us to go to Italy this summer... I need to be there..."

"So how about combining it with our visit to Israel?"

"Sorry... it's too late...you should have reminded me earlier..."

"What do you mean? We go to Europe every..."

"Don't start!"

"But ..."

"Enough!"

And at once his tone turns wintry black.

"Please Darien...please join us...only this once..."

"I haven't lost anything over there!"

My stomach churns with the bitterness of past promises and the dreams whispered in my ears when we'd first met. I start to understand the wrong choices I've made and feel sorry for the words which were never spoken out loud.

I was in a hurry to escape the things that pained me but failed to take the time to contemplate the route I'd chosen. I wanted to keep on running, distance myself from the ills and madness and get as far as I could from my home and from my past. At that point in time I failed to understand that there is no future without a past, and that prior to paving a new path and journeying into a new future, I must first comprehend my starting point. But something within me begins to awaken and I understand that Darien grasps our togetherness and the family concept very differently from me. It echoes within me old-new fears and plants seedlings of fresh new thoughts, but at this point I'm too scared to even contemplate another existence.

It's our last week in Illinois. Darien calls me.

"I miss you..." he whispers.

I stare at the receiver.

"Did something happen?"

He laughs.

"I'm horny ...and I'm dying to come home... but I've still got so much work...I can't stop thinking about you. I'll try to come home early...I've got to run ...speak to you later..."

The receiver is still in my hand. I shut my eyes and try to understand what exactly was said.

Darien returns home wearing a big smile.

"This is our last summer in Illinois. At the end of our vacation we'll fly straight to Dallas so I thought we should go visit The Colony one last time."

There's always a hidden agenda behind Darien's sudden suggestions, but I decide to let it go and not try to figure it out.

Our local restaurant, The Colony, is located within the only hotel in town and caters primarily to the young families and their children. It was built, at the time, for the local tycoons who enjoyed dining within its formidable surroundings.

As soon as we're seated Darien announces.

"I'll be right back ... don't wait for me .... go ahead and order..."

He disappears in the direction of the private rooms in back.

I order food and the three of us eat and drink and enjoy the after dinner ice cream with hot fudge.

An hour later Darien rushes in.

"I'm sorry..." his face is flushed.

"Where did you go to?"

"Oh... it doesn't matter anymore..." he releases an afterthought, "I was hoping to see Kalb Thornton from Hutchinson's...the one who replaced Dave Bell...I was told he'd be here tonight..."

I feel cheated. The bitterness within me is released at home.

"How could you be so manipulative... and use us for your own needs?! You could have gone there by yourself ..."

Our back and forth's continue long after the kids are already in bed.

I go upstairs leaving Darien with a glass of Chivas.

The Chivas is always there. And there's plenty of it.

***

The four of us fly to Italy where we meet up with Helmut and Stella. Three weeks later we part our ways: I continue to Israel with both kids spending two months with mother and dad in Bo-Acha Yam and Darien flies directly to Texas.

The two months go by swiftly.

"I don't want to leave," Oz cries when he sees the suitcases.

Sevan clutches my hand.

It's past midnight. The five of us are at the airport and it's time to say goodbye.

Sevan cries and Oz is all angled and strange and I wipe my wet cheeks.

The ground hostess helps me through the security-check and onto the plane. Oz' white face is strained. I prepare the bags, towels and cold water with the emergency kit nearby. Oz says the airplane smells bad and he doesn't like it and I know he means that he doesn't like going away and leaving behind his favorite people.

We take off to our new home in Texas and I can only hope for a positive change in our future.

The house in Dallas is beautiful and very spacious but the three of us are exhausted and go straight to bed.

The familiar noise forces me out of bed. It takes me a second to regain my senses and recall that I'm in a new house. I rush into Oz' room and listen to his familiar heavy breathing. His small body feels like an oven. I shut my eyes and imagine the beach as I try to hold off the fearful reality for a few more seconds. It's three in the morning and I don't know a local physician or neurologist and I'm not familiar with the city or its hospitals. It's been only ten hours since we've landed and I'm confused trying to figure out if I should dial for help and all at once I lose sight of who I am, where and why. I try to wake up Darien.

"Oz' is having a seizure... I don't know anyone here..."

But Darien doesn't respond, not even when I shake him and speak into his ear.

I dial the emergency number and drive Oz to the nearest hospital where I make the acquaintance of a new neurologist.

And that's how we spend our first night in our new home within our new surroundings.

Our house is located in the town of Highland Park, a refined alcove founded in the early 1920's within the city of Dallas. Aided by ingenious vision and sufficient financial backing to execute its abstraction, the community blossomed into an exclusive town while retaining the natural beauty of the land with the windings of Turtle Creek. Its borders, bound by crepe myrtle, red buds and thickly rooted sweet gum bushes, add to the luscious lawns and parks that green the entire community. Large estates framed by stunning landscapes emerged along both its banks, extending, over the years to include University Park, a ball throw away from the prestigious Southern Methodist University and its Cowboys heroes. Very old oak and magnolia trees cast heavy shadows over the wide sidewalks, lending majestic air to the seven square miles of exorbitant real estate famed throughout the States.

The spotless parks are in abundance and provide the whitest of playgrounds with the cleanest of white sands and the largest of play sets, tennis courts and a rich assortment of color coordinated blooms manicured to perfection by armies of gardeners. The parks welcome all, including the battalions of maids all dressed in white uniforms and allowed to rest on its comfortable benches. The humble, well meaning ladies are entrusted with the teachings of the younger generations within the Park Cities as they sound Spanish or lame English or both, leaving the mothers who employ them, with ample time to do what they do best: charity for the less fortunate.

The public library, neatly situated within a Spanish styled building, contains the latest of the latests and for those with extra finely tuned ears, the jet swifts and globetrotters of the community, a well-stacked variety of digital technology. The fire and police stations boast record response time for emergency calls: two minutes and ten seconds. Each.

The four elementary schools, one middle school and one high school enjoy the luxury of a near infinite budget allocated, primarily, to the enhancement of sports. A bird's view of the lushly green area would, undoubtedly, register countless church turrets and twice as many feminine heads wearing identical platinum colored hair, their delicate figures squeezed into dresses sized zero.

The town was blessed with twelve hundred or so executives residing within its boundaries that make up the financial pillars of the metropolis and beyond. All aspire to be beautiful, joyful and rich.

Darien is in love with the nonchalant atmosphere that omits any direct reference to money. The men's Porches and ladies' Mercedes speak loudest as do the breathtaking mansions and smiley air everyone exudes. Life seems happy all around and I'm beginning to wonder if Darien is wrong when he says that money is the only thing that counts in life.

I see larger than life mansions with matching swimming pools and tennis courts and backyards that stretch further than the eye can see. Most women look as though they've just stepped out of fashion magazines as they breeze through the infinite boutiques and tagged shops and restaurants galore volunteering their precious time to charity. They cling to each other in the plush restaurants with big smiles and glittering teeth but shy from any food intakes. They're all absorbed in socializing and creating glitzy social gatherings to satisfy their admirers that feed off their photographs in the local papers.

By creating an endless joyous party for all, they ensure the livelihood of a vast number of organizations and religious groups and if that's what money can do then I'm all for it.

But when I'm alone with Darien, other important things surface, those that money can't buy. I try loving him and I wish he could touch my heart and arouse the woman within me, but he distances himself from me and from the children.

"I want us to create a different togetherness... share our parenthood...it makes me want you..."

"What the hell are you talking about, woman?! You're sick in the head!"

When he touches me I shut my eyes and pretend. Then I slip into one of my silent drawers and pick out a memory from my past, a reminder of other touches, the manly kind able to cast a velvety drape over my eyes.

"I love you Tara..."

And I watch him exhale smilingly and keep my silent drawer open for the next time and the next soft touch. I know he feels something is amiss but he doesn't say a word. Not a word. And I, too, don't know what to say in order to make him understand.

***

A year has gone by and once again we're in Belgium on one of our routine summer vacations with Helmut and Stella.

The summer season is as fickle as usual; draped in typical European weather of brutal cold, summer ignores its titled name creating vicious winds with continuous rains that force us indoors throughout our entire vacation.

The children are still young but it doesn't stop Stella from checking their every move at all hours of the day and demanding they follow her strict rules and lengthy ceremonies that accompany each meal. Helmut, as per his habit, mumbles and complains and bursts out shouting whenever something isn't to his liking.

Oz wets his pant and Sevan doesn't stop crying.

Darien is furious. He takes Oz to the side and warns him to stop wetting himself but it only aggravates the situation. When Sevan refuses to eat he explodes and everything turns into a tumult.

Our nights are just as predictable.

"I'll miss you ..." Darien reaches for my hand.

We're in bed tucked under heavy blankets.

"Come here..." he squeezes my hand several times and uses small touches to tell me how much he'll miss me. When I don't respond he pulls me over to his side.

"Will you miss me?" he whispers.

He rubs his hands on my arms as though trying to erase them.

"Stop...please don't do that..."

"It's not nice of you Tara..." he uses a baby voice.

"But I don't like it...it doesn't feel good..."

"I won't see you for the next two months..."

"You can still change your mind and join us tomorrow..."

"Come here..." his deep voice turns husky.

And for reasons other than love I hold onto him and imagine

myself elsewhere hugging someone else, a kind man who doesn't shout or beg...

"Tell me Tara... tell me you love me..."

...a strong and gentle man...and when I'll meet him I'll wash him with words of love and cover his body with mine ...

"I want to hear you say it...say it Tara... tell me you love me... "

...and shower him with love... give in to my hidden lusts... and thank him for protecting us from demeaning words and painful humiliations ...

I hug him again and again but I can't bring myself to say what I don't feel.

The following morning Darien drives us to the airport where we say our goodbyes and part our different ways. Darien flies to Germany and the three of us board a plane to Israel. Five hours later the skies are blue and the air is warm and the kids are swamped by grand-love and kisses given by mother and dad.

***

Now that Naomi is married and living in New York and baby Bilha is elsewhere working for the government, Oz and Sevan get all the hugs that we've never known in childhood.

Dad, as always, touches the tiny souls gently. He takes both kids to the porch fronting the sea, seats Sevan on his wide shoulders and helps Oz onto a chair next to him. Hugging each other and gazing at the fiery sun as it dives into the Mediterranean Sea, the children are mesmerized by dad's soft voice and the ancient Greek tales about waxen wings and lost fleeces.

Once a week, Darien calls.

"I'm so busy ... good thing you're not here now...I have so much work ..."

"The kids would like to speak with you..."

"Maybe next week ...I'm in a hurry... on my way to an important dinner..."

At the end of two months filled with lots of hugging love and kisses, we return to Dallas.

Darien picks us up from the airport.

"So...how was it?" he asks the children who haven't slept since we'd left Israel. Looking confused they trudge slowly towards the car.

"Don't put your bag here! It's 'gonna mess up my car!" he threatens Oz with his voice.

"But..."

"You landed a minute ago and you already have a BUT?!"

"Come on Darien...leave them alone. You see they're exhausted. Nothing's 'gonna happen to your car if Oz..."

"Why are you meddling?! Maybe it's acceptable in Israel but not here! Now get this fucking thing out of here!" he growls.

The car is heavy with silence.

"I'm thirsty mom."

"Here. Take this," I hand Sevan a bottle of water.

"Hold it! How many times did we have this discussion?! No one eats or drinks inside my car!"

"But she's..."

"Which part of what I just said don't you understand?!"

The next hour is drenched with the familiar murky atmosphere.

Summer in Texas is long, stretching beyond its borders well into fall and lengthening the sun's warming hugs. Darien smiles then jumps into the pool taking Oz and Sevan with him. I near the water's edge bend down then kiss him. I tell him that it warms my heart and thrills me to see him with both kids and watch the way he fathers them, but from the look on his face I understand that he finds my words baffling.

"What's the big deal? It's only a short swim!" he hurries out of the pool.

Winter sneaks in at the end of October showing off its forceful powers. It seems that everything is larger and stronger in Texas, including the rains that lash out with gusty might accompanied by freezing storms that release orange-sized balls of hale. The large balls plunge into the pool scrambling its waters and turning it into a small ocean with a white blanket spread all around it on the ground.

Life's routines include daily therapies for Oz, medical checkups to monitor his various medications and evaluations that never seem to end. The waiting rooms available at the various therapists are spacious allowing me to pay full attention to Sevan. I open a large bag and let her choose a game, a book or any other item that arouses her curiosity.

We're at the dentist for a routine checkup.

"I don't want to alarm you Mrs. Schmidt but... Oz has a lesion on his tongue which must be removed..."

The following day Oz is wheeled into the operating room. I kiss his cute dimples and promise to be there when he wakes up. He puts both arms around my neck and kisses my cheek.

An hour and a half later the dentist explains.

"It was quite large ... but I doubt that it's malignant... of course, we'll have to wait for the pathology report ... it might even be caused by his medications... so I'm afraid I can't discard any future lesions ..."

Oz' recovery is slow and painful with nine stitches crisscrossing his small tongue. He tries to sift liquids and bursts out crying.

"I love you Ozzie..." I cradle him in my arms, "I wish I could make the pain disappear..."

Darien loves puns in French and German and enjoys just as much practicing the cusses he'd learned from his father.

I don't react anymore when he calls me a stupid cow. I don't argue. I simply give in and don't demand a thing. I find myself taking up less space, shrinking within my own world and caring only for both children.

Oz' relentless fevers continue into their fourth year and the doctors are at a loss unable to find a reason or a solution for the situation. The nights are long and frightful with sudden high temperatures that trigger seizures. Days and nights get confused and affect my moodiness. I'm permanently exhausted feeling dreary and burdened by a heavy melancholy with a sense of desperation but I'm still hopeful for some sort of friendship with Darien.

My hopes take me back to my childhood days and the fireplace scent that ignited within me a dire want for the family warmth that I've never known; a heartwarming feel resembling what I was hoping to find in Darien, a quiver of sorts that slipped away from me.

Perhaps I was hoping for things which I wasn't able to define sharply enough, vague wants and wishes that got confused along the way and were affected by the sadness reflected in his eyes.

I do my best to balance Oz' required daily treatments and therapies, while allowing both children fun and joyful mischief. Guided by the therapists, I drive to the various parks scattered throughout the city of Dallas that are best suited for his needs, and take advantage of the diversified equipment installed in each. It allows him to practice his balance, equilibrium and coordination in a playful environment. Being extraordinarily agile and fast, Sevan helps Oz climb ladders and cross long wooden bridges stretched over creeks. They go up and down twisted slides using the various apparatus scattered around the park, rocking and swinging at dizzying speeds.

Next to the rucksack that contains foods and drinks, is the emergency kit that's always with me.

On the way home from the park, we stop next to an open field carpeted with the blinding beauty of sunflowers, dandelions and daisies, a dazzling carnival of colorful flowers. Oz and Sevan cut through the wild field covered with the brassy coppers of firewheels and catch golden fragments of yellows and reds and greens speckled with blue and purple smiles.

I hug them to my heart and cover their faces with kisses.

"I love you so much..."

On our way home the car is filled with songs and laughter and perfumed with the scent of flowers and good humor.

Only Stella, always a phone call away, refuses to let go.

"If you won't look for trouble, Oz won't have any, eh Tara?"

***

"The repair guy is coming tomorrow at nine sharp. Make sure the bathroom looks descent!" Darien releases in my direction on his way out to the office.

By the time he returns home that evening, the kids are already fast asleep.

The familiar noises wake me up. Seconds later I find Oz in bed with a raging fever. His body tremors and his eyes are glazed. I hurry with the towels and the cold water but by the time I'm back he's already unconscious. I pick him up in my arms and enter our bedroom. Darien is in a deep state of sleep and doesn't react. I call the hospital and follow their instructions and half an hour later Oz' body is exhausted but calm. There's nothing else to be done now except wait for him to wake up from his deep sleep.

I lie down on the carpet next to his bed.

Around eight Oz begins to shift in bed. He moves restlessly then bursts out crying. I pick him up and rush to the nearest bathroom because I already know what's coming and I don't want him to throw up in bed. Darien stands in the doorway and blocks the entrance.

"You can't go in there now! I just finished cleaning it up for the repair guy! He'll be here in an hour."

"Move out of my way!"

Oz snorts.

"MOVE!"

Darien pushes me back.

"BITCH!"

The blow lands on my back.

And as always, late at night, Darien mumbles his sorry words.

***

There's a new lesion on Oz' tongue. The dentist is concerned and asks that we see him the following day.

Around noon I leave the house with two-year-old Sevan napping in my arms only to find out that Darien had taken my car, along with the baby seat, to the repair shop that same morning. I have no choice but to place Sevan's smallness on the back seat of Darien's large Mercedes, buckle her snugly with both safety belts and get onto the highway in the direction of Oz' kindergarten.

The drive on Central Expressway is smooth with sunny rays of late October. Traffic is sparse. Sevan lets out a cry. I glance in the rear view mirror and within a split second things change.

The noise is deafening with glass exploding all around. I'm overwhelmed with fear and confusion. The air is filled with shrieks and cries. I squeeze the breaks with all my strength but I can't stop the car from smashing into the metal in front of it or stopping the raining glass. The sudden silence is horrific. I open my eyes and find myself inside a strange car. It's hard to breathe. Everything around me is cloudy. Sevan lets out a piercing shriek. I'm all confused. I try to open the door but my hands shake so badly I keep missing the release button. I can't remember where I am or how I got there. The car fills with cries and shrieks. I manage to rid myself of the safety belt, force open the door and hurry to the back seat. It's red. I pick up Sevan and hug her tiny body. She's all wet with blood thumping rhythmically out of her ear. I hug her tighter.

"Get out of the car! Get out! I'll drive you to the hospital..." someone shouts.

I don't budge.

"Lady! Get in the car! Move it! Hurry!"

"Please...my baby is dying...she's losing blood...please drive faster..."

I keep my hands tightly around Sevan. She's fast asleep but her ear keeps thumping. My hands are sticky and blood keeps dripping in between my fingers.

We reach the emergency room at Presbyterian Hospital. I'm confused and I still don't understand why Sevan is so red. People stare. A strange hand grabs her. I feel a sudden urge to urinate and ask the nurse what I should do but her words don't make sense and I find myself in the next cubicle behind green curtains. I shut my eyes and try to figure out what I'm doing there. When I reopen them I realize my shirt and pants are painted red and at once I remember Oz. I go to the nurses' station and try to dial the kindergarten but I keep missing the numbers. The nurse says she'll call Darien but I'm not sure he'll want to come and see the bloody mess.

Someone says he's in Chicago and I feel a relief. Brad, a colleague of his appears and sits next to me. The nurse says we need to wait. I don't feel tired but my eyes keep shutting. When I open them again I see my hands are still red. Red and sticky.

A doctor appears.

"I'm sorry...I'm afraid her condition is unstable..."

I feel dizzy and grab a white coat.

"Here...drink this..." a nurse hands me a small cup.

The liquid has a strange taste. Again I try to figure things out but nothing makes sense. A policeman appears. He wants to know what happened but I don't know so he tells me.

"You were hit from the rear...propelled into the car in front of you ...hit the car ahead of him that propelled..."

I can't keep track of who did what to which car but the uniformed man is gentle and says I'm not to blame.

"It was a yellow cab...he rammed into you...didn't keep his distance..."

I don't ask any questions. Sevan's bleeding face keeps floating in front of me. But Sevan is gone. She's not near me. I shiver and retch. I try to vomit out the fear.

A sharp pain cuts through my upper chest.

"It's from the seat belt...it was fastened real tight.... " the doctor says.

Once again I'm reminded of Oz. The nurse dials Leslie, my neighbor, who picks him up from kindergarten. More time passes before the nurse gives me a green bathrobe.

"Here...put this on. Your son is here."

Leslie walks in holding Oz' hand. He smiles and points with his finger.

"It's red, Ima."

I look at the stain poking out.

Leslie promises to take care of Oz until Darien's return. She gives me another quick hug and they're off.

I have no idea of the time. Brad says we've been here for over six hours.

The door opens again and the doctor says.

"We need to transfer her to another hospital...she's unstable...it's a head injury... serious condition..."

Inside the ambulance I try to memorize.

"Unstable...serious condition," the doctor said.

I'm almost certain that's what he said.

The children's trauma unit located in Parkland Hospital holds five beds. The large rectangular shaped waiting room has blue chairs arranged along its white walls.

At the far end of the room is a metal door with a digital box attached to it. I'm given a code to be used once every four hours restricting each visit to five minutes. In a separate corner of the room is a small table with a coffee machine next to two recliner-sofas.

When it's my turn, I punch in the code and step inside the unit.

After crossing the large entrance I count four beds hemmed behind green curtains. I step hesitantly and at once, out of nowhere, my baby's face from five years ago floats by. An awful nausea takes hold of me flooding my eyes and making me feel as though, once again, I'm in hell.

I take a few more steps. Behind the fifth curtain I find Sevan. Her tiny body is covered with countless monitors. She cries and stretches her small arms towards me.

"Ima..." her voice comes out in tiny squeaks "Ima...."

I hold Sevan's small hands in mine and kiss them over and over and over again. I kiss her forehead and the free spaces on her arms and my five minutes are up.

"I promise to be back soon, Sevanie... please don't cry...I need to wait outside... I'll be back soon..."

On my way out a curtain opens slightly and I see a small black silhouette.

I'm back in the waiting room. There're a dozen or so blacks holding bibles. They sit and pray and every so often chant. My eyes are on the big clock. Another four hours less ten minutes until my next visit.

The singing subsides and a woman gets up and hands me a clean shirt. I look at mine and burst out crying. It's already two in the morning and the place is as quiet and as calm as the woman. When she hears I'm from the Holy Land, her fallen face turns into a smile.

158

"Fate...ist fate that landed us two n'same pit 'o sorrow...fate by higher power..."

The entire congregation joins in and promises to hold a special prayer for Sevan.

It's already five. A short black man bent in half and accompanied by several new members, appears. I listen to their prayers and wipe my eyes at the sound of Sevan's name.

The kind woman follows with her own story.

"My daudew's but sixteen... had her last surgery in Mayo Clinic and on de way home in de car she lose consciousness...faith's kept us togetha ...alive...as family ..."

I nod my head.

"You've someone close 'pray with? The fadher... daudew's fadher...is he 'round?"

I cry. I can't stop crying. The kind woman wraps her arms around my shoulders and sings. The entire group joins and sways sideways. And I just keep crying.

"Mrs. Schmidt!" the doctor calls out my name.

I hurry to the door.

"Sevan is unconscious and she's not doing very well...she sustained a fractured skull and a punctured eardrum... we'll have to watch her ...only time will tell..." the physician mouths the familiar words.

I move my head up and down because I'm supposed to understand.

The people in the waiting room are singing again. I don't care how they choose to name their God, I'm just grateful for their human warmth, their compassion and kindness and for holding my hand and telling me that things will be okay even though I know they're only trying to make me feel better.

It's six in the morning. Darien arrives straight from the airport wearing a three-piece hand tailored suit. After a small hug and a peck on my forehead he inquires about the accident and adds.

"I need a few hours' sleep... I have a hectic schedule tomorrow..." he takes a taxi and goes home to sleep.

My eyes are again on the clock. Two more hours until my next visit with Sevan. I can't stand the waiting so I go to the door and punch in the code. A nurse appears.

"Please...please let me see Sevan again..." I cry.

"I'll see what I can do..."

The door shuts. Seconds later it reopens.

"You can come in Mrs. Schmidt...but only for two minutes ..."

I'm swallowed inside, find the tiny hand and plant a forest full of kisses on it.

'Sevani...you've got to get well... then we can chase wild flowers and bugs ...please Sevani... please..."

My two minutes of grace are up.

The next time I go in to see Sevan she's better and the following day she stops crying and starts asking questions. At night I hurry home, take a quick shower and plant several small kisses on Oz' head then I rush back to the hospital with a bag full of fresh clothes.

There are only empty chairs now in the waiting room. The congregation is gone and so is the kind woman whose daughter died but the old frail man returns. He speaks softly and promises to pray for Sevan until she gets stronger. I hug him through tearful eyes and thank you's.

Ten days later Sevan is released from the hospital with specific instructions.

"She can return home on the condition that she's kept in total isolation for two months...we need to ensure that she doesn't contract a virus...or develop an intercranial infection..."

We return home to a front porch decorated by caring neighbors and friends and to a fridge stuffed with food. The small table outside the door is heaped with cookies and cakes and best wishes for a quick recovery.

The colorful letters strung above the front door announce.

"Welcome Home Sevan"

The isolation period with both children is long and exhausting. Sevan recovers slowly and begins to let go of her haunting memories.

I'm so consumed with worries that I keep neglecting the fierce pain in my left arm.

"It's muscle strain... probably from the tight safety belt and from pushing hard against the steering wheel ..." the doctor repeats.

I'm glad it's nothing more.

***

Oz is six when he asks to choose his own shoes.

We enter the store.

"I want this."

Oz points to a pair of laced shoes.

"Dumb choice! I won't allow it! You know damn well he can't lace!" Darien growls.

I feel tingling at the tips of my fingers.

"I want Oz to learn how to lace."

"I see you're out to frustrate him, eh?! Are you doing this to be annoying or are you just plain stupid?! Don't you understand that he'll never be able to lace?!" his puffed cheeks are red with anger.

"Ozzi, are you sure you want shoes with laces?"

"Yes."

"So you've got to promise me..." I bend down, hug him and whisper familiar words into his ear then add, "I want you to promise me that no matter how long it takes ... you'll keep trying until you learn how to lace them... promise me that you'll never give up trying... promise?"

"I promise, Ima."

My eyes are on Darien.

"Oz promised me he'd try to learn how to lace them."

"So what if he promised?! It only makes it all the worse! Don't you understand that you're asking him to do something that he'll never be able to do?!"

I smile at Oz.

"You can have the shoes with the laces ...", again I hug him, "It doesn't matter how long it takes you to learn, Ozzi ...as long as you'll do your best," I cover his dimples with tiny kisses.

"Stupid cow!" Darien storms out of the store.

Later, at home, we sit on the carpeted floor in Oz' room and practice tying knots. Three year old Sevan sits close by and follows our every move.

"One lace...over the other... chasing each other under the bridge..." I hum a tune I've put together especially for tying knots.

The songs are always with us. Oz loves music and his memory is sharp when it comes to learning melodies. He's quick to recite new tunes and retains them. There are various tunes for doing math calculations, gathering words, reading, sequencing days of the week, the months or any other events and remembrances that are required.

Oz is unable to retain a focused gaze on both laces. His weak muscles force his eyes to roam sideways much like his hands with their slight tremble and soft fingers that lack strength. When he tries to hold both laces together, they twist and fall apart. We practice again and again and again but they always give in and fall apart.

The anti seizure medications also affect his motor skills and make it so much harder to control. There are moments when I actually doubt some of the things I've said to Oz but then I again think of his future. I look at the years ahead and the life that awaits him and I know that I mustn't give in to the sense of self pity that threatens to overwhelm me.

Several weeks go by with countless hours of repetitive humming of ups and downs and underneaths.

Oz walks around the house carrying the new shoe in his hand. He keeps trying over and over to cross both laces until I hear him say.

"Ima, I don't know how to tie a knot."

I hug him.

"It's okay Oz... let's put the shoe away...let's gives it a rest...we'll try again later on..."

He leans his head on me. My eyes sting. I hug him and let another day and another week pass.

A few days later I'm in the kitchen preparing dinner. Oz comes over, hands me the shoe and I spot a tiny beginning of a knot, two laces that loosely cross each other. The pride on his face makes my eyes water. We laugh with joy and clap hands and Sevan rushes over and hugs him and it's his first success in crossing two laces and tying a knot.

The following day we set out to learn about loops.

The left one is especially difficult because of the weakness of his hand and the angled way in which he holds his head. We practice elephant ears, lollipops, butterfly wings, ostrich eyes, fish bowls and any other round shaped object he can think of. Oz tries his hardest to move both laces with his soft hands and create a loop but fails each time. We spend several long weeks working on the loops and again I make him promise.

"Never say I can't, Ozzi, because you can always try again."

"I promise you, Ima."

But sometimes he forgets.

"I can't do this..."

I tell him that if he'll break his promise, all the knots and loops he'd already learned will leave him and go to someone else.

"But I'm trying, Ima ..."

I hug him with a silent prayer.

"And you'll make it!" I hold him tight, "you'll see...you'll make it at the end!"

Several more days pass by.

It's early afternoon and I'm busy in the kitchen. Oz is crouched in the corner of his room busy with his shoe. Sevan is nearby, building an entire city out of Lego blocks.

Moments later Oz toddles towards me with eyes glued to the floor. His left foot is bare. Only his right one is inside the shoe that's not so new anymore.

"Look Ima. I tied it."

I look at the awkward loops with the loose ears and I can't hold back my joyful tears.

We make cupcakes and the kids decorate them and the three of us celebrate Oz' victory.

"I'm so, so proud of you, Ozzi! You've kept your promise and you didn't give up! I'm so proud of you... And of you too, Sevani...I'm so proud that you learned from Oz how to tie your own laces..."

***

Mother calls to say that Bilha and Chris are getting married. They've been dating for the past two years and I'm happy for them, but doubt I'll be able to make it for the wedding. Darien is on his way to Japan.

"Don't expect me to take care of the kids while you fly half way across the world for a stupid wedding ceremony!"

I give Bilha and Chris a call and wish them Mazel Tov.

Darien phones from Japan and says that he's busy and doesn't have the time to call them.

"I'll do it when I return," he promises but when he's back he finds other excuses and by the time Bilha's first child is born Darien is already angry.

"Stop nudging me! If I'll want to call them I know how to dial!"

164

But Darien never dials leaving an unpleasantness between us that only intensifies over the years.

***

Oz is in his last extended year of kindergarten and requires a new school setting for the following year.

Over the past three years I've been actively involved in promoting special education within our school district, but it's clear that I won't receive any special privileges concerning the A.R.D. (*Admission, Review and Dismissal*) committee, scheduled to meet in two week's time. The role of the committee, as stated by law, is to determine the I.E.P. (*Individualized Education Program*) and related services required for special education students. The rules guiding the committee are identical on the federal level but differ in every state and residential area, ensuring the parents' rights to make the final decision pertaining to the services and placement of their child.

Darien is immersed in his weekend newspaper.

"I'd like you to join me to the A.R.D. meeting...I'm afraid they won't approve all the services that Oz requires."

"So he probably doesn't require them!"

"But he'll soon turn seven and he still can't read..."

"Has it occurred to you that THEY'RE the experts and not you?!"

"But Oz IS capable of learning!"

"Aren't you sick and tired of listening to yourself?! Why do you always fight them?!"

"You're his father. You should also fight for him!"

"I don't need a thing! I listen to the experts and act accordingly!"

"But if I'd listened to them in the past when they said that he'll never learn how to walk or talk or ride a bike... and all the other things... what do you think would have happened?!"

"The difference is that I listen! But I don't expect someone like you to understand!"

"BUT OZ IS CAPABLE OF LEARNING!"

My words turn into a painful cry that fills the space inside the large living room where the two of us are seated at both ends of the couch.

"If he were capable of learning how to read and write, it would have already happened!"

My cheeks are wet with angry tears.

"Oz is slow...he does everything in a slow pace...but that doesn't mean that he can't do it!"

"Save me your stupidity!"

"But if WE give up on him he won't stand a chance! He's got to learn to read!"

"It's all in your head! Just don't ask for my help when your plan back fires!"

He returns to his newspaper and mumbles.

"Dumb wit!"

From my seat at the long table, I'm able to see all twelve professionals. I feel nauseous.

The long list of services I intend to request for Oz is based on the thick Parents' Advocacy guidance book dedicated in its entirety to the legal rights of special education students within the state of Texas. First on my list and the most important issue, is the placement of Oz in a regular first grade class for the sake of allowing him social integration. And though I've read and re-read it carefully and am familiar with the eligibility criteria and terminologies, I face the committee with a churning stomach knowing that Darien isn't supportive of my requests.

The table, set widthwise inside the large meeting room, is crowded with the kindergarten teacher, first grade homeroom and special education teachers, educational counselor next to the psychologist, speech, occupational and physical therapists in addition to three administrative representatives instructed on behalf of the school district to attend the meeting ensuring that my demands are kept to a minimum in order to save the expenses involved.

My marked seat places me at its head next to the principal.

The setting is charged.

"I'd like to start the meeting by thanking Mrs. Schmidt."

The principal releases a sour smile in my direction and continues.

"I salute your much appreciated volunteer work and your continued efforts to advocate for special education students within the community. Your hard work throughout the year has certainly made an impact..." he scouts the table with a sly smile.

The principal is careful with his words. The administrators are tuned into his every word, making sure that he doesn't stray from the guidelines dictated to him in advance. At the end of the day, all special services and therapeutic sessions approved by the committee are binding by law and translate into hourly costs.

"Mrs. Schmidt," he goes on, "we're here to discuss Oz' IEP for the next school year. I'd like to start off by hearing what the kindergarten teacher and the other professionals, who've worked with him this past year, have to say."

A barrage of summaries and statistics based on year long evaluations are thrown into the air demanding that Oz be placed in a special self contained classroom with students who are severely mentally retarded.

I listen to their words and feel rage bubbling within me. Memories of my own childhood begin to stir and at once my nausea is replaced by a strong sense of defiance and anger.

It's now my turn to fight for my son.

"I brought this tape recorder," I place it on the table and push a black button, "I'll make it easier on all of us to remember what's been said and agreed..."

"But Mrs. Schmidt," one of the administrators is quick to interrupt, "Everything is documented ..."

I detect a vague smile on one of the teacher's faces. I understand the dilemma the principal now faces and his somewhat embarrassing situation. He knows he's being scrutinized by the administrators who gawk at him so that he doesn't exceed the services dictated by the system but I have no intention of giving in.

"Today is October 17, 1991 A.R.D. meeting for Oz Schmidt. Present are..." I call out the names of all seated.

"You're doing great Tara! You should try conducting an orchestra!"

The principal's words trigger laughter. Sweat trickles down my back.

"I'd like to start off by focusing on my son's abilities and achievements proven over the past three years. He's shown an improvement in his motor skills and academics and he can even hold a pencil and form letters... Oz has shown impressive progress in speech and is able to express himself clearly. He has a sweet and kind personality ... he's a great kid with a great sense of humor... he's funny and goodhearted and he always helps others and encourages those who are weaker than him. He tries to connect with everyone and his perseverance and determination are impressive... he never gives up and he's polite and well behaved and doesn't disrupt the class but... Yes! He's also slow and, Yes! He requires help... but the fact that he's slow doesn't mean that he can't be placed in a regular class room the way you're all trying to argue! Oz is a kid who can fail or succeed. It depends strictly on your decision... and the help you'll allow him. It's in your hands..." I finalize my well-rehearsed speech by specifying the various services and therapies he requires.

"Mrs. Schmidt, are you sure you're doing the right thing when you insist on placing Oz in a regular classroom?"

"Absolutely! I wouldn't advocate for something that he wasn't capable of. I'm not out to frustrate him but I ask that you recognize his abilities and allow him to advance and far as he possibly can."

"We're worried about the difficulties he's encountering in academics... we're not sure he'll be able to achieve the goals you're setting for him..."

"I really appreciate your concerns," my eyes circle the table making contact with each of the participants.

Over the years I've had several private conversations with Oz' teachers and therapists outside the school setting, regarding the special education programs offered throughout the district.

They were all very supportive of my involvement and shared with me specifics about the A.R.D. meetings adding insightful information they were prohibited from voicing openly in the meetings.

"My outlook differs from yours. As Oz' mother I must ensure that my son learns how to read and write otherwise he won't reach independence as an adult. I know you're all supportive of each and every special education student and strive to enable him to function independently in the future ... especially you, as principal. Only last week you told me that if every parent invested as much as I did in their child, there'd be fewer special education students in the class ...so how can you now refuse me? I'm asking all of you to help my child ... for his benefit ...as well as that of the entire community..."

Two hours later I leave the meeting totally exhausted but proud. Oz has been guaranteed a placement in a regular first grade class with full social integration and academic assistance throughout the day, in addition to all the other services and therapies I'd requested.

Next month we're planning a visit to Israel and I'm determined to find a solution to Oz' reading difficulties.

"When Oz tries to concentrate on each of the letters, they sort of... jump in front of his eyes...kind of separately and that prevents him from seeing it as one word... but it's only a question of practice Tara... he needs to continue practicing..." the therapist again repeats.

As soon as we reach Israel I decide to take advantage of Moti's chicken coup.

Twice a day I take Oz to collect chicken eggs. Oz loves it and is excited and thrilled to be able to do it himself. Once the tray is stable on his arm, I ask him to pick carefully each egg and place it from left to right, one after the other, much like gathering individual letters in English. It's hard at the beginning. His arms tremble and he finds it difficult to concentrate on the precise placement of each egg but he strains and tries again and continues until the tray is full. A week passes by, then two weeks and three but even after a month the task is still challenging much like the identification of the letters and their grouping into words.

The change occurs unexpectedly, during one of mother's after lunch siestas, as Oz snuggles next to her on the bed holding a book and begins reading out loud.

"Tara! Come quick!" mother hollers and at once we're all around the bed, clapping hands and celebrating with laughter.

"I'm so proud of you Ozzi! You're reading! You know how to read! I'm so proud of you..." I can't let go of his dimples.

Four weeks later Oz turns seven. He enters first grade able to put together letters and read words.

*   *   *

A year has gone by since the accident.

It seems as though Sevan has made a full recovery, though she still requires follow ups. Her nightmares are gone and with them her drawings in black and red. I'm glad for every additional day that distances us from the traumatic event.

One morning I wake up with a strange tingling in my left thumb. When it persists I go see Dr. Aalsveer, a stern looking bearded hulk of a man. He grabs hold of my arm and hits my elbow with his small hammer. There's no reaction. In a voice resembling a hoarse parrot he pecks his short sentences.

"It's from the accident. No question about it."

"What do you mean?"

"Trauma Mrs. Schmidt! Trauma! Surgery is the only solution. You don't have any reflexes here!"

He again grabs my arm and hits my elbow.

"I know you don't believe me," he chirps, "so go see a few more doctors. I insist!"

I feel like chirping back at him but I respect his reputation as one of Dallas' top neurologists.

I follow his advice and visit another neurologist.

"You've shattered three discs... and you're risking permanent neurological damage... if you were my wife I'd send you straight into surgery..."

The following week two additional physicians confirm similar verdicts and by now my situation is worse. The smallest movement of my arm triggers a sharp pain that vibrates inside my brain.

Oz' fever shoots up again. The pediatrician calls me.

"The last x-rays show that Oz has a serious sinus infection and the E.N.T. specialist recommends urgent surgery...the tonsils and adenoids must be taken out and his sinuses cleaned...he has a chronic infection that's liable to spread to his entire head. It's a risky situation Mrs. Shmidt..."

I feel lonelier than ever, debating between O'z surgery and mine.

That evening Darien calls from somewhere.

"Oz needs urgent surgery..." I burst out crying.

"Tcha... what's so urgent?"

"He's got a serious sinus infection... that's what's causing his fevers..."

"Can we discuss this on Wednesday? My clients are already in the lobby...it's 'gonna have to wait."

I pick up a pillow, wrap my arms around it and cry.

The constant pain in my arm is fierce and nauseating; when I try to lie down it only worsens so I spend my nights sitting on an arm chair in the living room.

Three additional neurologists have now confirmed Dr. Aalsveer's diagnosis. I have no choice but to postpone Oz' surgery.

Darien is in Beverly Hills.

"If you need anything give me a call..."

Crazy thoughts pop into my head, topping the list is my wish to leave him but it's not something I can do right now.

A week later, Dr. Aalsveer checks my arm again.

"The steroids aren't helping. You need to undergo surgery immediately. You're thirty-eight years old with two small children. You should also know it's a very risky surgery..."

There's one more test left before surgery.

The cervical myelogram is meant to detect compressed nerves in my spinal cord.

I lie fully clothed on a narrow metal x-ray table with my face down and chin hard against its cold surface. Both arms are at my sides with palms up though I have no control over my left arm that continues to tremble.

"It takes about thirty minutes...just don't move Tara ...whatever happens make sure not to move..." the team of physicians warn me.

The needle with its thirty or so centimeters of sharp steeled edge is inserted behind my left ear releasing a liquid that seeps into the spine in a maddeningly slow pace. Someone dries my tears.

"You're doing great Tara... great...just don't move..."

Time comes to a standstill as the tears continue to tickle down my cheeks.

"Great! Great Tara, we're already half way there...only five more minutes... hold on...we're nearly there...don't move...hold still..."

There's a tense atmosphere inside the room. Someone wipes my tears again.

"Just don't move...just a bit longer...only two more minutes..." and then again, "Don't move. We're now going to take several x-rays. You won't feel a thing ...just make sure not to move...whatever happens ...just don't move..."

I can hear people running in and out of the room. They circle the narrow table and call out angles and numbers. Every so often someone says.

"You're doing great Tara...just don't move... keep still..."

I try to imagine myself escaping the room with a thirty centimeter long needle stuck behind my ear.

"Don't move...we're nearly done...you're doing great..."

When the x-rays are over the needle, once again, crawls out in a furiously slow pace.

As soon as the metal point is out, eight arms grab and topple me forcefully into a sitting position.

"You've got to keep your head in an upright position for the next twelve hours because of the substance injected into your spine... it can cause severe headaches and other complications..."

Within minutes I'm given the test results.

"Your nerves are totally compressed. We need to operate immediately otherwise you're liable to sustain irreversible nerve damage..."

It's already Thursday afternoon. Surgery is scheduled for the following Monday.

The pain is horrific. Maddening. My left arm feels like a lump of frozen rubber unable to hold itself. My right hand helps carry it everywhere. Mother and dad have been notified and are scheduled to arrive on Monday. I make lists of physicians, medications, friends, and neighbors but try to postpone the hardest.

"Dear mom and dad,
It's difficult for me to write. There are so many things I want to say but there's little time left. I'm scared, terrified that I'll never get to see Oz and Sevan again. You've been good grandparents to both. I know that if I don't make it Darien simply won't have the time with all his travels and long hours. Naomi can't handle it and neither can Bilha with her own family. I just hope you'll

figure out a way for both children to stay together. I'd like them to stay with you because you're the ones they're closest to. It's important that Oz stay with Sevan. They have a really good and close relationship and with love and patience he'll do okay. I don't want him sent out somewhere. He deserves his dignity to grow up with Sevan. I've saved some small souvenirs of the kids. They're next to the family albums inside a large plastic bag. Please take good care of them. I'd like the children to have them one day when they're older.

I hope to see you on Monday. Kiss the kids for me and tell them I love them. I miss them already."

I add information about the money I've stashed inside the bag. I want both children to have it.

It's Saturday evening. Darien and I are in the living room.

"It's a good thing your parents are coming on Monday...they'll be here on time for the funeral."

He cackles.

"Can you please make me a cup of tea?"

Darien points his finger in the direction of the kitchen.

"The kitchen is right there. Go ahead!"

On Sunday we drive to Medical City hospital. I hold Oz' and Sevan's small hands as we cross the entrance and go through the registration process. Darien holds my bag and hands it over to the receptionist.

"I got you a new bathrobe with matching slippers... from Neiman's, of course with the original tags still on ... make sure not to remove them just in case you don't make it ... that way I'll be able to return them..."

I hug Oz aged seven and four year old Sevan.

"You can come visit me tomorrow with Saba and Safta."

I give them another kiss and two little hugs.

Darien pecks my forehead.

"Would you like me to wait outside the surgery room tomorrow?"

My shoulders go up and down.

"I asked if you'd like me to wait in the hospital or go to work and come visit you later on with your parents?"

'Whatever's convenient for you."

It's Monday. Around noon.

"How are you feeling?"

Dr. Aalsveer is standing at the foot of my bed in line with my eyes.

"When's the surgery?

"You've already had it. It's now two in the afternoon. You were there for over three hours."

Dr. Aalsveer asks if I can move my arm and I raise it and he smiles and we exchange words but I don't really understand what he's talking about. My eyes are heavy and my lids keep shutting.

"I need to use the bathroom."

"I'm glad to hear it," he points to the door, "go right ahead."

"I can't."

"Of course you can! It's all in your head! Mind over matter! You told me you needed to get well soon because of your son's surgery. So the sooner you start walking the sooner you'll be out of here!"

He leaves the room with instructions for the nurse who explains about the stitches across my throat.

"Why did they go into my spine through my throat?"

"Because they had to get to the upper vertebrae... it's a bit like stuffing a turkey," she smiles, "you make a slit, go inside and shift the windpipe sideways to get to the back and stuff it with the new disc replacement..."

"And the scar?" I point to a large cut on my hip bone with several stitches.

"They took out a piece of your thigh bone, re-shaped it and used it to replace your crushed spinal discs. Your leg is now paralyzed but once you start walking it'll loosen up... just like the stitches across your throat..."

A week later I'm released from the hospital with a bottle full of painkillers.

"Take one of these only when you absolutely can't tolerate the pain...you can easily become addicted to them..." The doctor warns me.

When we reach home, I hug and kiss Oz and Sevan then walk into the bathroom with the bottle and flush all ninety-six pills down the toilet.

The following morning mother helps me out of bed and into my clothes. Dad drives Oz to school then takes Sevan to kindergarten.

"How did you sleep?" Darien asks.

"With a strange new spine." I smile.

"What's so funny?"

"You'll never guess what the surgeon told me just before he released me...he said I'm allowed to resume sexual activity... with caution!"

Darien laughs and kisses me lightly on my forehead.

"It's good to see you smile... I knew you'd make it!"

Later that afternoon he moves next to me on the couch.

"Would you mind if I go to London tomorrow for a seminar? It's not urgent or anything...and it's only for three weeks...I'd never leave you alone, of course, but... now that your parents are here ... it's an opportunity..."

The following day Darien leaves for London and returns the day prior to my parents' departure.

***

A month past my surgery I'm on my way to the hospital with Oz.

I hug him and whisper soothing words in his small ear then I kiss his dimples and together we cross the long white corridor to the nurses' post. Oz blows me kisses and disappears behind the door.

Two hours later the doctor comes out.

"Everything is fine Mrs. Schmidt... the adenoids are out and so are the tonsils... and we've cleaned out the sinuses ...it's now only a question of time..."

I'm grateful to the nurses who are considerate of my fragile new spine and go out of their way to assist me. I hold Oz' hands throughout the night, trying to chase away his fears and distance him from his aches and pains by telling him stories of faraway places splashed with sunshines and blue skies with soft sand and cute animals that like helping kind children.

Now that his brain is receiving oxygen more efficiently, I hope his world will be less confused. I dream he no longer stares into space or bumps into people and objects. In my dreams he's already able to count to twenty and run with the speed of a seven-year-old without flapping his arms or tripping and his smiley face understands the words he reads without requiring help.

He wraps his small arms around my neck and gives me a kiss and my heart melts.

Oz and Sevan are in the park busy inside the sand box. I watch them from a distance and see Sevan's tiny hand reach over to Oz and all I wish for is that they stay just like now, close enough within touching distance. I sometimes wonder about the future but I have no reason to imagine that I'm staring at an image that will crumple and fade within a few short years.

The weeks that follow are fever free and I can't get over how easy a fever-less existence is for eight year old Oz. His overall health is much improved and he forgets about coughs and runny noses and headaches and seizures though he still requires daily medications, therapies and special instruction and the gap between him and Sevan only widens.

One evening shortly after both children are in bed, Sevan hollers. I race up stairs to her room and find her sitting in bed with a beaming face.

"Look Ima...Look...I just figured it out! Look!"

I watch her small hands. They move real fast in tiny notches.

"If I have five packs of bubble gums and I put three bubble gums in each pack and I take one pack and then another and another like that five times it makes fifteen all together!"

"I'm so proud of you Sevanni...you're not even five and you've already figured out multiplication... I'm so proud of you..." my eyes well.

My heart feels like exploding. I hold her tight and I don't want to let go.

"I love you, Ima" she wraps her arms around my neck and kisses me.

I kiss her golden crown.

Oz still finds it hard to figure out the number of fingers he's got on both hands.

Oz returns home from school crying.

"I want a friend... I don't have any friends...and no one wants to play with me..."

I hug him to my heart and try to calm him but I'm lost for answers.

"I try, Ima...I do everything you tell me, Ima...but no one wants to be my friend...I want a friend...I want someone to invite me to his house...just a friend..."

A few days later Oz again returns home with a tearful face.

"Bryan broke my glasses."

Oz is full of wounds and scratches and I know that his life, too, will be filled with hurts and stings. The public school is limited in what it can offer children with social difficulties, and what's offered isn't effective.

Darien, too, offers solutions all of which are dictated from afar.

"You need to let him solve his own problems!"

"What's there to solve when three kids gang up on him and break his glasses?!"

"Maybe that'll teach him what he needs to learn!"

"But that's precisely the point! He's incapable of learning from examples or implementing things he's already been shown!"

"Whatever! I need to run! They're waiting for me! I'll call you tomorrow!"

Oz tries sports activities but can't fit in with the group. It saddens Sevan.

"What's wrong Sevanni? Why are you sad?"

"Do you think that...maybe...maybe you can...I don't know how to say it, Ima... maybe you can help Oz," the tears pour out of her, "his brain...maybe there's something like...a machine or a screwdriver... maybe you can put something inside his head and fix his brain?"

Both of us remain seated on the couch, hugging each other.

Darien surprises me when he calls from somewhere and says.

"I'm willing to do you a favor and go to a marriage counselor... but only for one session! Only one!"

We meet with Dr. Bernie Gillford, the counselor. At the end of our session he hands each of us an envelope.

"I have here a questionnaire with approximately four hundred questions for each of you to fill out separately. The questions are identical but not all are easy to answer so I'd like to suggest that you devote some thought and time to answering them."

Two weeks later the envelopes are returned and Bernie schedules another appointment.

At the start of the session Bernie explains.

"Before going over and evaluating the questionnaires I'd like each of you to specify the one thing you'd like to ask of your partner... it can be something that bothers you ...or something you'd like your partner to change... like a specific request... or anything you'd like to ask... on any subject ..."

Darien smirks.

"I have something to say," he points in my direction, "I'd like her to stop bitching about her problems and the children's problems and whatever it is that makes her sad and whatever it is she wants from me ...."

"I've asked to state only one thing," Bernie interrupts.

"She constantly bitches and..."

"One thing, Darien. Only one!"

"I'd like her to stop bitching!"

Bernie turns to me. I wipe my tears and look at Darien.

"I'd ...I'd like you...to be my friend..." my choky voice is tiny.

A long silence follows.

"Do you understand what Tara is asking?" he asks Darien gently.

Darien's palm resembles a butterfly trying to escape from side to side.

"Not really," his voice is soft, "not really..."

My hand reaches for the tissue box.

Bernie pauses for a minute then continues.

"I'd like to refer now to the questionnaire you each filled out. In order to consider the possibility of treating you as a couple, I had to get a general idea of each of your personalities. There were four possible answers to each of the questions... each answer reflecting a different facet of your personality pointing to your way of thinking... rationalizing etc, so that at the end I could come to certain conclusions. Now...you both answered all questions...but only one of you chose not to respond emotionally to any of the four hundred questions. I'm mentioning this because it points to certain emotional difficulties... and is reflective of someone who finds it hard to comprehend someone else's emotions. It also means that... that person will have to undergo intense therapy and work with me separately prior to treating both of you as a couple... because right now it's not even an option."

Darien points a finger in my direction.

"That's exactly what I meant!"

Bernie's eyes are on Darien.

"But the problem is with you, Darien...you have a lot of emotional issues."

The air within the room stalls but within seconds Darien regains his composure.

"I think it says something about your questionnaire! I suggest you do your homework and re-write it from scratch!"

It was the last time Darien agreed to see the counselor.

***

The situation at school only worsens and by now Oz returns home with daily blues and scratches on his arms and legs. I try to imagine a different school setting, another kind of approach with emphasize on the enhancement of social skills alongside academics.

My imagination takes me to faraway places. I contact countless universities around the nation and probe PhD students and professors who are smarter and more experienced than me in all aspects of social skills. Several months go by before I reach the understanding that perhaps the only way to improve Oz' social skills, is by practicing them on a daily basis. But that's precisely the problem: by being rejected socially, Oz doesn't get the opportunity to practice the very thing he lacks.

I spend the next year thinking about all the "what-ifs" and "how's", making changes and working on my vision until I find the solutions. When the final program is complete and I'm holding the printed copy in my hand, I call the school and ask for an appointment with Dr. Dowell, the principal.

I've been volunteering at his school for several years and am well acquainted with the students the staff and how the system works from within. I also know that I must get Dr. Dowell's support and decide to gamble on his love of conspiracies and gossip and his adoration of the concept of honor.

He catches a glimpse of me standing near his open door.

"Come in, come in. What can I do for you, Tara?" His forced smile reminds me of tar.

"May I shut the door?"

"Yes... yes... of course," he jumps out of his seat to oblige.

"I've come up with an idea that's bound to interest the superintended... and earn you credit."

His eyes flare up. He leans forward from behind his wide desk both hands clasped under his chin and swallows my every word. I outline briefly the program I've developed and watch the smile spread over his face.

"Of course I'll make sure that you get all the credit for the program... I'm only interested in implementing it ..."

He now leans against the chair trying to figure out its weak spots. He digs deeper and probes into hypothetical questions demanding answers to all the "what if's" until he reaches the crucial one.

"And if it fails?"

"I'll take full responsibility for its failure."

We shake hands and the deal is sealed.

I implement A.S.A.P.© known as the After School Arts Program in all five schools within the HPISD (Highland Park Independent School District) involving nearly two hundred students over a period of two years. All thirteen instructors employed in the program are renowned artists from Texas carefully chosen by me and supportive of the goals of the program which strives to integrate students with social difficulties into the mainstream of society.

The program proves an immediate success and within four months is recognized by The National Honor Society enabling high-school students who take part in it to gain credits when applying to Ivy League universities.

The local press is full of praise for the program, for Dr. Dowell's initiative and for enabling its implementation. When asked, I make sure to note Dr. Dowell's wit and vision and predict his future as the next superintendent.

The offers soon trickle in. I get calls from school districts nationwide and all at once everyone is interested in seeing the program expand and implemented on a national scale.

Everyone, except Darien.

He picks up the morning paper, sees my name on its front page and doesn't say a word. Not a word.

Following the success of the program I get a call from the editorial board of the country's largest newspaper asking to meet with them. Two days later I meet an enthused Chief Editor who updates me.

"The President's wife is planning a visit to the Park Cities in two weeks...part of her husband's re-election campaign. She's very involved with special education and expressed an interest in your program. We'd like your permission for the article... five pages long... in chrome... with your profile and photograph in the weekend magazine followed, a month later, by a coast-to-coast TV interview. Special education is hot and trendy. We'd like to use this opportunity to expose the program nationwide. You'll find yourself in the limelight ...with profits that are bound to soar...."

I listen to his words and think of Darien and the back and forth's that passed between us last night.

"I want a divorce, Darien!"

"Do you really think you'll find someone better than me?! Someone who'll want somebody like you?!"

I take a deep breath and thank the Chief Editor.

"Time is crucial, Tara!"

"I understand... I'll call you back within a week."

I walk out of the meeting confused, feeling happy and sad at the same time.

When I reach home Darien calls.

"I've decided not to fly tonight. I've got an awful headache ... I've already taken several pills but it's not helping so I'm seeing the doctor at five..."

It's six and already dark outside. The wide sidewalks are bubbling with small children all dressed as witches and ghosts, tiny images of Halloween holding small orange colored buckets shaped as pumpkins. Oz and Sevan are dressed as cute baby ghosts cloaked in white sheets with beady dangly eyes that I've sewn onto them. They hold each other's hand eager to start the adventurous 'trick or treat'. The camera flashes and we're on our way.

Darien's car breaks to a halt on the arched driveway adorning the front yard.

"I just came to say that I'll catch up with you later. Radio Shack is having a sale and I don't want to miss it."

"I thought you weren't feeling well...."

"That's right...but I postponed the appointment. I want to make it to the store on time."

Within seconds he and his silver Porsche disappear.

The streets are flooded with children in costumes accompanied by family members. The three of us join the crowds and stop at every door along the way until both buckets are overflowing with candies and chocolates and tiny trinkets. By nine the children have had their fill and are tired.

We return home to find Darien asleep in his leather recliner.

"Oh ...you're already back?"

"Daddy... daddy... look how many candies we have...." Sevan runs proudly towards him holding her bucket.

"Don't touch me! And stop shouting! I have a splitting headache. I couldn't even make it to the doctor..."

Sevan moves to the side.

"Good night dad ... I hope you feel better."

"I love you dad."

There's no response.

After both children are safely tucked in bed I'm left with my own thoughts as I try to digest the incredible offer I'd received only hours ago from the editor.

Darien wakes me up. I switch on the light. It's three in the morning.

"This pain...it's awful, it's killing me...I can't stand it!"

Darien's face is twisted with pain as he holds his head in both hands.

I call the physician on duty who prescribes something strong. I rush to the drug store and when I return I find Darien downstairs in his chair cradling his head in his hands.

"I can't take the pain...I can't bear it..."

I've never seen Darien in such a state. He takes two pills and remains seated in his armchair.

The following morning he's on his way to see the doctor.

I busy myself with the children and school and when I return home around noon I find Darien slumped in his chair. His face is pale.

"What did the doctor say?"

"They ran some tests... I'm expecting a call any minute."

Just then the phone rings.

"Mrs. Schmidt this is Dr. Windham your husband's neurosurgeon. The CT shows he has a leaking aneurysm in his brain stem... he needs to come urgently to the neurosurgery department ...."

Darien calls out angrily from his chair.

"What are you making such a big fuss over anu...aurism? How... what's the name?"

"There's a hemorrhage in your brain."

"Where do you get your ideas from?!"

I call Leslie and give her a brief explanation. She says not to worry. She'll take care of both children, and if need be keep them over night.

Twenty minutes later we're at Presbyterian hospital inside a waiting room I seem to recognize.

Darien leans back on the chair.

"I don't feel well ..."

At once I recall Dr. Windham's name. I'd seen him four years earlier at the insistence of my insurance company for a second opinion, prior to my spine surgery.

"Miz. Schmidt?" Dr. Windham's bearded face appears to my left. "This way..here, I'll help you..."

He helps Darien to a narrow bed.

"Is this better?"

"No! It hurts!" he again cradles his head in his hands.

"I'll be right back."

Dr. Windham motions to me and we move to the adjacent room. He tilts his head sideways while his eyes roam the desk

"Look Miz Schmidt... I'll say it straight out. Your husband is in real bad shape. He can go any minute!" he snaps his fingers, "Just like that! So ... let's get it over and done with quickly... you need to sign here ...it's the consent forms for the surgery. I'll take care of the rest. There's no time now for any explanations...we'll begin the surgery in two... three hours," his hand covers a yawn.

"I'm sorry but...I'd like at least a second opinion, maybe even..."

Dr. Windham raises his eyes and voice.

"A second opinion?! Sure! You can have a second and even a third one! You can also kill your husband in the process! But I don't suppose you've thought about that, have you?!"

I step out of the room and check on Darien.

"I don't feel well."

Dr. Windham joins us.

"Listen! Your wife here won't sign the permission to operate so I'm afraid I can't help you."

"Excuse me, Dr. Windham, but... I'd like a word alone with my husband..."

"Sure, sure...you've got all the time in the world!"

He flaps his hands sideways and exits the room angrily.

"I don't trust him, Darien...there's something..."

"Since when are you authorized to voice an opinion?! Are you out to kill me?!"

"I want a second opinion and a third one, if need be. He wants to go into your brain without any explanations or tests...he didn't even ask for an MRI ... he told me he doesn't have time to explain ..."

"Stupid cow! It's my brain and I'll decide! I want you to sign the darn paper or I'll sign it myself!"

"I refuse to sign it! I won't take the responsibility!"

Dr. Windham re-enters the room.

"Have you made up your mind?"

"I told her I'd sign if she won't."

"Sorry but you can't. Only she can sign it. If anything happened to you it wouldn't hold in court."

Darien hesitates. He eyes me for a few seconds then shuts his eyes.

"Okay ... get a second opinion."

Dr. Windham again checks his pulse.

"He's not doing so well. I want him in neuro- ICU. Now!"

Dr. Windham helps Darien into a wheelchair while directing me to the unit located at the far south wing of the hospital. I place the small suitcase on Darien's lap and wheel him through a long maze of tunnels. Darien is dizzy. His head drops to the side. The underpasses, reserved for medical staff, are long and windy packed with medical teams and white coats. I continue rolling the chair carefully, but Darien's heavy body slumps and threatens to slip off the chair. Two men wearing white coats rush over and wheel his hundred plus kilos into the ICU unit.

Darien is placed in a bed while I speed back home and start calling a list of highly reputable neurosurgeons located throughout the nation.

The phone rings. It's the nurse from ICU.

"Dr. Windham's decided to postpone your husband's surgery 'till seven tomorrow morning."

I thank her and continue with my list of calls.

Spread on the table in front of me is a stack of pages in which I've summarized the main points of my conversations with the various surgeons, each one with his approach and impression of Darien's situation.

After reading them several times over, I go back to Dr. Lowenthal's words.

"Before you make a final decision I'd like to go over it with you, carefully, once more. There's no place for any misunderstandings. There are two very different approaches to handling such a leaking aneurysm. One says to go into the brain and operate immediately as Dr. Windham suggests. The other calls for complete rest prior to penetrating the brain and clamping the blood vessel. You see... the brain right now is angry ... and swollen ...and its texture's changed. Surgery is risky and the cells can be damaged if touched by hand.... and we don't want any fingerprints left on them. I would recommend sedating the patient and suppressing most bodily functions for the duration of nine to ten days and only then operating. From what you've told me about your husband's condition I'd insist on an MRI and uphold any further comments until after I've looked at it. You must understand, Mrs. Schmidt... even moving him by ambulance is very risky. It can exacerbate the mild leakage and cause it to rapture ...he can die within seconds ..."

Dr. Lowenthal's words make sense and I decide to opt for his opinion.

At eleven a clock I call the ICU unit.

"I'd like to cancel the surgery scheduled for tomorrow morning with Dr. Windham."

The nurse's voice is hesitant.

"I'm sorry, Mrs. Schmidt, but you'll have to call Dr. Windham yourself...I can't call him at this hour..."

I dial Dr. Windham's home number. I hold the receiver in one hand and cover my face with the other. On the fifth ring a sleepy voice answers.

"Dr. Widham, this is Mrs. Schmidt. I'm sorry to wake you up but the nurse asked that I call you directly. I've made arrangements to transfer my husband elsewhere tomorrow morning. There'll be no surgery."

"Thank you."

I'm exhausted from all the calls, deliberations and indecisions that keep haunting me.

Have I made the right decision?!

I go upstairs to our bedroom, sit at the edge of our life's bed and stare at its empty half. Darien's half. A creaseless white sheet reminiscent of a shroud is spread on it, emphasizing the void of our creaseless existence. Darien's face is alive and breathing, but it comes and goes like a ray of sun on a wintry day. I kiss him gently and move my hand over the tightly spread sheet. Tears flood my face.

And I cry.

I cry over merciless nights with wounded prides that knew shame and humiliation. I cry for Oz and Sevan who've never known a father's pride or felt the delicate touch of a father's warm love and compassion. I weep for the things we never had, the moments we missed and the emptiness and loneliness of our pasts. I cry for the love that eluded us, for our hidden passions and the softness of words and secrets that we kept from each other. I weep for the boy-man too weak to stand by and support me and for the walls we've erected between us. I pain over the long years we've spent alone within the void of our togetherness and I want him to know of the sadness within me, the pain for the things that we failed to hold close to our hearts, the important moments we missed, and the fateful seconds that could have changed the course of our lives had we not failed to recognize their importance.

And I cry for want to understand where we went wrong.

Have I made the right choice?! Again I wonder.

I don't have a clue as to how things will ultimately end but whatever happens, I know I'm the one that will be held accountable.

My stomach hurts and I feel dizzy. It occurs to me that I haven't eaten since lunch. I go downstairs to the kitchen, open the fridge, take out a chocolate bar and gnaw at it slowly until the cuckoo clock strikes five.

At six Darien is transferred by ambulance to Medical City hospital and placed in Dr. Lowenthal's care.

Darien survives the complicated brain surgery and recovers quickly but I'm left with hesitations and conflicting ponderings all tangled with hubris.

Unending thoughts loop back and forth inside my head leading me to believe that Darien's life was saved thanks to me, to my resourcefulness and to my insistence on additional medical opinions. An enormous sized EGO lacking all boundaries takes hold of me and demands recognition.

Hurray, Tara! You handled it smartly, stood your ground, demanded other opinions and even had the courage to move him to another hospital.

The sinful paths of Hubris are convoluted, camouflaged by sophisticated manipulations aimed at diverting the line of thought from the heart of matters. But the heart of matters lies in Fate's hands and forever out of our control. The "why's" and "why not's" remain as inexplicable as the new thoughts that carve within me new paths of understandings, routes that I've never fully comprehended until now.

I begin burrowing into the reasons and circumstances that led us both on our common path of life; for there were so many landmarks along the course of our lives that pointed to unanswered questions, open mouthed hesitations that were neglected along the main track. Unspoken subjects brushed aside by harsh rules: the unraveled worlds of our childhoods, the hearts of our beliefs and essence of life, our wants, our dreams and above all the constant grayness of our daily existence which hovered from above dispensing mistrust and lies camouflaged by colorful rainbows.

It takes me a while to sift through our past and reach clarity of feeling and thought. I realize that we've spent our entire lives wearing masks. We used them to hide our lack of confidence, cover up lies and pretenses and primarily mask our inability to cross life's path together.

A month and a half past his surgery, Darien walks downstairs all freshened up and perfumed wearing a new suit with a new shirt and a new tie, drinks his morning coffee then drives off to the office as if nothing's happened.

The only hint left of his encounter with Dr. Lowenthal's hands, is a hair thin scar most of which is hidden under his silky mane.

Several days later, when I open the weekend magazine, I recall the editor's offer from two months ago. It feels strange, and years remote from me.

The sequenced events that followed are freshly etched in my mind despite the long years that have since lapsed; and though Fate's ugly smirk was already watching us from afar and hinting of things to come, I failed to recognize its foreboding winks.

LONELINESS

At the end of May Darien surprises me.

"I'd like to take the kids to visit my parents. They're planning on coming to Belgium and renting an apartment in Knokke for two weeks ... they suggested that the three of us spend time together. So why don't you enjoy some free time over here by yourself and join us in two weeks for the weekend ...then you and the kids can continue from there to Israel..."

I'm stupefied by his suggestion. In the past, Darien has always found excuses to avoid spending time with the children. I was hoping that perhaps his near death experience had triggered a change in him or awakened a sincere wish to work on our relationship.

I land in Belgium on a gray rainy morning.

"What d'you think?" Darien smiles hesitantly, pecks my forehead and moves a finger over his newly sprouted mustache.

The drive to Knokke is slow. The silence in the car is louder than the thundering rain. We sit inside the muted space and listen to the noisy beatings on the car and watch the constant no-no's of the windshield wipers. An hour and a half later we reach Knokke. When the door opens I meet a gray-faced Stella and Helmut. Oz and Sevan remain standing to the side.

"I missed you," I bend down and hug Sevan's smallness.

She's frozen in place.

"What's wrong, Sevannie?"

Her small arms tighten around my neck but she's silent.

"I missed you Ozzi," I hug him.

Oz too is restrained and releases only a faint smile.

I hold onto both their hands wondering about their odd silence and at once I sense an inexplicable fear. It takes some time before they shake off their strangeness and hug me.

After lunch we join the long line of vacationers that swamp the elegantly plush resort town of Knokke, sprawled along the beaches of the North Sea and its neighboring Holland. The promenade is spectacular with its natural curves that follow the sea coast closely and twist over several kilometers.

At the end of a long walk we reach a well fostered nature reserve with wooden thickets alongside trails for biking and hiking. Helmut, as usual, disappears on his mountain bike promising to meet us inside the coffee shop planted in the midst of a forest and surrounded by a large open spaced playground.

The place is packed with families and children of all ages, a large crowd bubbling in an assortment of languages all enjoying the wooden play houses set between the tall trees, with bridges and ladders next to swings and slides. The children have fun finding their way out of the wooden mazes. We enjoy the traditional pastries with coffees and hot chocolates then return to the apartment exhausted and ravished.

Stella hurries into the kitchen. Helmut is in the living room with its glassed wide wall fronting the black waters of the North Sea. He plucks his wispy mustache and stares with his bleary eyes at the sudden storm that burst out of nowhere. Both kids are slouched quietly on the couch.

Darien releases a command.

"Oz! Set the table!"

"I'm tired...I don't feel like it," he answers with the naiveté of an eleven year old.

"I'll show you what I-don't-feel-like means!" Darien roars.

He jumps out of his chair pushes Oz to the floor then grabs hold of his ankle and drags him on his back all the way through the living room and into the corridor that dead ends in the back room where I'm busy unpacking the suitcase.

"It hurts...it hurts..." Oz cries out.

I step into the corridor.

"Why are you dragging him like that?! It's undignified! Let him walk!"

Helmut appears out of nowhere. He crosses the corridor wildly with his six foot two gallops in my direction and smashes his fist into my head. Oz is facing me. His mouth is wide open. Sevan's eyes stare at the blood that squirts out of my eye. Helmut smashes again and again. Oz screams and Sevan cries. I shriek like mad but Darien remains standing in the doorway staring at me. He only stares. I jump back squeezing myself into the room while trying to shut the door. I know the apartment is on the fifth floor and the wall behind me is all glass and I'm scared of it as much as I'm scared of Helmut's hands. One more step and the door slams shut. I quickly turn the key leaving Helmut's face on the other side, with Oz and Sevan.

My head is bursting and everything is muddled. I try to think. I need to get the children out of the apartment. I've got to get them out and escape this hellish place...passports... money...I need to find the children's passports...and money...I need money.

I move my hand across my wet face disregarding the red that sticks to my fingers. My hands are shaking so hard that I can't find anything inside the suitcase.

Get the children out... I've got to get them out of the apartment...

I hear an awful shriek. Oz' voice echoes.

"That hurts! Don't...please don't..."

I tear open my door and launch at the one across from mine. It's locked.

"Open the door! Let the kids out!"

"I will open the door when the children are quiet!" Stella chirps.

Sevan bursts out crying.

"But no...grandma don't...it hurts..."

Again I bang on the door.

"Open this door! Let them out!"

"First they must to be quiet, eh?"

I step into the corridor and see Helmut resting calmly on a leathered armchair, his arms and legs crossed over. Darien is sitting opposite him, cross-legged reading a newspaper.

"How could you..." is all I manage before Helmut springs again out of his chair and loses control. He kicks my legs pulls my hair and uses fists to bash my head and make my eye disappear. I try to protect my head and escape into the room. The door locks behind me. It's hard to breathe. My knees tremble and my throat releases small sounds. My hands are again inside the suitcase prying at clothes and looking for the passports but I can't find a thing. I take a deep breath and wipe red tears. The clock on the wall keeps ticking. Another minute. And another. Then another.

The apartment is silent.

Hesitantly I unlock the door and reach for the door handle across the corridor.

"Open the door!"

The key turns and the door opens. Oz is standing in the far corner with Stella's arm against his chest. Sevan is next to him. I jump inside, grab Oz and Sevan and pull them out. And now both kids are glued to me. Oz' ear is purple and swollen.

"What have you done to him?!" I holler into the face in front of me.

"They must to learn to listen better, eh?!"

I hug both kids tightly and hurry into the corridor.

"Don't worry...we're getting out of here."

The three of us are like a tightly strung rope. We cross the corridor hurriedly, disregarding Helmut and Darien who remain seated in the living room, then turn right and exit the apartment straight into the elevator.

I kiss Oz and Sevan and hold them close to my heart.

"I love you," tears wash over us.

Oz holds his purple ear. I kiss it. It burns.

Outside is a vicious summer storm with freezing temperatures and unrelenting rain.

"Here, Ima...I'll clean the blood," Sevan holds out a tissue and wets it under the rain then carefully wipes my eye, "it's...your eye is scary, Ima..."

I hug Oz and Sevan and the three of us now stand on the deserted sidewalk under the ruthless rain and cry. We just stand and cry in the rain.

"Let's find a phone..."

The apartment building is situated on the waterfront, a leisurely stroll to the elegant center with its plush boutiques and appetizing restaurants. But on this horrible evening there's no one walking the wide sidewalks of Knokke. No one but us.

I hold both their hands and at once we're in the heart of the storm.

The northern wind is wickedly vicious, whipping the rain sideways at an angle aimed to pierce; sharpened needles lash forcefully in our direction tearing wildly at the light summer clothes the three of us are wearing.

We hug each other tight, shivering and fighting against the ferocious wind as we search for a phone booth suited for international calls. We pass one booth then another and another until we find one that works.

Wet and chilled to our bones, we huddle together inside the steamy booth and wait.

Mother picks up.

"Ima... Helmut attacked me...he beat me up ...I'm here with the kids..." tears choke my words.

"Why?! What have you done?!"

The words escape me.

"Here...speak to dad."

Dad listens.

"And how are you feeling now? And the kids? Are they okay?"

I cry but I don't have to say anything else, not to dad.

"I'm catching the first flight to Belgium tomorrow morning and bringing you over here..."

"No dad...it's okay...I just want to get out of here... our flight is in two days...we'll be okay until then..."

Dad is relentless. He refuses to let go and wants to make sure that we'll manage to find a safe place until the day after tomorrow.

"What about the police? Can you..."

"The laws here are different... I'm just my husband's wife... I belong to him according to the law! They'll never intervene in my favor. On the contrary...they might even take the kids away from me..."

"So I'm definitely coming tomorrow!"

"No dad... really...I'll be okay...and the children too...no one will touch us now...I'm sure..."

"Are you sure? How far are you from the apartment?"

"About twenty minutes."

"Listen...I know you're very upset now...but... I'll call you in exactly thirty minutes. If you don't answer I'm calling the police and catching the first flight tomorrow morning. You can count on me! I'm coming tomorrow and helping you with the kids!"

We're on our way back to the apartment. The children cry and the three of us are once again huddled into each other.

"I won't let anyone touch you. I promise. I love you."

We hold each other and cry against the wind and the rain, trying to wash away the fears and the horrors.

We reach the building all drenched. I hold a child under each wing as we step into the elevator.

"I love you..." I tell them over and over.

Within seconds we reach the fifth floor. I leave the children next to the elevator.

The door of the apartment is slightly open. I push it hesitantly with my foot and at once Darien appears.

"Don't worry. My dad moved out to a hotel. He's not coming back..."

I take the kids to the bathroom, help them out of their wet clothes and fix each a hot drink.

The phone rings. Darien answers and it's obvious he's talking to dad. They exchange a few words before Darien calls me over.

"Dad..." my voice breaks.

"Are you okay? And the kids? How are they?"

"Yes, we're all okay...what did you talk about?"

"He told me his father moved out of the apartment into a hotel and that you don't need to worry. Are you sure you don't want me to come tomorrow? I'll take the first flight..."

"No, it's okay dad... yes, I'm sure ... what did you say to him?"

"I told him that violence breeds violence. He understood me perfectly well."

Late at night the two of us walk down to the beach only yards away from the apartment building. We've been together now for nineteen years but it's the first time I get to hear about Darien's childhood, his abusive father, and the constant trail of terror that accompanied his childhood. He speaks of his loneliness and of his mother who never protected him and barely survived his father's ruthless hands.

We remain on the beach over long hours. Darien doesn't hold back his tears and I listen and hold him next to me.

We return to the apartment exhausted and emotionally rattled.

It's obvious that we've reached a crucial crossroad in our relationship and we must now decide about our future.

The next hours are bitter and I can't fall asleep. Darien's hand, the confused butterfly in Bernie's room, keeps flickering in front of my eyes.

The following day Darien leaves the apartment and returns in the evening to say good night to the children.

It takes them a while to open up and tell me about the two weeks they'd spent alone with Stella and Helmut prior to my arrival in Knokke.

"They only spoke German and they didn't allow us to speak English... and grandma was really mean to us...it was scary, Ima..."

"I was also scared," Oz adds, "and I wanted to call you but dad wouldn't let us..."

The next day, Darien drives us to the airport but refuses to join us.

***

We've been in Israel now for the past three weeks trying to put behind us the Knokke events. I'm worried about the children's emotional state. Oz refuses to let go of dad's hand. Dad tries to sooth Oz' heart and rid him of his fears by taking him on his red tractor to the orange grove. Sevan seeks mother's company. She cooks and bakes with her and from time to time returns to her drawings of a woman's face with red tears dripping from her swollen eye and a large gaping wound on her cheek.

Another month goes by and by now it's the end of July.

The phone rings. It's Stella. Her cricket like voice can be heard through the receiver as she chats with mother.

"So... how are the kids? They enjoying the sun? It was so cold for us in Knokke..."

Mother as usual tries to clear any bumps along the way by disregarding words and past events. I'm standing next to her and can hear every word. I feel a gush of anger rise from within.

"...but Tara claims that Helmut punched her..."

"Non...mais non... he just to move his hand and hit, eh? He didn't mean, eh? With his elbow... like dat, eh? But he so sorry, eh? Maybe you speak to Tara and say he so sorry and dat's it! eh?"

"Look Stella... I wasn't there so I don't really know what happened ... but...yes... I'm willing to try and find out...maybe Tara will agree to accept his apology..."

I'm angry at mother's words and outraged by her conduct.

It's the beginning of August. Next week we're scheduled to leave Israel and return to Dallas and to our routine lives though I have no idea what that routine will look like now that its frame has been violently shuttered.

Over the course of our first years of marriage Darien enjoyed joking that if I'd ever want to leave I'd have to pay him.

"One hundred thousand dollars as compensation for the act of kindness I showed your father when I agreed to take you off his hands."

My worth, valued roughly at five hundred eighty eight dollars per centimeter, was based on my height of one meter and seventy centimeters. At the time Darien's teasing sounded meaningless, serving merely as amusing decor to his witty humor.

Perhaps because we sought laughter and wanted to escape our own selves, forget the ugly scars of our pasts singed deeply into our souls, flee our own homes and own families that forced us into craving other things. I sought to escape the madness and chaos of our home, break loose from the crazed nauseating tumult and find refuge in the family portrait Darien drew for me, a picture of perfection with soft comfort and caring loving European parents, a place where I could relax.

Darien wished to embrace the very same things from which I

longed to escape. He was drawn to the noisiness that filled our home and the wild seesaw rides which he translated in his own mind as mere childhood games and brotherly fun.

We both craved wants that differed greatly from those we knew in our respective homes.

Using our imagination we each elaborated on our own wishes transforming them into masterful tapestries of perfection that had little to do with reality.

Saying goodbye to my parents is harder than ever.

"I miss you too much, Saba," Oz cries bitterly and refuses to let go of dad's hand.

Sevan cries as she hugs mother.

"I want to stay with you, Safta."

"Call me if you need help," mother says.

Dad hugs me then kisses my head and whispers in my ear.

"I'll speak to you soon. I want to make sure you and the kids are okay."

The flight back home is longer than usual.

My thoughts keep churning as I try to think of something we could latch onto as a couple, figure out a solution that would offer a way of guarding our frail marriage.

Darien picks us up from the airport and within minutes the car is loud with mean remarks and angry silences.

When we reach home Darien declares.

"I don't need any help because I don't have any problems...so do whatever you want with the kids."

I take both children to Bernie.

"What do you feel?" he asks Oz.

"That my dad wasn't good to my mom. A dad needs to be strong. He needs to protect mom. She's our Ima..."

Oz refuses to let go and demands answers even after we return home.

"Why didn't you help mom? Why didn't you protect her?"

"Enough! You've already asked that question twenty times! Now shut your trap!" Darien roars.

Sevan is locked deep inside her own inner sphere and refuses to talk about it. Only her drawings release hints of her shuttered world. She uses red ink to draw smashed faces and heads of women with black tears oozing from their eyes. Her nights are restless and she often wakes up with nightmares.

My mother's basic assumption remains in place and continues to echo inside my head.

"Tara's to blame! And it doesn't really matter what happened exactly. I wasn't there so I don't know all the details... but something happened... for sure. Tara must have done something..."

***

Next week school resumes marking Oz' first year in middle school. Once again I check the list of therapeutic services and individualized tutoring as detailed in the last A.R.D. meeting shortly before our trip to Knokke.

Sevan's school is a twenty-minute car ride away from our community and caters to students whose achievements equal hers. The entire campus with its spacious classrooms was built on a privately owned land greening with lawns and lush vegetation next to old dignified looking trees with fostered gardens. A family of peacocks had taken ownership of the green hilly site and claimed it their own long before the school grounds were established. The birds were left to roam the grounds freely and show off their stunning feathers becoming an integral part of the school setting. The unique atmosphere encourages curiosity and creativity and is challenging academically helping Sevan alleviate some of her fears and anxieties as she tries to overcome the horrifying experiences of the summer.

She hugs me and refuses to let go yet represses the events.

"I don't want to think about it."

I wrap her small hands in mine and sense her fearful heart.

But four more years will pass before I dare ask her.

"Do you remember our last visit to Knokke?"

"No," she says.

I leave it at that, though the memories that are deeply rooted in her soul refuse to leave.

**

The process of separating from Darien began long before the divorce itself, as an ongoing painful hemorrhage that slowly gnawed at the very frame of our lives.

Things seemed to happen on their own; a small event followed by a pinch and another slap to the soul washed away by a misunderstanding and abusive name callings. Its rhythm seemed effortless. Like wild grass that roots itself slowly with intentions to deepen its hold, our marriage wallowed in a permanently shattered state even before the Knokke events. The attack and its aftermath only marked the final breaking point of our relationship, simply because Darien refused to deal with his parents and with the harrowing events that took place or seek help for himself and for us as a couple. He found his comfort in Chivas. Soon thereafter the atmosphere at home sunk into a bubble of sadness and a deep sense of disappointment that clouded my soul and forced me to address the future.

It was over one of those rare evenings together that I tried to speak with Darien.

"I'd like to return to Israel and be near my parents...I'd like them to help me."

"What makes you think they'll help you?!" he smiles with contempt, picks up the newspaper and continues reading.

Darien is away from home most days, but even when he's present he refuses to discuss our future as a couple or apart. Every so often he releases a few words.

"When we get there, our attorneys will decide what to do and how to proceed ..."

"I know it's only October ...but..."

"So why are you starting again?!"

"It's important because of Oz' school...we need to be in Israel no later than May."

"You can leave today as far as I'm concerned!"

But there are times when he tries to glue together the broken pieces and revive its leftovers.

"I love you Tara...I want you to stay with me..."

"So please join me to Bernie's... it's important for me...for us... for the kids..."

"I've already told you. If you won't create problems, we won't have problems. It's all inside your head."

"But we need to address the issue in front of the kids...get them ready for the future. We must talk about it ..."

"I don't want you to discuss the future with them!"

"But they keep asking me if we're getting a divorce. D'you really think they're blind and deaf and that they don't understand what's going on?!"

"Don't even think of talking to them about it until I say so! I'm warning you! It'll work against you if you do!"

And there were other days and nights.

"You're so stubborn!" Darien holds my head in both hands

shaking it sideways, "If you just weren't so stubborn!" he repeats over and over again.

Tears choke me. And my voice is hoarse.

"Maybe... maybe I'd be willing to stay with you but...only if you'd agree to take care of Oz. Why won't you do it?" I again ask.

"If you decide to stay here after we divorce, I'm willing to go on paying for Sevan's school. Sevan is a good investment. I don't have a problem paying the twenty or so grand a year. But Oz?! He's simply not worth it! He can go on at the local school."

"But next year the local school will no longer provide for his needs...this year he's in a regular class with a special teacher who sits by him and helps him with his academics ... but next year he'll be moved into a self contained class with severely mentally retarded students. There isn't another option at school ... and he won't receive any help with his academics. It'll only limit him. Oz is capable of so much more. Please Darien...please agree to move him to a private school..."

"Stupid cow!" he mumbles, "save yourself the words! I'm not paying for any private school for Oz! Forget it! He's not worth the investment! As far as I'm concerned, take him to Israel and find a solution for him over there! I'm done with the subject!"

On a sad November weekend I made another effort to find a way to his heart. Saturday morning was gray and wet with a relentless drizzle. The children busied themselves downstairs in the living room.

Darien was still in bed. I sat next to him.

"Do you remember your first visit to Bo-Acha Yam when you helped me pack the suitcase for our trip to Belgium? My clothes were scattered on the bed. You picked up a black shirt that was on the bed and asked me if I really intended wearing it and I told you that it was there by mistake. Remember?"

"Aha...."

"It was my only new shirt," tears wet my face, "after I'd spent all

206

my savings on the ticket I barely had any money left... so I went to the market and bought the one shirt I could afford... the black one..."

I lay down beside him, placed my head on his chest and let myself be me.

His eyes filled with tears. I felt relief wash over me. We just lay there, quietly, hugging each other, and for the first time in our lives as a couple I felt a moment of keen friendship, a sense of true honesty and sincerity, a remarkable moment that I've never known with Darien before. And the more words were added, the warmer I felt in my heart with a flare of hope that maybe, despite everything, we could still mend the broken parts and create a new togetherness.

In those vulnerable moments, I wasn't afraid of sharing with him my painful memories, entrusting him with the truth about my wretched past, unraveling my weaknesses and faultiness over the long years of my childhood, drenched with aches and pains and a sense of hollowness, hoping he'd be willing to accept me despite everything. It was an exalted moment of intimacy, a tiny universe created by the two of us based on trust and a deep sense of caring friendship.

"I don't know what to do now...what should I do?"

His face soaked with tears.

I could have tilted his heart, fed it promises, manipulated his soul and forced him to make commitments he'd never fulfill, but I understood that a true change must rely solely on one's own free choice and desire so do so. Only he could choose to change things. I kept hoping he'd favor me and the kids and be willing to accept help, but he didn't.

Within minutes the magic fizzled out and once again we became two separate entities, each planted deep in its own alcoved world.

And that's how we remained: a powerless twosome lacking a firm strong backbone and unable to navigate ourselves as we parted from each other.

***

The daily routines stabilize our lives and assist me.

Sevan continues with her piano lessons, sculpting and drama and Oz enjoys his piano lessons combined with music therapy, drama and a marionettes class offered within my A.S.A.P.© program for the second consecutive year. I understand the importance of retaining the thin balance of our tiresome daily routines and guard them fiercely so that they guard us.

November ushers in Thanksgiving with an invitation for the entire family to attend the play at Sevan's school.

Sevan wraps her small hands around my neck.

"I'm so excited, Ima."

I kiss her beautiful head and sense within the painful sadness of the future that's about to unfold.

"I want dad to come see the play."

I hug her and promise he'll come.

That same evening Darien updates me.

"I'm flying to Chicago for two days."

"Can you maybe postpone it? The day after tomorrow is Sevan's Thanksgiving play and she's so excited...she's been waiting for it since the beginning of the year... and she's been reher..."

"You'll manage the kids and I'll manage myself!"

"Please Darien... don't let her down. She especially asked that you ..."

"Stop nudging me!"

The two days pass quickly.

"Dad's coming home today, right mom?"

"Dad will come," Oz hugs her and smiles with both dimples, "Good luck little sister," he kisses her forehead.

I hug her and all I can do is hope that she isn't disappointed.

It's evening. Oz and I are seated inside the school auditorium. Darien is nowhere to be seen.

The play is lovely and Sevan recites her part beautifully. When the play is over the audience stands up and applauds. I catch a glimpse of Darien squirming his way into the large hall from behind the left side of the stage.

I wave to him and he climbs the steps and reaches us.

"So...what do think of Sevan? How was she?" He raffles Oz' hair.

The students walk off stage. Sevan sees us and hurries over, her face beaming with pride. She hurries in Darien's direction.

"I'm so happy you came daddy..." she wants to hug him, "I knew you'd come..."

"Watch it! Don't touch me with those dirty hands of yours! I'm wearing a new suit!"

He moves away sharply.

Sevan is rooted in place.

"Daddy...daddy..." she again tries.

I hug my little girl and sense her hurt and disappointment and do my best to suppress the disgust I feel brewing within.

***

"By the way," Darien releases an afterthought one evening while holding a magazine in front of his face and speaking to it, "this year's conference will take place in Horseshoe Bay."

"When?"

"In two weeks."

"So why did you wait until now to let me know?"

"I forgot." He turns a page.

The weeklong yearly hospitality conference held outside the city of Austin is the culmination of Darien's year long efforts invested in the relationships with his clientele. It's the perfect stance for someone who thrives on control allowing Darien to serve as its organizer and ultimate orchestrator. With the patience of a woodpecker, he dedicates all hours, including weekends, to ameliorate these relationships ensuring his efforts come to fruition.

The luxury resort located northwest of Austin is sprawled over ten square miles of hilly country with hidden paths amidst rocky hills and beautiful wild trails that cut through a natural forest surrounding the area. The place gained its reputation following the president's visit to the bay. It has some of the world's best golf courses next to adventurous hiking paths that twist between thickets with free roaming deer. Spiraling waterfalls with breathtaking swimming pools carved into the giant rocks hold arresting sights tended to by fleets of landscaping architects and gardeners.

The end of the year, shadowed by the nearing divorce, frames the horizon.

I'm hesitant whether or not to join Darien and decide to raise the issue with the therapist.

At the end of our session Bernie sums up.

"Darien is now very vulnerable and lacks the skills to restore his relationship with you or with his parents. It's a fragile situation … which he's not equipped to resolve… but if you're willing to give it another chance… knowing that it might fail, I'd recommend trying one last time in a calm atmosphere away from the children. The place itself is beautiful and can contribute… but it must be your decision. Do you want to give your marriage one last chance?"

My head and heart hold stormy doubts.

Much like the ever-changing reflective mirrors of a kaleidoscope, I too longed to recreate the relationship with my mother by marrying Darien, her mirrored image. I wanted him to like me, a childlike twisted notion to undo and repair all the things that were displeasing to my mother. I was occupied with my efforts, desperate to gain his acceptance and approval, the same way I've always longed to be approved and accepted by my mother. I didn't stop to consider my motives and ignored the basic fact that Darien and my mother were molded out of similar substances that always mixed well regardless of weather conditions.

After teary eyes and many thoughts and deliberations I decide to give it another try.

As Darien's wife I'm expected to serve as hostesses at the opening night and entertain throughout the week the wives of the chairman and some special guests.

"You won't have to worry about a thing...you'll have a car with a driver at your disposal, and you'll enjoy the surrounding towns ...yes, there're lots of nice little antique shops with arts and crafts and coffee shops like in Europe...oh, and we're arranging for a hot air balloon and other interesting activities..."

One of Oz' teachers agrees to stay with both children and supervise Oz' medications.

After setting aside the clothes that will serve me throughout the week, I decide to purchase two evening gowns and drive to a plush shopping center lined with some of the most extravagant stores in the state of Texas.

Starring in Neiman's display window is a mannequin resembling a Parisian demoiselle, similar to those splashed on the covers of the fashion magazines Stella loves scouting. The doll is wearing a black coquettish evening dress with a shapely décolletage. Around her neck is an exquisite onyx necklace combined with white diamonds and droplets of gold. A pair of black high heeled shoes accentuates her well curved legs and cements her in place.

"Look, look Darien," I imagine Stella's squeaky voice, "Look how nice the dress fits Tara, eh?"

Darien responds with a spoiled little smile.

"Does it come with the boobs?"

"Ooo! Malicieux!" she cackles, "I don't think you have to moch complain, eh?"

I near the window study the mannequin closely and respond silently.

"It's absolutely charming, especially the décolletage. It reveals what's required yet retains its elegance."

I can see Darie's smile and I know how he'd react.

"I prefer to keep nice things for myself."

I enter the store, move straight to the luxury department, try on the dress with the necklace and matching earrings and ask that they wrap it all up for me.

Darien, who'd already left two days earlier, calls me shortly before my scheduled flight.

"There's a problem... someone forgot to put you on the direct flight to Austin and by now it's full... so you'll have to land elsewhere and a driver will pick you up..."

The luxurious limo awaits me outside the entrance to the terminal.

I'm somewhat embarrassed and ask the driver to leave the glassed partition open. The drive is two hours long and I get to see the beautiful area known for its stunning views and hear about its history.

At the end of the ride the driver says.

"I'll wish you good luck...from the little you've told me about your husband you're bound to have a challenging week."

The hut is a luxury suite the size of an apartment that holds within ravishing elegance in soft creamy colors to create a leisurely sensuous atmosphere. The bathroom makes up for half the size of the entire suite and matches the wooden elements in the large bedroom with its stunning décor linens and beddings. There's a lush feel of a well balanced harmony throughout the place with vases holding bouquets of colorful flowers and wheat stalks in every corner. The background music is soft and caressing, blending well with the fireplace and the silky lights that flow from tiny crevices in the ceiling. The atmosphere within the hut arouses sentimental thoughts that wink from every corner.

After freshening up and changing clothes I look in the mirror. The evening dress accentuates the contours of my figure and makes me smile in contentment. I open the door, step into the fresh air and at once I'm on the main path decorated with antique styled lanterns.

"Good evening Mrs. Schmidt," a man wearing a white uniform appears from nowhere, "My name's Brian. Mr. Schmidt asked me to escort you to the ball room. He apologizes he couldn't come himself... said he'll find you once you get there ...but he wanted you to have this," he offers me the white flower and his arm, "I understand your flight was delayed..."

Sprawling lawns next to flowery bushes frame the wide path. Within minutes we reach the main building.

"It's been a pleasure, ma'am... enjoy your evening."

I thank him and step inside.

The dazzling ballroom is bustling with laughter and loud banter from every corner. Waiters in blindingly white uniforms and matching gloves roam among the hundreds of guests holding heavy trays filled with wine glasses and champagne. The perfumed air is bursting with excitement. At the far end of the vast room is a small stage with a live band sounding soft background music, a pleasant accompaniment to the swishing sounds of the women's long evening gowns. They circle around holding wine glasses that never empty, mingling with each other and wearing white smiles with giggly sounds. The men in elegant evening jackets congregate in large groups trumpeting their overly joyous deep laughter matched only by the ice cubes rattling in their glasses.

"Tara! You look great! I can't believe it's really you!"

The wife of the CEO spots me and swishes around in her long plum colored taffeta gown. I offer my cheek and meet hers at the right angle. She stares at me with the eyes of a woman who finds it difficult to conceal her jealousy.

"Oh! My!" her eyes grow large, "I've never ...I mean ...you look so ... where have you hidden it all these years?!" her demanding tone sounds fake as she draws an imaginary line along my dress with her free hand.

Her husband joins in.

"Is that you, Tara?!" his eyes are fixed on the décolletage in front of him.

My hand is choking a glass of soda with a slice of lemon. I smile.

"Oh boy... wait until Darien sees you!" he again smiles and squeezes my shoulder.

"Is he nearby? I can't see him."

I take small steps and move away.

"Tara! How are you?" the VP's wife with her husband in toe head in my direction, "You look so... so different...is it the haircut?"

"I'll tell you what it is," her husband joins in giving me a tight squeeze, "it's a special recipe! We need to ask Darien about it!"

Everyone bursts out laughing.

"I see you finally made it?! Darien's deep voice sounds from behind.

I turn around and meet his surprised look.

"Is it really my beautiful wife?! I barely recognize you."

His arms hold onto my shoulders. He moves his head close to mine and in a repulsed tone whispers into my ear.

"Where the fuck did you find that dress?!" his arm retains our distance. He smiles and kisses my cheek.

The circle around us grows with the giggles and laughter. Everyone moves close to introduce themselves. The women compliment me on the dress and the matching jewelry; the men stare at the cleavage fronting the exquisitely tailored gown that takes advantage of all the delicate parts that Darien always forces me to hide.

"You're my wife and you need to dress accordingly! Now button your shirt all the way to the top! That's it! And the sleeve must come down to here!" he touches my wrist, "and the skirt shouldn't be shorter than this!" his finger draws a line on my knee.

The guests are called to their designated tables. Our own table, set at the head of the room, hosts the president of the company and his second in command accompanied by their wives and a special client who flew for the occasion all the way from Japan. The meal that follows is a culinary delight much like the drinks and wines handpicked by Darien ensuring that no glass remains empty. Darien requests that the band pause gets upstage and delivers a brilliantly eloquent speech without ever missing a dot, a star, a spark or any other small speck that might stand in his way of reaching the sky with an applauding chorus.

Scouting the nearby tables I meet smiles of admiration all focused on Darien, the hero and winner of hearts and minds. Three hundred eyes stare at the man who now stands in front of them with his white smile releasing witty jokes meant to entertain and impress them. Loud laughter and applauds interrupt his words. Oz' and Sevan's faces float in front of my eyes. I look at their shamed faces and hear the degrading words unleashed only days ago by Darien and it's the same voice that now sounds inside this beautiful room; and for the millionth time I wonder, if there's something faulty within me, something that prevents me from admiring the man who stood and watched his father bash my face with his bare hands and chose not to protect me or his children. If only the children were here to witness the waves of admiration vibrating throughout the hall; if they could feel a father's pride, see his good and fun sides all hidden and camouflaged under loud laughter and charming smiles, perhaps they could be proud of him and not have to carry their shoulders in fear and shame.

"No!" I strengthen my inner voice, "there's nothing faulty inside of me. The man now standing on stage is the same man who didn't protect you and the same one who will never stand up to support you."

At the end of the meal the band strums sentiments to hearts. Darien gets up and offers me his hand. He holds me tight on the dance floor in view of all those staring eyes as he smiles and tightens his grip on my back.

"You look like a slut! Where the hell did you find this dress?!"

I smile.

"At Neimans...and it costs accordingly! I like it!"

At the end of the long evening, after the food and the drinks and the speeches and the dances and the fake smiles and giggles, Darien demands my presence next to him at the entrance door to see the guests off. Most of them, who've already lost their sharpness of tongue and equilibrium, get into a long line to thank us. Several unidentified faces pass by me, stopping long enough to shake our hands, say their thanks and meet our cheeks in mid air. My facial muscles ache from the hours-long smiles.

Robert the VP wobbles in our direction with his wife holding firmly onto his arm.

"Well...keep doin' what you're doin' Darien... seems like it's workin' great on your wife!"

A strong, nauseating stench of alcohol mixed with the sour odor of a sweaty body clouds him.

I know about Robert's past from Darien's stories and am aware of his boundless appetite for drinking and women that got him into trouble in the past. He grabs both my hands and tries to pull me towards him.

"Tara... I'd ...I'd really like..."

Robert's eyes rest on my necklace and the valley below. I readjust my extended hand and allow him to plant a kiss on its back.

He smiles at Darien then eyes me allowing the words to ooze crookedly out of his mouth.

"I hope Darien appreciates you, Tara...'cause...you're not only beautiful...you also...you also understand things..." he winks at me, his eyes lingering longingly on my décolletage.

It's past two am by the time we're on the path in the direction of the hut.

I recall Bernie's words.

"This week can really be of help, especially with romance...you'll be in a beautiful setting...and you'll have a chance to work on your togetherness..."

Darien's voice breaks the silence.

"What was that thing ...with Robert?! You know he's my boss! So what if he wanted a kiss?!"

"He stunk of alcohol! It sickened me!"

"But he's my boss! What's wrong with a kiss? You should have given him what he wanted!"

"So fucking me for dessert would have also been okay with you?!"

We keep our pace and silence as we enter the hut.

The air inside vibrates. Natural woodland scents blend with the fragrances of wild flowers caressing each other to the tune of the soft background melody. Together they arouse magic that yearns for lovemaking. The wide bed lies naked. Its spread has been removed and now glows under the mesmerizing lights of the fireplace. A small heart shaped chocolate has been placed on each of the pillows.

I move slowly in Darien's direction, step out of my shoes, turn my back and lean into him.

"Can you please unzip me?"

I can feel his hands shake. The long zipper is undone and the dress drops to the floor. I turn around and let his eyes brief my body. I wrap both arms around his neck and move into him. He lowers his head towards me, kisses my forehead and steps away.

"Eh....I've got to return to the bar ...to update Brian... he's leaving tomorrow morning to London... I'll be back shortly."

And he's gone.

***

In January I initiate the divorce proceedings and begin checking into the various schooling options available in Israel. Following countless phone calls and conversations with people who are well acquainted with the different settings, I choose the appropriate placements for Oz and Sevan. Their polarized educational requirements will ultimately dictate our future place of residence. I end up settling on a small town with a reputation for educational excellence, located half-an-hour's drive from my parents where Oz will be bussed daily to and from school. The school's unique setting aims to integrate its graduates into the main stream of society by allowing them daily practice of social skills alongside a vocational program to ensure their full independent living. A different school offering special classes for the talented and gifted will provide for Sevan's needs.

I call mother and share with her my decision but her words take me back to my early childhood days.

"Why plan ahead of time?! Once you're here you can figure things out..."

My heart beats fast. I concentrate on the one question I've been practicing for a long time.

"What's wrong? Why are you quiet, Tara?! Have you changed your mind? D'you prefer to stay in America?"

"I want to know," I swallow the pain with the fear and the shame, "I want to know if..."

"What?! What do you want to ask?!"

And again from the distance of the Knokke events I hear her protesting voice.

"WHAT HAVE YOU DONE TO HIM, TARA?!"

"I want to ask if you... and dad...if you'll be able to help me when I get there...?"

The tears that follow my question reflect the many disappointments I've known throughout my childhood and teenaged years. I lived with the understanding that I mustn't burden my parents, mustn't ask for their help or add to their difficulties with Naomi and Bilha.

"Why even ask such a question?!" mother responds.

In March the divorce proceedings begin, assisted by two mediators.

"I'm telling you right now that it's not 'gonna work out with her!" Darien points in my direction, "It's a total waste of money. We're getting a divorce!"

The attorneys smile in agreement and from that moment on Darien's money is siphoned into their pockets much like his nightly Chivas.

We're both seated on opposite sides of a long table, each with our own attorney and own mediator.

"I'd like this process to be over with as quickly as possible so that I can register Oz on time for his school in Israel."

"What's the deadline for registration?" Darien's attorney inquires.

"The end of May."

The attorney scribbles something on the writing pad and Darien smiles.

The attorneys' sole purpose is to stretch the proceedings as long as possible while clocking the hours and loading as many additional expenses as possible. They take apart every sentence, erase every dot and move every comma, defining from scratch every word in the English language and reinventing new ones as they exercise creativity. Darien is sharper than his attorney: he sits opposite me with his head held high and demands to erase definitions add appendixes and move paragraphs, all aimed at making it as difficult as possible to bring the process to an end.

Over the break I approach him.

"Let's finish it in good spirits...I don't want the kids to be hurt more than they..."

"You should have thought about it before you acted stupidly!" he growls.

"But maybe we can..."

"Save your words! I'm not compromising on anything!"

It's the middle of May when Oz' teacher calls me at night.

"I apologize for the late hour," she explains, "But I thought I should update you. I just found out that Oz is getting a special award tomorrow."

"An award?!What kind of an award?"

"Well...every year there's a ceremony at school with several categories...the first, of course, is for academic excellence... but there's also a special award initiated by the community for exceptional students who stand out for reasons other than academics... students who serve as examples to others...it's a surprise, of course, so... please don't say a word to Oz ...I just wanted you to know so that you can make plans to be there..."

"Thank you... thanks so much for letting me know ... I really appreciate it! Yes...of course I'll be there! Yes...I'll let his dad know too..."

I call Darien and update him.

"I'm sure you're 'gonna be there!"

"But don't you want to come for Oz'...?"

"I'm busy!"

He slams the phone.

The large auditorium is packed with students. Short speeches are delivered followed by musical and vocal performances and joined by the school's choir. The principal returns to the podium and begins calling out the names of the award winners.

The first to be called up stage and receive a certificate of excellence are students praised for their academic achievements. Each in turn shakes hands with the principal and the teaching staff then reaches out for the certificate. I listen to the other categories and scout the auditorium with the hope of seeing Darien.

"And now for the special award," the principal announces, "this year we've decided to give it to a very deserving student... someone who's shown empathy and kindness to all... someone who always offers assistance to others... even to those outside his own class.

It's someone who doesn't excel academically... you could even say that at times he finds academics difficult, but he never gives up. He always carries a positive attitude and is very considerate of others. Yet he's stubborn," he releases a chuckle, "Yes! But a healthy kind of stubbornness. He's tenacious, diligent, never gives up and isn't afraid of hard work and giving it a second try... he doesn't know the meaning of 'I can't' and if he fails he tries again. It's an honor for me to ask up stage the award winning student whose diligence and perseverance stand out! Give a big one to Oz Schmidt!"

The thunderous applause deafens my crying. I spot Oz sitting in the first row closest to the stage. Seated around him are students who cheer him on.

"Get up, Oz! Get up! You've been called up stage...you're getting an award. You need to go up stage now."

Oz is confused. It takes him a while to reach the podium. He bows slightly. A short chuckle swishes through the auditorium.

"Oz, it's an honor to present you with this award on behalf of the school," the principal extends his hand, "You've earned it because of who you are. You deserve this special award. You've set an example for students who excel in areas other than academics. Well done Oz! Well done!"

Oz is overwhelmed with excitement. He holds the certificate with both hands lowers his head and allows the principal to place a medal around his neck. Moments later, when the ceremony is over, I reach the entrance to the auditorium and hug him.

"I'm so proud of you, Ozzie! You're so special...so wonderfully special..." I hold him close to my heart.

***

The month of June is nearing its end but Darien continues to wear down the attorneys and mediators by refusing to sign the final agreement for divorce.

"I'll sign it on our anniversary. That way you'll always remember me!" he chuckles.

The agreement is finally signed at the beginning of July 1994.

That evening Naomi calls.

"I'm with Darien! He's absolutely right! You're just plain dumb! You're even too stupid to realize that you've made the worse decision of your life by asking to divorce him! Who'll even want you with those two defective kids of yours?!"

Moments before departing to the airport, Darien stops by and whispers in my ear.

"You only wanted the children...you didn't really want me..."

"I DID want you... but I wanted you WITH the children... and sometimes I felt that you...that you didn't..."

He holds me tighter now. Tears choke me.

"Sometimes... I even thought...it seemed...I even thought that... maybe you're sorry we ever had kids..."

"Tcha...there's something to it..." he strokes my hair, "there's something to it..."

Five days later the three of us land in Israel.

***

As soon as we arrive I contact Oz' designated school but registration is already closed. I explain our reasons for being late and beg them to accept him but they refuse. I have no choice but to place Oz in a self contained class within the local school.

The education system is ill equipped to handle students with diversified handicapping conditions, forcing all thirty-three students, some developmentally delayed others with behavioral or emotional issues, inside the same classroom with only one teacher to address their individualized educational needs.

I approach the teacher for help but she directs me to the principal.

"This is all we can offer! And don't tell me what Oz had in

America! This is not America! What did you expect when you decided to return to Israel?!"

Sevan also finds it hard to adapt to school. Her Hebrew is fluent, with no traces of a foreign accent but the basic differences between both schools are vast.

"I couldn't even use the bathroom ...it's dirty ... disgusting ... you can't even go in... and the kids make fun of me...they're mean ... they keep telling me I should go back to America... why did you bring us over here?!"

I speak with her homeroom teacher who offers help.

I see the great changes that have taken place in the country of my childhood, not all of them for the better. The newspapers and television are full of sensational headlines announcing the arrival of an assortment of foreign goods and fast food eateries replacing the high quality local products. I take Oz and Sevan on long trips and acquaint them with the natural beauty of my birth country but seeing its rapidly changing face pains me.

I find myself wondering if I haven't made a mistake by bringing my children to a place so very different from that which I'd remembered and share my thoughts with dad who often joins us on our trips.

True to her habits, mother demands that I adhere to her dictates.

"You'll come here with the kids on Friday directly after school... and stay over through Saturday..."

"But we're only half an hour away. Besides, it's important that they get to know other kids in our neighborhood and befriend them... especially Oz...so we'll come on Friday or on Saturday... ...."

"Whatever! But don't complain later on!"

"Complain about what?"

"Oh...I'm sure you'll find what to complain about!"

***

Chris and Bilha view my return to Israel with both children as a threat. Chris is especially perturbed. After being pampered and supported by my parents for the past several years, he's fearful that our presence will consume all my parents' time and rob him and his children of the exclusive attention they've enjoyed all these years.

I'm in the back yard, next to the open kitchen window, when I hear Chris complain.

"They bother our kids... I think it's better if Tara stops coming here every week... maybe you can go visit them instead..."

"Well... what can I can do about it?!" mother replies.

But the situation only worsens.

Chris and Bilha's children, who grew up with my parents in the same yard, taunt Oz and Sevan.

"We don't want you here! It's our house and our grandparents! They're only ours! Go back home! Go back to America!"

As soon as I mention this to Chris and to my parents, mother goes into action. She meddles in every conversation taking sides and interfering in the children's interactions, as she's always done throughout our childhood.

She calls me at night.

"Chris is complaining about your kids... and we're absolutely devastated ... I really don't know what to do because he's right, of course... we spent our entire time with them until you got here...it's not easy for us...I hope you appreciate all we're doing for you..."

Things only get worse after I walk unexpectedly into the kitchen and hear Chris' words.

"I wish Tara hadn't returned to Israel..." he blurts out loud.

"Well...there's nothing we can do about it now... she's already here!"

I see my mother's arm stretched into the air, just like Grandma Perla's arm behind Naomi's back.

Following the divorce Darien uses silence to express his anger and frustration. He waits two months before calling the kids for the first time.

"I'm busy! So speak quickly!" his voice is angry.

Oz is speechless.

Sevan takes advantage of the momentary silence and grabs the receiver.

"Daddy...I miss you daddy..." she whimpers in a childish voice.

"Make it short Sevan! I'm on my way out with clients."

"When can we see you daddy? When daddy? I miss you..."

"You should have thought about it before joining your mother!"

Sevan stares at me.

"But I..."

"Save me your excuses. I'll try to call again soon. Bye."

It's now October, three months since our arrival. My upcoming birthday coincides with the holiday of Sukkot (Tabernacles) soon to be celebrated for the first time in Israel. I call mother ahead of time to plan for the festive meal and mention the special decorations prepared excitedly by both children.

"Naomi will be here for the holiday...but we don't want any problems or quarrels," she announces.

"What problems are you talking about?"

"Come on Tara! I don't have the patience for your games! Naomi needs peace and quiet... she's sick and she doesn't want to quarrel so... so it's better if you don't come at all!"

I ask a friend to join us for the holiday meal and together we put up a Sukkah and hang up the children's decorations. But despite my efforts to disregard my mother's painful rejection, within a few short months my parents' house turns into a place of constant friction and I find myself without any family support.

Naomi, who's always sheltered Bilha under her wing, now orders her not to communicate with me or my children. She flies over several times a year, always landing unexpectedly for extended visits and uses her talents to rekindle old disputes carried over from our childhood. She meddles in Bilha's and Chris' affairs, forbids them and their children to have any contact with us, restricts our visits to my parents' house and basically ostracizes the three of us. Her manipulations work wonders and soon my parents are also drawn into her crazed hallucinatory world igniting the familiar conflicts of our past.

"We don't want any fights like in childhood!" mother repeats over the phone, "and besides... Naomi's always been closer to Bilha... she comes especially to visit her and the kids! So why fuss if she doesn't want to see you here?!"

But Bilha, who is now slightly damaged, is somewhat different from the sharp witty girl she once was and doesn't understand Naomi's manipulations. She embraces her presence whenever Naomi's in Israel and allows her to manage the household and her children as she sees fit.

"I'll back up Bilha every single time!" Naomi declares, "And I don't want that stinking carcass to defile the atmosphere with her defective kids! As long as I'm here I don't want to see Tara's face! That's all there is to it!"

***

Within six months my relationship with Bilha and Chris dissolves into nothingness.

Mother follows Naomi's orders, mixing lies with secrets kneading them together and creating walls to keep us apart; she meddles in everyone's daily schedule, watches Bilha's and her children's every move, cleans their house, cooks and bakes for them, decides who goes where and when, controls my father's movements and whereabouts, dictates his daily outings and goes as far as telling him when he can visit us. Mother becomes Naomi's extension, a busy body whose sole occupation is managing other family member's lives as she sees fit.

At the end of our first year in Israel Oz is accepted to his designated school, Sevan's situation improves and she's socially involved and well integrated with her friends at school. I'm very proud of my children's achievements as they continue their daily private lessons to improve their Hebrew and catch up with the required subjects at school. I find a secretarial position with flexible hours and concentrate on strengthening the family bondage of the three of us.

Next week is the traditional school band procession that marches through the main street of town. Sevan is very excited and looks forward to taking part in it.

"So you're coming tomorrow to see Sevan play the trumpet, right?" I ask mother.

"Well...now that you mention it...I'm not really sure...dad needs to drive Bilha's youngest to an after school activity...I'll have to get back to you."

"Please mother... it's important for Sevan...please come... for her sake..."

My parents arrive late. They stand next to me on the sidewalk as the band marches by. Ten minutes later mother announces.

"Okay! Time to go! We're in a hurry to get back home. Dad needs to pick up the little one...I don't want him to be late ..."

"But can't you at least wait until Sevan finishes..."

"I really don't want to be late for the little one...never mind...we'll call Sevan later on tonight..."

As soon as the band is dispersed, Sevan comes running.

"Where's Saba and Safta?"

And all I can do is hug her.

***

Re-threading past connections with friends and acquaintances resembles an artful masterpiece of intricate knots woven together carefully to bridge the gap of past times. I seek every opportunity to try and re-connect with people whom I haven't seen in many years and go out of my way to meet new ones.

I bump into Eddie, a past family friend who knows my parents and happens to live nearby.

"We haven't seen you in ages, Tara. Why don't you come visit us with the kids?"

Over the weekend I take Oz and Sevan and the three of us spend the day with Eddie and his family.

Mother calls me that evening.

"Where've you been all day?! I tried reaching you ..."

"We had a great time with Eddie and his family...it was really nice after all those years ...and the kids enjoyed it... he sends warm regards..."

"Eddie?! How could you! He behaved miserably after Bilha's accident! Shame on you?!"

"What's wrong? What did he do?"

"He came only ONCE to visit her in the hospital! ONCE! And he had the audacity to bring her canned corn as a get well present! Who brings a can of corn to someone who's hospitalized?! And after all we've done for him in the past..."

"But what's all that got to do with me?!"

"Shame on you, Tara! Shame! What exactly don't you understand?! Eddie behaved in such a disgraceful way... and now you're teaming up with him as if he's done nothing wrong!"

"But...I still...can you explain to me how all this is connected to our visit...?"

"If you didn't get what I said, you probably never will! Shame on you! Shame on you, Tara!"

Dad visits us as often as he can. His presence, in our lives, serves as a stabilizing force we all lean on. Following dinner he moves with both kids to the couch in the living room, wraps his arms lovingly around them, chats, inquires and takes a keen interest in their young lives acting his usual funny and silly and spreading good humor all around. Oz adores dad, his kindness and softness of heart and the fact that he always avails himself to his every phone call and question.

From being the best dad he's becomes the best granddad for my children.

As I watch both children tucked under his strong arms, mesmerized by the calmness of his voice and the stories he tells them, I smile at the sweet memories of those same ones we listened to as children.

***

Twice a year, as detailed in the divorce agreement, Darien sends the children plane tickets to meet him in the States or elsewhere in Europe. I'm perturbed by the fact that Helmut and Stella intend joining them but there's nothing I can do to prevent it.

It's December now and the children are preparing to visit Darien.

After checking the route I call him.

"How are you?"

"I'm fine."

"And how ..."

"Let's skip the small talk and get to the point. Why are you calling?"

"I got the tickets you sent the kids with the two stopovers in Europe and in the States ..."

"That's right! They were the cheapest tickets I could get."

"I'm afraid of letting them fly alone all the way to Texas with two connections ...It's 'gonna stretch over twenty-four hours... and I'm thinking about Oz' medications..."

"Then YOU have a problem!"

True to our choppy style of communication, things quickly get out of hand and turn into chaos. Within seconds we're drowning in a whirlpool of words that get thrashed back and forth scorching us like the darn couch grass of my childhood that pestered my small hands.

"I'm not sure Oz..."

"Mind your own business!"

"But the children ARE my business! It's OUR children! Why make them suffer? They're 'gonna have to spend long hours sitting and waiting in terminals..."

"They DON'T HAVE to come!"

"But they miss you..."

"So explain to them that it's YOUR fault! YOU'RE the one who chose to divorce and move to the other side of the world! If you hadn't been so stubborn and kept your mouth shut we wouldn't have had any problems to begin with!"

And as always, our dialogues end up as one long monologue trumpeted by Darien and accompanied by threats that if I don't go along with his suggestions, the children won't get to see him.

Careful planning is required prior to every flight. Oz' anti seizure drugs must be taken punctually at precise intervals but because he can't tell the time, Sevan has no choice but to take on the responsibility. After landing, the children are met by a ground hostess who takes them to a secluded area where they spend endless boring hours doing nothing but wait for the next leg of their trip. Oz doesn't travel well. He throws up which in turn causes Sevan to become anxious. Worried about his medications and concerned for his welfare, Sevan carries a sense of responsibility long after the flight is over. By the time the children finally get to meet Darien, they're all shaken up, confused, jet lagged and totally disoriented.

The visits vary, lasting seven to twelve days depending on Darien's momentary whims.

"It's inconvenient to have them land here on Monday...I'll just be returning from another trip ...and then I'm scheduled for an important meeting..."

"But it's your kids! Don't you miss them? They haven't seen you in over six months..."

"That's none of your business! So don't stick your nose into my affairs!"

Sevan calls up Darien.

"I miss you daddy. Can we please stay with you for longer than just a week?"

"No! I'm busy! As it is I hardly have the time for you."

"But I miss you so much, daddy..."

"I miss you too but there's nothing I can do about it."

"Can you maybe talk to your boss... explain to him...you can tell him that you have a little girl that misses her daddy so much..." Her small voice breaks, "One week isn't enough for me... I'm sure he'll give you extra time... please daddy..."

"A week! That's all I can spare!"

"But I miss you more than just a week... I even miss you more than you miss me, daddy..." she's now crying.

"I've got to run! I have a meeting!"

The children are tense, they don't know when they'll be able to see their father or for how long.

After returning home, both are very quiet and reserved for several weeks. Only years later will they open up and share with me what they've gone through during those visits.

"Oz fell from his bike and lost consciousness...then the ambulance came and took him to the hospital..."

"And where was dad all this time?!" I ask Sevan.

"We were in a forest on top of a mountain and there were huts and bicycle trails. Dad stayed separately in a hut with his wife... and he told us to go ride our bikes and not to disturb him ...so Oz went all the way up and after he fell, dad didn't answer the phone so I had to go all by myself with Oz in the ambulance ..."

And there was another visit when Oz kept throwing up during the flight. When he finally saw his father and asked to hug him, Darien pushed him away.

"You stink like a dog that hasn't been washed in years!"

Shortly after our divorce Darien remarried a divorcee with two children from a previous marriage and together they relocated to another state. Her abusive son, who was Oz' age, enjoyed beating up on him and enticed his younger sister to join forces. Soon the two began taunting and teasing Oz and Sevan at every opportunity.

When they first visited their father's new home, Darien instructed the children.

"I want you to pay attention. This is our entire house but it's divided into two parts with two separate entrances. Here's where you'll stay for the next three weeks...this entire section is yours. We're staying in the other part so you won't have a reason to fight with each other. Now ... I'm going to lock up your door from the outside and you're 'gonna stay inside until I come pick you up. See... over here...there's everything you'll need ... a kitchen...with plenty of food...everything...there's plenty until tomorrow morning!"

As time went on there were other visits, when the kids were still allowed to keep in touch with me.

"I'm scared...I don't want to stay here...I want to go home... Scott hits me ...and Liz too ...and dad isn't even here... I don't feel good Ima," Oz cries on the phone but Darien refuses to take my calls and I can't help the children from afar. I can only refuse to send them over again. It takes both children several weeks to calm down and overcome their emotional turmoil and by then it's time to re-visit Darien.

During one of their visits, Sevan calls me in the middle of the night.

"Why are you whispering, Sevanni?"

"Dad doesn't allow us to call you... I miss you, Ima...and your food...it's no fun over here. Dad is at work all day...and we're bored. He brought us a baby sitter but she just sits there... I'm sad, Ima..."

Sevan is distraught long after their return home and keeps to herself.

***

We've been in Israel now for three years.

Over one of my weekend visits with my parents, dad says.

"Tara... I'm going out to water the back yard...'wann'a join?"

I understand that he wants us to talk.

"I really don't trust Darien and I have no idea what he's capable of... so I've decided to keep the children's new German passports with me over here... all this sudden interest in them ...they have their American passports... sounds to me like he's planning to kidnap them."

"No way!" I release a nervous laughter, "No way! The kids don't even interest him!"

"But issuing new passports... that really bothers me...I think he's capable of anything..."

"Darien?! Capable of kidnapping?! "

My father's image now floats in front of my eyes. I feel a painful pinch in my heart for failing to heed his warnings.

My children's passports are still with me to date.

Two years later, my father is diagnosed with a benign brain tumor and undergoes surgery.

Bilha uses mother to deliver messages.

"Now that dad's hospitalized I want Tara to share the load and take on a few shifts."

Mother is in the center of things, spinning words back and forth and unleashing operational instructions.

I'm quick to respond.

"I don't need Bilha to remind me about dad... I've already been to the hospital last night! And even if Bilha doesn't want me there I intend visiting him every single night after the kids are in bed!"

But mother is relentless.

"Eh...but Bilha and Chris are planning to visit him later this evening... so you can save your trip tonight..."

It's an ordinary evening at home. Sevan's friends exchange witty banters and kid around filling the air with the loud giggling sounds of teenagers. Oz is in his room with one of his friends from school. I'm in the kitchen preparing food. Stirring inside my head are thoughts of the things we now have and remembrances of those we've left behind in America; and as though set apart from my hands, my fingers knead memories this way and that way reminding me of the world we once knew, a faraway place, life-times removed from where we are now.

Faint longings from the past sprout from nowhere but within a split of a wink they vanish and I find myself happy with the small family of three that I've managed to keep together. I shut my eyes for one long second staring smilingly into the here and now of my life, blinded by pride and self contentment much like a duped sheep a hairline away from having its throat slit.

"I'm starved!" Sevan clings to me, "Everyone is just waiting for the food! Can I already set the table?"

"I'm proud of you," I wrap my arms around her slenderness, "I'm so proud of you."

"What about?"

"Oh... everything Sevanni... everything..." I hold her tight and I don't want to let go.

Within minutes the entire group is seated around the table,

six giggling teenagers sharing momentary peaceful crumbs of life, benign events that make up their youthful lives, worlds removed from the future happenings that are about to unfold at our doorstep.

Every Tuesday Oz' five friends from school join us for dinner.

Oz, who'd never experienced friendships before he'd entered school, feels proud and wants to help me prepare the meal.

"They only want your food, Ima."

"I'm so proud of you Ozzie...you have friends who really like you... and care for you." I hug him.

Sevan helps set the table and after dinner we all sit and watch the movie 'Forrest Gump.'

Several minutes into the film Oz whispers.

"Ima, am I like Forrest Gump?"

"Is that how you feel Ozzie?" I swallow hard.

"Sometimes..., "he says, "sometimes..."

After his friends leave Oz' hands move up and down his chest.

"I feel so good, Ima...my friends make me feel like... I feel warm in my heart ..."

I return his hug, a tight hug, without realizing his hugs are numbered.

***

It's the end of the school year. We're all very concerned and fearful about dad's deteriorating condition and sit over long hours outside the ICU.

Oz has now completed his twelfth's year of schooling and is very excited about the upcoming final year. He's already taken his matriculation exam in computers and anxiously awaits the results. His teacher encourages him and promises to work with him on a special project the following year.

I receive a letter from Oz' school.

"Please sign your agreement for Oz' next year's curriculum as detailed below..."

My attorney advises me to request a guardianship past the age of eighteen.

"You'll need it in order to sign next year's curriculum... and to continue caring for him ... do you have any medical documents attesting to his cognitive state?"

I share with him two medical opinions: one from the neurologist in Dallas who treated Oz until the day we'd left the States and another assessed by the pediatrician in Israel who's been taking care of him for the past six years.

After studying both documents the attorney fills out the forms.

"Why did you tick here the word 'retarded'?!" I point to the form.

"Because the court demands a reason for requesting a guardianship and this is the only option. I agree with you that it could have been phrased differently, but there's no other option here... and anyway...it's for his own good... you'll be able to sign all future forms from school and it'll protect him when he goes to visit his father... you never know..."

My father's voice echoes in my head.

I ask the attorney to explain the forms to Oz.

The following day Oz is in his office.

"So... do you understand why your mother is asking for this guardianship?"

"Not exactly..." Oz fans the palm of his hand sideways, "but I trust my Ima."

The attorney prepares the documents and the request is forwarded to the Israeli court.

We're all edgy given Dad's fading condition.

Darien happens to call that evening.

"How are you?"

"I'm okay thanks...how about you?"

"Good, good...I'd like to speak with Sevan."

Sevan is silent. She debates a while before picking up the receiver.

At the end of the long conversation Sevan is shrouded in an odd but familiar silence, one that I recognize from her past, an anxiously reserved stillness that always followed the aftermath of Darien's reprimanding voice.

She releases her words later on, after several other phone exchanges.

"Dad wants me to move to France and study at the Sorbonne ... I told him I can't because I'm in the middle of high school so he tried to convince me that I should try it anyway... he even offered to pay for a friend to join me. I thought he meant that I should study French during the summer ...but then he said that it's for at least two years. Why would I want to quit high school over here when I'm nearing my graduation?!"

I wondered what could have triggered Darien's sudden interest in Sevan's schooling and his suggestion to send her to France but it was already too late to consult with dad.

At the beginning of December 1999 the court grants me the guardianship.

I translate it into English and mail it to Darien.

A week later dad passes away.

The funeral procession leaves my parents' house in the direction of the cemetery, a short walking distance. Bilha and Naomi support mother on both sides. I walk behind her with both children. Oz clings to me; he holds my hand and can't stop crying. Sevan hugs me and wipes her tears. As we stand above the open grave Sevan drops in a letter she wrote with a chocolate bar attached to it, dad's favored sweet. Oz adds his own letter and now the three of us are standing together hugging each other and wiping our tears.

"I miss Saba," Oz' voice keeps breaking, "I miss Saba so much..."

I'm nailed to the ground. I stare at the freshly dug earth trying desperately to preserve the memory of dad's eyes, but they're extinguished. I make an effort to block Naomi's nutty mumblings and wonder about dad's void and how it will affect Oz and Sevan and our future lives as a family.

In the past mother enjoyed planning her own gardens but demanded that dad execute her instructions. It was dad who watered the softest of plants, stroked new blooms and gulped from nature's intoxicating fragrances. His steadfast hands weeded stubborn couch grass and tamed the lawn that threatened to choke the citrus trees. Dad was the one who cleaned flowerbeds and plucked stray thorny shoots. He encouraged curiosity and imagination and over the years was even able to tame Naomi's entangled flower bed.

Mother's hands birthed delicious foods, knits and amazing embroideries but she saved the best of her talents for the cloudy days that followed dad's death during that awful December month.

Overnight mother lost her inner balance by supporting the monster she helped grow, giving in to her every whim and serving as Naomi's battered floor rag.

***

At the end of that terribly sad December the children fly to Belgium and spend a week with Darien. When they return Oz is very upset.

"Dad told me that you wrote that I'm retarded! He showed me the papers that you wrote it!"

I sit with Oz and, once again, go over each of the clauses.

"When you ask the court for guardianship you have to give them a reason, Ozzie. Remember we spoke about it with the attorney? There are different reasons for requesting a guardianship... a guardianship of a person or of an estate. I asked for the guardianship so that I could sign my agreement of your lesson plans. When we lived in Dallas I did the same thing. Each year I attended an A.R.D. meeting and then signed my agreement of your lesson plans, but now that you're over the age of eighteen, I need to have a special guardianship that will allow me to continue signing on your behalf. Do you see the difference?"

"But you wrote that I'm a retard."

"Because there's no other option on the form. Look here, Ozzie... look what it says..."

Oz finds it hard to comprehend. It takes him long to sort things through but he's left feeling very hurt.

Darien calls again and asks to speak with Oz. As the conversation continues Oz' face crumples and he bursts out crying.

"Dad says that you're the only one that thinks I'm a retard because you want to manage my life and boss me around...you want this paper so that you can boss me... and tell me what to do...you didn't have to write that I'm a retard...dad doesn't think I'm a retard...he told me so..."

Despite all my efforts to clarify the situation and terminologies, Oz remains cautious and grows suspicious of me.

We mourn the loss of dad, but guard within the memory of his soft voice and good hearted eyes. The children enjoy telling stories and short anecdotes about the last five years they've spent in his company. Dad was more than just an extraordinary grandpa; he was an extraordinary human being, a kind, loving, sensitive, soft hearted and very compassionate person, full of humor with an amazingly sharp mind. He loved Oz and Sevan unconditionally and served as a father and trusted guide to both.

Over the weekends the three of us visit mother, but Bilha's and Chris' home, located just a few yards from my parents' house, remains shut.

In April, Oz' class enjoys a three day trip to Eilat. Oz returns home glowing with pride and happiness.

"Ayala kissed me...it was so...so good...it made me feel so warm in here," his hand rests on his chest.

I hug him tightly.

"I can feel your happiness...and I'm so happy for you, Ozzie."

"I don't want to go to dad...I want to stay here with Ayala."

"But dad misses you, Ozzie...he hasn't seen you in over six months..."

"But I'm afraid to go to him."

"Why?"

"Because I'm afraid I won't know what to say ...dad always says things to me and I don't know how to answer him."

"But it's only for three weeks, Ozzie...and you're going with Sevan... time will pass quickly..."

Again I find myself calming Oz and on some level, myself as well.

In June, as part of the special school's tradition reserved for students who've completed twelfth grade and are preparing for their next final graduating year, Oz's class sets sail to Cypress. The excitement is overwhelming. The marina platform in Herzlia is crowded with cheering family members and friends. Sevan stands next to me as we follow the sail boat until its silhouette is swallowed in the horizon.

Five days later Oz returns. He can't contain his excitement.

"It was so much fun, Ima...I enjoyed it so, so, so much..." he repeats over and over and over again as he hands me a decorative keychain for a present.

To this day, I still treasure the keychain.

A week later the school holds a special event for those who sailed to Cypress and their families. At the end of the evening the principal announces.

"Don't forget the special party in two weeks...it's not every day that you graduate twelfth grade!"

There's laughter and cheering with the crowd standing up and applauding.

Oz is radiantly ecstatic. I've never seen him look happier. Mother informed me earlier that she's not interested in joining us, so it's only me and Sevan who share Oz' special day. We take lots of photographs not realizing they'll be his last ones.

Before leaving I ask for a copy of the video of the sailing trip.

"We'll send it to you in the post," the homeroom teacher assures me.

The video is still with me.

Oz has never seen it.

***

July second, 2000, is the day of the children's flight. The three of us are at the airport. Oz is agitated and fearful.

"I'm scared of going, Ima," he again says, "I'm afraid I won't know what to say to dad ...he tells me things and I don't know what to say to him..."

I hug Oz and, as always, sooth him, promising he'll be back within three weeks.

It's nearly time to board the plane but there's nothing that hints of the late hour. The place is noisy and crowded. The loudspeaker announces a last minute delay of the flight.

"The camera! Where's the camera?" Oz asks.

I look inside my bag and realize I'd forgotten it at home.

"You won't remember me, Ima."

"There's no way I'll ever forget you, Ozzie!" I again hug him.

Oz if fidgety. He paces back and forth, worried about every small change.

"Why did you forget the camera, Ima?"

"I simply forgot it."

"But why mom? Why? You've got to photograph us."

"I promise to bring it next time, Ozzie."

"But you need to photograph us now! Now mom! You need to photograph us right now..."

Again I calm him down.

"There's no way on earth I'll ever forget the two of you. Besides, in three week's time you'll be back home ..."

But three weeks later only Sevan returns.

I feel I'm going mad, losing my mind while trying to understand why Oz hasn't returned with her. Sevan's words are laden with fear as she releases them slowly. She cries. I hold her tight and squeeze her to my heart.

"Dad locked Oz inside a room and didn't allow me inside...I tried to open the door but he yelled at me to get the hell away... only three-and-a-half hours later he let him out. Oz looked very strange... he kept pacing back and forth...you know how... like he always does when he's upset...and he didn't even talk to me. I asked him what's wrong and if he was okay but he kept quiet for a long time... and then he suddenly stopped and said that he's decided to stay with dad in America."

"And then?! What happened then?!"

"Nothing! Nothing happened! That's it!"

"What do you mean that's it?! Didn't you ask...or say something to him? Didn't you ..."

Sevan continues crying.

"I could have convinced him to return with me...I know I could have...but I didn't want to...I wanted him to stay there because... I wanted to stay alone with you, mom...only with you ...alone with you..."

I'm stunned. I hold her in my arms and at once grasp the depth of my daughter's distraught soul and its complexity which must have brewed within her over long years.

"Even if you would have tried, Sevannie... even if you would have tried...dad wouldn't have allowed him to leave..."

But my words don't help and since then Sevan's inner moral compass is all confused and tangled up.

Within a few weeks Sevan's overall behavior deteriorates; she skips classes, falls behind in school, returns home at odd hours and barely communicates with me. She refuses to share her aches and pains and I sense that I'm about to lose her.

In the days following the kidnapping I try to retain clarity of thought and function as normally as possible. I try to hold onto my sanity and not lose my mind. I tend to Sevan who'd just turned sixteen. I speak with her homeroom teacher who doesn't spare any efforts trying to help her. I reach out to the school counselor and to the principal and try to cling to my daily routines. I breathe. I go the office. I try to eat. I try to fall asleep. I try to survive the endless days and nights. I place the phone in bed next to my pillow hoping to hear from Oz, hoping he'll call, hoping he'll remember the phone number and somehow find a way to call me.

A month past the kidnapping is Oz' nineteenth birthday. I call Darien's home dozens of times and check with the international switchboard but there's no reply. The connection with Oz has been totally severed.

On the ninth of September at three in the morning the phone rings.

"What's wrong, Ozzie? Why are you crying?"

"I'm sad, Ima...and I don't feel good... I made a mistake... I shouldn't have told dad that I'll stay with him... I miss home..."

"Ozzie... Ozzie... I love you...you don't have to stay with dad if you don't feel good...but first ..."

"I want to go back home, Ima..."

243

"Calm down, Ozzie...calm down... you really don't have to stay there...but you need to calm down..."

"I don't feel good with dad...it doesn't feel good over here...I miss you and I want to see Ayala...and Billie...she'll forget me."

"Billie will never forget you. Remember when you first saw her at the dog pound? You picked her up and took good care of her...she's so cute now...but sad. She sits outside your room and yelps...she misses you ...she'll never forget you, Ozzie... never."

"But I also miss my teachers...and my friends."

"Did you tell dad that you want to return home?"

"Yes...and he said that if I want to go back home I need to find a job and earn the money and then I can buy a one way ticket. What does that mean, Ima?"

"Don't worry, Ozzie... I'll send you a ticket... don't worry...you'll soon return home...just try not to worry..."

Several more minutes pass before Oz is able to contain his crying and converse.

"Ozzie, I want you to be next to the phone tomorrow at ten in the morning. Can you remember to be there exactly at ten?"

"Yes, I'll ask dad about the time."

"Remember...the small hand stands on ten... and the big one on twelve. All right, Ozzie?"

The conversation goes on. An hour and twenty minutes later we say our goodbyes.

I remain with heavy fears, hoping that Oz will pick up the phone at the scheduled time. He doesn't wear a wrist watch and his memory isn't strong.

The following day at six pm Israel time, ten am by Oz, I dial.

"How are you feeling today, Ozzie?"

"I'm happy you called, Ima...I was afraid you'd forget to call me."

"How can I ever forget you, Ozzie? I miss you terribly and I want to see you."

"I also miss you."

"Are you feeling better today?"

"Yes."

"I'm glad to hear. I already ordered your ticket back home... but you need to listen real good...Oz? Are you there Oz?"

I hear muffled noises in the background. Someone seals the receiver.

"Oz! Can you hear me, Oz?"

"Dad...please...no...I want to speak..."

Oz! Are you still there? Talk to me! Oz!"

There's silence followed seconds later by Darien's voice.

"I want you to listen well, Tara! You better listen real well because I'm only 'gonna say it once! Don't you dare call this number again! Is that clear?! If you do, I'm 'gonna make sure my attorneys tear your ass apart for harassment! Got it?!"

"Let me speak to Oz!"

"Go to hell! Dumb shit!"

"Oz!!!"

My hands are shaking. The receiver drops. I don't know what to do or whom to call.

"Go to hell Darien! Let me speak to Oz!" I shriek at the walls, "Why?! Why?! Why?! Why?! Why are you doing this to Oz? Why now? You never cared about the kids! You were always mean to them! Bastard! How can you do this to Oz?! How can you?!"

I can see Oz. His head is lowered with both eyes staring at the floor. A battered child who's been slapped hard on his face.

"Why are you hurting him, Darien?! Now...when he's so successful at school...when he finally has a girlfriend?! Did you hear me?! He has a girlfriend! You should be happy for him! Why?! Tell me why?!"

My head feels like exploding. I rinse my face and dial again and again and again but I only get a recording.

And I can't stop crying.

Despite the many years that have since passed, Oz' voice is still with me.

***

Following Oz' kidnapping, Naomi takes center stage. She encourages mother to make up lies and spread distorted rumors surrounding Oz' sudden disappearance and even adds sickening elaborations of her own. Mother's so called self confidence, the weakened remnants that are still with her, regroup into a harrowing new state of flaccidity that succumbs to Naomi's dictates. She hurriedly sides up with Naomi and obeys her edicts and even adds warped vicious rumors of her own.

I'm pained. And shocked. The very delicate equilibrium dad has worked on his entire life to achieve, has now been violated, turning our family's garden into a heap of unruly wild terrain. Flowers are trampled, bushes are vandalized and the barbed wire fences which, up until now served as our family's stabling borders, have been buried under a thick layer of evil and madness. Dad's prior rules adhered to and abided by all, have been erased and all restrictions lifted. The fragile fabric that had once made up the core of our family has now changed and dissipated forever.

I turn to mother and ask for her help but she follows Naomi's instructions and responds with more lies, convincing herself and everyone around her that Oz chose out of his own volition to leave the house, quit school and move overnight to the States.

"What are you complaining about?! Oz always said he wanted to live with Darien...so what's your problem?!" her voice pierces my ears.

And Naomi is her usual self.

"I'm totally with Darien!" she declares blocking all communications between me and Oz. She calls up Darien and offers him help on the issue of vengeance, pumping hatred into his pained heart while encouraging him to avenge the years he'd been forced to suffer my presence.

As soon as I'd left the States Naomi began courting Darien. I guess it was the idleness in her life that made her want to stir in other people's lives; or perhaps the mental illness that afflicted her from childhood and fed into her hatred of me; or maybe her odd marriage to the man who agreed to marry her; or the knowledge that her former deviant pathways prevented her from ever bearing children.

Naomi sounds in Darien's ears all the right words that best suit his moodiness and painful heart. She spits out ugly words, wraps them with lies and plays with his injured soul the way we played with our marbles as children. She vilifies me for having dared leave him after twenty years of marriage, tells him that I didn't appreciate his hard work and that I neglected my love for him. She feeds him with bitterness then calls me.

"I'll see to it personally that you go down to your grave without ever seeing Oz!" she shrieks over the phone.

Darien is thrilled with her unexpected support and retains close contact with her.

Bilha, with her now frail memory, doesn't understand what's happening in front of her eyes and from the little that she does understand, is unable to sift the truth. Chris, too, isn't functioning so well. He listens to mother and prefers to keep his distance from anything remotely connected to Oz' disappearance.

Three teamed up and acted in vengeance: Darien, Naomi and my mother. And because of Oz' weaknesses and limitations he was chosen as victim, a good hearted, kind child with a soft, innocent soul and two beautiful dimples that always smile.

***

The day following Oz' phone call I contact a law firm in the United States and request legal assistance. Simultaneously I consider other options meant to help Oz in his current situation.

It takes me two months to reach someone who specializes in locating Israelis who've disappeared abroad. We exchange words and details and schedule a meeting aligned with the return of his crew from a complex rescue operation abroad. At his request, I again call him two days prior to our set meeting to ensure there are no changes, and casually mention the fact that I've received notification from the United States court to appear for a hearing in March.

"I'm sorry Tara but as of this moment our meeting is cancelled. If we get involved now in any way or get Oz out of the States, we risk being accused of kidnapping..."

My attorneys notify me that they've received a request from the court in the States.

"The court requests an affidavit from the Israeli court confirming the authenticity of the guardianship granted to the mother...you are hereby given a six month's extension to produce the document..."

My Israeli attorney requests the Israeli court to produce the routinely issued Affidavit but the judge doesn't respond, even after she's faxed a second request.

Several weeks later she faxes my attorney her response.

"I will look into it and release my final decision at a later date when I'm ready!"

Time ticks by quickly but I remain frozen and paralyzed. I can barely breathe during the day and spend the long nights cuddled with the little dog on the couch in the living room. My Israeli attorney and the judge drag their feet and basically ignore the court's dead line request. Six months later the case is automatically entered into the American court system and now the only way to free Oz relies totally on the processing system of the United States courts.

The final decision from the Israeli judge is received only a year later.

"The family court hereby instructs to conduct a survey into the matter of ... in the presence of a social worker ..."

"But Oz has been kidnapped for over a year now! He's in America!" I cry but there's no one listening to me inside the empty room.

The case embarks on a five year long path, filled with pits and holes of legal obstacles that slowly crawl and pave their way through the various court hierarchies. Over those grueling years I make some unsuccessful attempts to reach Oz and let him know that he's a free person and is allowed to return to Israel as he sees fit.

***

Weeks pass by, months come and go, but the pain of Oz' absence only increases.

I hug Sevan and support her but she refuses to talk about anything that has to do with Oz. I refrain from discussing the situation, but beg her to get professional help and even suggest that the two of us go together, but she adamantly refuses either option.

It's Saturday, around lunch time. Sevan is still in bed.

"Sevannie..."

"I don't want anything from you! Get out of my room!"

"We need to talk... this can't go on..."

"I want to be left alone!"

"But..."

"What exactly didn't you understand?!"

"I understand that ..."

"You don't understand a thing! You only care about Oz. Oz. Oz. You cry because you lost him but I lost more than just my brother! I also lost my dad!"

"I under ..."

"Stop saying that you understand because you don't! No one can understand! Especially not you! You only think about Oz, not about me..."

I call mother and I cry. It hurts me to see what Sevan is going through.

"Yes," she says, "She's really miserable...but you caught me at a bad time...I'm in the middle of cooking...I'm preparing a big pot for Bilha and the kids so we'll have to talk another time..."

I continue sharing my hesitations with the school counselor, the home room teacher and others involved and keep them updated; I also turn to mother in an effort to find some support, while encouraging Sevan to visit her more often.

Within a short span of time, my efforts, albeit successful, prove a curse.

Mother, with her black and white mindset, is supportive of Darien's distorted principles; she weaves her spool of poison and manipulates Sevan into choosing sides.

"Oz is happy in America. Don't let mom tell you otherwise..."

But at this point in time, I'm blinded by pain and worries and am totally unaware of my mother's meddling behind my back. I'm only thinking about Sevan.

At one point I sense that Sevan is confused and conflicted and assume that it has to do with mother's refusal to help me, so I keep encouraging her.

"Don't let her behavior towards me affect your relationship with her. She's your grandmother, Sevannie, and you should keep calling and visiting her. She loves you..."

But despite all the counseling and my well intended encouragement and care and devotion and love, the tight knit relationship with Sevan begins to weaken and within a few years fades out altogether. Sevan wraps herself in silence. She refuses to mention Oz or her father and distances herself from me and only retains a close relationship with my mother.

"Sevan claims that you only care about Oz... and not about what she's going through..."

"And what do you say to her?"

"Actually... I don't really know what happened with Oz...you see...I wasn't there..."

I refuse to take part in my mother's manipulative games. She tries desperately to hold onto her magic wand, an imaginary scepter with which she hopes to retain her crowned position as head of the family, the one thing that makes her feel strong.

"Have you heard anything from Oz?" I again ask her.

"Yes, but he doesn't say much."

"But ... what DOES he say?"

"Truth is... he's quite boring...it's always the same words...that he doesn't like school, and that he's studying horticulture... and it's difficult... and that he doesn't have any friends ...and that he misses me..."

Conversing with her only makes it harder on me but I have no choice but to speak with her and exchange words with the woman who enjoys hearing how much she's hurting me. She's a mean, heartless woman with a twisted soul identical to that of her crazy daughter, the one whom she equally and simultaneously adores and fears.

"Naomi is trying so hard...really... I take my hat off to her. She spends so much time on the phone with Oz ...and he just blabbers along and wastes her time. Poor girl... I wish she'd have kids of her own..."

I'm worried and perturbed about Sevan's overall wellbeing and consult with her teachers. Her matriculation exam is scheduled to take place on the same date as my court appearance in the States. It's already February and I'm set to appear there next month.

Sevan continues to refuse any professional help and basically withdraws. In the evenings she goes out and meets with friends and returns home long after midnight. The counselor suggests that I let her be and not push her.

"She's grieving the loss of her brother and that of her father. After all ...her father was the one who severed all ties with her so she really lost both of them at the same time..."

Darien refuses to answer Sevan's calls. He writes her a short note clarifying that she now belongs to THAT part of the family, the one in Israel, which is why he refuses to have anything to do with her.

Sevan is mourning her losses and I'm hurting for both my children and feeling lost. Utterly lost. Sevan insists on taking the matriculation exam on the scheduled date and asks that I attend the court session without her.

I turn to mother for help.

"She's only sixteen ...and I'm worried about leaving her alone at home..."

"She'll manage. Bilha's kids need me more."

Sevan remains home by herself.

***

As per information obtained through a private investigator, Oz' horticultural instruction classes take place at the local nursery where I'm hoping to see him. Easter vacation is a week prior to the scheduled court date which means, that if I want to see Oz I must get to him before his class is let out on vacation.

I'm concerned that once the court session is over, Darien will immediately eliminate him and I won't get another chance to see him.

I reach Ben Gurion airport and find myself in the midst of utter chaos. The Israel Airport Authority is on strike and all outgoing flights are cancelled. I have no choice but to return home and depart two and a half days later. As a consequence, all flights are backed up and delayed and I end up missing the connecting flight and find myself in an overnight layover in New York. Four days have been wasted and by the time I reach Oz' school, they've already been let out for the Easter vacation.

I remain an entire week in an empty hotel room. I call Sevan several times a day, listen to her words and wipe my tears. Again I ask her if she'd like to join me but she prefers to remain home and take her exam.

The following week I'm in court, scared to look directly at Oz. I don't trust myself to control my emotions, fearful that I might cross the short distance that separates us within the small court room, run towards him and hug him and never let go. My attorneys warn me not to be carried away for fear of causing legal complications. I heed their advice, give my testimony and walk out into the long corridor where I wait outside the door.

An hour later the door re-opens and I'm asked inside.

"You have precisely five minutes to communicate with your son. But in English! Only in English!"

I look at my son. He's frightened and gaunt looking. His eyes keep bouncing between me and the judge. I hug him and whisper in his ear.

"I love you Oz...I miss you so much..."

Within seconds my words fizzle and disappear and I'm again torn away from him.

My five minutes are over.

Since that split second encounter with Oz, my conscience keeps gnawing at my soul. I wake up at night all panicky, look at Oz' tearful eyes and for the life of me I can't understand what caused my terrible paralysis and what stopped me from wrapping his hand in mine the way dad would have done and say to him: "Come Ozzie... let's go home... you're free to come home with me...no one can stop you..." and simply walked out of the court room with him.

How could I?! How could I have kept silent?!

I find it hard to succumb to the reality of the situation and to the very slow and abrasive process of the American court system. In between each level of court hierarchy, there's a near year-long-silence before a final ruling is released. Only then does the case move up to a higher court level.

I try to find alternative ways to contact Oz. I write to members of the Knesset and ask for their assistance but they all try to shake off the powerlessness of the guardianship laws regarding adults that have been abducted abroad.

"The law pertaining to this issue is still lacking the firmness required for deliberation ..." a well appreciated Knesset member replies limply.

"I'm currently occupied with other issues...," another member replies.

Newspaper reporters and editors prefer not to raise the specific subject for fear that it might spark media turmoil or ignite an interest in a subject that currently has no legal solution.

My letter to the President goes unanswered as does my plea to the International Court of Justice in The Hague that decides on all legal outcomes of abducted minors on the planet.

When my attorney approached them following the abduction, the highly regarded and sanctimonious institution found all the reasons in the world why the international laws don't apply to our specific case as they're limited to minors under the age of eighteen.

"But Oz requires assistance beyond the age of eighteen!" my attorney argues, "and the mother holds a guardianship to that affect!"

"But we only help minors up to the age of eighteen. Adults must fend for themselves."

"And if they're unable to do so?!"

"We're sorry."

"And if it's an aging adult who requires assistance?!"

"We've already answered that. There's no need to insist further!"

***

Nearly five years went by from the day Oz was kidnapped until the final verdict was issued by the Supreme Court in the state he was abducted.

Throughout these tormenting years, as my attorneys battled the courts in an effort to return Oz home, they witnessed Darien's manipulations and abusive behavior towards his son. It was obvious he was only trying to get back at me to avenge his injured pride.

My attorneys' only efforts ultimately failed due to a procedural issue as evidenced in the publically published Dissenting Opinion.

It took an entire year for the first level court, where the lawsuit was originally entered, to release its verdict. The court granted me a guardianship within the state where the case was filed, so that Oz could return immediately to his home in Israel. But following Darien's request for appeal the process was stopped and held up.

The case was moved to the next level of courts. Nine months later it issued its verdict confirming the prior lower court's verdict that granted me the guardianship.

Once again Darien appealed and the legal proceedings came to a halt.

By now, more than three years have gone by.

The case reached the Superior court. Seven months later its verdict reversed the previous two rulings in Darien's favor. It was clear that certain exchanges were involved.

"We've been trying to fight corruption for years ... but unfortunately it still exists..." my attorneys explained.

The fourth and final ruling argued by the three Supreme Court judges was received ten months later.

The Majority opinion reflects the Supreme Court's unanimous opinion and verdict.

The Concurring opinion reflects its disagreements with the rationale behind the Majority opinion.

The Dissenting opinion reflects the reasons and disagreements the judge may have with the Court's verdict and allows for his opinion.

Such opinions are meant to clarify or even remedy similar situations which may appear in future cases, and can even go as far as getting Congress to correct certain issues by making changes in the way the laws are written (as reflected in the Uniform Act of Adult Guardianships and Protective Proceedings Jurisdiction which has undergone changes allowing local US courts the discretion to treat a foreign guardianship the same way as though it was granted in the States).

The Dissenting opinion (part of which is quoted from the original verdict) sums up the case:

"...It is unwise and ironic to dispose of the appeal upon procedural grounds..." the judge writes explaining that due to the "...sensitive issues and... complexity of the law..." within the specific state, the court is forced to disregard the Israeli guardianship and cannot allow for a just and moral ruling in the case.

"...the court ... failed to make a determination on a full and fair hearing... concerning ...the present status and best interest of... Oz'..."

He goes on to say that although the court is aware of the injustice in this case and the grave long term consequences it will have on Oz' future, it is unfortunate that the court lacks the laws with which to address the issue of extradition based on a guardianship granted in a foreign country outside the United States... and is unable to complete the process of extraditing Oz to his rightful home in Israel.

I'm totally lost and desperate to find help wherever I can.

***

Over one of my conversations with mother I ask her about Oz and unwittingly she says.

"I've asked Oz to call you when he first visited Naomi... but by then he'd already refused to talk to you."

"When did he visit Naomi?!"

"Two months after he decided to remain in the States. Darien took him to visit Naomi in New York and she let him call me. It was nice of her to do so, don't you think?"

"How come you never told me about it?!"

"What difference does it make? He didn't want to talk to you anyway..."

"Did you even ask him? And why didn't you ask Naomi to connect him with me? I'm his MOTHER!"

"But I'm his GRANDMOTHER! I tried to calm him down. I told him that you miss him... and that you want what's best for him... so he said that he thinks the best would be if he stayed with his dad. What did you want me to say to him?!"

***

I spot an article in the newspaper about an attorney who specializes in rescuing Israelis that are imprisoned in various countries.

> *"I seek to free only pure and untarnished Jewish souls who were unjustly imprisoned ... any Jewish soul that landed unjustly in the wrong place ..."*

I contact him and following a brief explanation he asks that we meet in his office on Saturday night.

"Please make sure to be here exactly at eleven thirty...yes, at night...during the day I'm busy studying Torah...and especially on Shabbat ...but as soon as Shabbat is over I return to my sacred work. I'm used to working on Saturday nights...oh, and you should also bring a check book with you ...no, I have no idea at this time. Once you get here we'll discuss it and decide what needs to be done. There's also the delicate issue of... the redemption of souls...I'm sure you understand? I work well with various organizations that fight over each and every Jewish soul...but don't worry...for the time being you can put aside the issue of money ... the most important thing is that you be here on time..."

Sevan joins me and at the appointed time the two of us stand at the entrance of a sky scraper that towers above the rest of the city buildings. The elevator flies us up to one of the top floors. The doors fling open and now both of us are staring at a glassed door with the attorney's name engraved on it in large letters.

It's eleven twenty. I ring the bell.

"Come in, Tara."

The place is busy and noisy with beeping faxes and constant ringing phones. A man wearing a Jewish skullcap and tzitzityot (fringes) walks over to us.

"Good evening, Tara, I'm glad you made it on time. Is this your daughter?"

He stares at Sevan.

"Yes, that's my daughter Sevan."

"She's very beautiful...very beautiful," his eyes are glued to her, "unfortunately we have an emergency situation here... so it'll take a few minutes. Please feel at home," he points in the direction of his office, "I'll join you shortly."

We cross the large hall towards his office. On our way we pass several work cubicles all partitioned into small spaces and equipped with computers and telephones.

"Look at all this...you'd think it's the middle of the day," I whisper in Sevan's ear.

"It's a strange place, Ima..."

"I agree...but let's at least hear what he has to say."

Within minutes the attorney joins us in his room.

"Sorry for the slight delay," he explains briefly what detained him, pushes a button and asks someone to join him.

"My partner is also an attorney... but she usually handles the more sensitive cases," he points in the direction of a tall, elegantly dressed woman who enters his room and shakes my hand.

"Yes...I've been working with the attorney for yeas... so I'm the one that will personally handle your case, Tara."

The two of them are now seated across from us behind a very large desk heaped with documents and three phones that ring relentlessly.

"Don't pay attention...just go on," he says to her and continues his phone conversation.

"I want to hear every single detail," she eyes us, "how exactly did Oz disappear... when and why it happened. The more details you can provide, the more helpful it will be for us."

Holding a pen in her hand she listens carefully and records our words.

At the end of Sevan's recollection of the events and my responses, the two attorneys exchange words in Russian. They continue speaking for quite a while until the attorney summarizes.

"Look...it's not an easy case and I'll explain why. Oz disappeared in America. If such a thing would have happened in any other European country we could have already started the process. But here we have a different story. We'll have to invest an awful lot of efforts just to locate him, and only then we'll be able to start thinking on how we can get him out of there..."

"I'm willing to pay whatever it takes... I understand that there are also charity organizations involved that cover some of the expenses..."

"Look, I'm an honest guy... as you can see," he rests his hand on his chest, "I won't ask for a penny more than the actual cost, but the truth is... I have no idea how much it'll be. That's the problem. Now look...if I wasn't a decent, honest guy I'd tell you to pay me this and that...and then I'd disappear with the money, but you can see what's going on here," his arms point in the direction of the large hall with the cubicles and the people who occupy them.

"So ... what are you suggesting?"

"Well...usually people who come here deposit checks...yes...they simply leave me checks. They trust me. They know that I'm here to save souls. There hasn't been one soul that I haven't saved! Not even one! There were even souls that I was sorry I'd saved," he smiles, "all sorts of types...you know what I mean? But here we're dealing with a dear soul, a tender soul... of a child, a pure soul that was kidnapped by his gentile father! Oy oy ...! We have to bring him back! We must!"

"So you want me to give you a check?"

"If you have one with you... it can certainly get things moving..."

I take out my check book.

"How much are we talking about?"

"Well... again...I'm trying to explain... at this point I have no idea how much it'll cost..."

"So... you want me to give you a blank check... and you'll fill out the amount? I need to know approximately...how much will it ...?"

"Look! You either trust me or you don't! And if you don't, then I can't help you! I feel pressured by you! You need to understand... there're so many people that need my help... I've got to know that you trust me one hundred percent!"

I tear out a check.

"To whom should I make out the check?"

"Nah...leave it open. It makes no difference anyway..."

I sign the check without specifying an amount or name and hand it to him.

"Good...very good Tara... I'm putting it right here...look...inside my drawer and I promise to start working on it immediately. You'll hear from me within a day or two..."

He walks us to the door. Once again his eyes are pinned on Sevan.

"Do you know how beautiful you are? You've probably heard it before...but you're so beautiful."

It's an awkward moment. Sevan doesn't respond and the two of us walk out.

The following morning I call my attorney.

"A blank check?! You gave him a blank check?! What's wrong with you Tara?! The man's a notorious crook! How could you do such a thing...?!"

His words rattle me. I immediately contact my bank, put a stop to the check and send a formal letter to the soul saving attorney.

But my own shocking actions haunt me for days to come.

***

I'm standing on the blackened veranda outside the living room. The air is cold. A sudden breeze makes me shiver. I wrap my arms around my shoulders raise my head up and stare at the crispy air above. The sky is pure, clear of any clouds and void of the tiniest of lights, allowing only for the magical moon light to tantalize the universe. I concentrate on its silvering smiley face and speak to it, begging to let Oz know that I love him and miss him. I ask that it guide him and whisper in his ear; I want Oz to know about the empty nights and the passage of life, about my broken motherhood and pains. I beg for its delicate light to stroke him, lighten up his passage, guard him, and deliver my words of love to him, let him know that I'll always be here for him, and ask that he please return home.

"I love you, Ozzie...please take care of yourself...take care of who you are..."

I wipe my tears.

"Just a while longer, Ozzie, just a few more hours before the silvery orb reaches you... sailing across the waters and continents that separate us...its magic light will smile and speak to you... whisper words in your ears and tell you of my longings...of my painful tears, and help you understand... help pass my love onto you as it lights your path back home..." magical glow above.

When I stare at the maddening beam of light and pin my eyes on it, I recognize two dimples with smiling eyes. And now I'm smiling and hugging Oz and my tears mingle with my inner happiness and I hold it tight to my heart ...and all I want is for its light to last...and never end ...and never disappear...please...please don't wane in the sky...

***

Time passes. Another day. And another night. And a week. And a month. And by now an entire year has gone by adding to a total of six years that Oz is missing from our lives. Again I fall into a pit of depression that pulls me into dark, hopeless places.

It was during one of those heavy painful evenings that I watched a television report about the worldwide activities of Chabad (Hassidic sect of Judaism).

The following day I schedule an appointment with the local Rabbi.

As I exit the apartment dressed in suitable attire, I meet Sevan outside the elevator door.

"What's this?" she checks me up and down.

"I'm going to meet a Chabad Rabbi."

Her face twists.

"Good luck, Ima."

I hug her tightly.

I must have passed the dilapidated building located in the midst of the city hundreds of times without noticing it. The entrance is lit by a flickering neon light. A young child wearing a skullcap and the traditional Jewish fringes hops on the stairway.

"Is this Chabad?" I stare at the peeling paint.

"Yes... up there." He points in the direction of the stairwell.

I climb up the filthy stairs avoiding touching the wall to my left. A choky heavy smell fills the staircase and its stained walls. When I reach the second floor I see a wide open door with a handful of praying men inside a room. I wait a while until someone notices and approaches me.

"I have an appointment with the Rabbi."

"Oh, yes... Mrs. Schmidt, right? We spoke on the phone...come... please come in, as you can see there's very little space here..."

The Rabbi points to a white plastic chair.

"So let's talk... why are you here?"

I tell him in a nutshell about Oz' kidnapping.

"Yes...yes...children are precious, there's nothing as precious as children...which is why I'll say what I have to say very carefully... so... it's like this, Mrs. Schmidt. I can certainly send a fax to the local Chabad members near Oz' residence in Texas...But! But! And this is a big but! I have no idea who will actually get his hands on the fax. Do you understand what I'm saying to you? We're a very big organization, very big...and sometimes...it's unavoidable, someone might see this fax and actually hold it in his hands and decide to do something about it... even though he's not the right person to do it. Do you understand what I'm trying to tell you? They're plenty of hooligans in Chabad... and I'm saying this cautiously...and only here... inside this room... and only between you and me, but...yes, I'm sorry to say that it can happen. And so we must weigh things very carefully and decide if that's really what we want to do... because if a hooligan decides to do something...from that moment on no one will have any control over it...and your son might even end up where you wouldn't want him to be."

"What do you mean?"

"Look Mrs. Schmidt... they're some very extreme organizations... very extreme... you've probably heard of them... the kind that can literally eliminate your son within a split of a second ... places like Mea Shearim (an extreme orthodox Jewish sect in Jerusalem) or in similar places in America...and there he'll be subjected to a deep brain washing process ...and he might never want to see you again. I know of such cases...that's why I'm warning you."

I return home with a heavy heart. A very heavy heart.

My children's photos stare at me from the wooden shelves spread throughout the living room. All around is a threatening silence, except for Darien's deep voice that surfaces from the shadowy past.

"Are you an idiot or just a retard?! What possessed you to spill the wooden blocks on the floor?!"

From where I'm standing at the bottom of the staircase, I can see Oz's small figure wobble over the top stair. Darien's fingers are closed around his neck as he shakes him like a bitch holding her puppies.

"I asked you a question!"

Oz' fingers are trying to loosen the painful hold. I climb slowly, careful not to make Darien drop Oz. When I'm two stairs away, I reach with my arm and at once grab Oz, pull him towards me then hug him with all my might and try to calm him. Darien's eyes look to smash my face.

The sights move to Sevan. I'm on the second floor overlooking the swimming pool in the back yard. Sevan is sitting quietly, her small body bent in half as she waits for Darien to let go of the hunting dog. He keeps throwing the Frisbee into the water and for the thousandth time commands the dog to retrieve it.

"Daddy, can I..."

"Stop nudging! You need to learn to be patient!"

An hour passes. It's already dark around the pool.

"Daddy, can I please go in now? Please daddy?" she dares a tiny voice.

"If you make a big fuss over it I won't let you swim with us!" he again strokes the dog's tired head.

When he finally avails himself, Sevan quickly jumps into the pool.

"Let's play a game," he catches her foot and tickles it and doesn't let go even when her giggles turn into hysterical cries.

"Stop...no ...dad... please...d...d...I can...can't br...I'm chok..."

The small body is forced flat on the water, her arms battle wildly as her head fights to stay above the water. She cries and gags, chokes, swallows water then gags again.

I run outside, pull her out of the pool and hold her tight.

"Why are you meddling?!" Darien roars.

"She asked you to stop!"

There are so many wretched remembrances, a cemetery full of tomb stones that hold witness to the humiliations Darien enjoyed trampling and his disrespect for human dignity. My head spins with heavy weighted thoughts that refuse to leave. I confront them and try to rid their presence but they refuse to let go and cling strongly to me.

***

Time passes, creeping in slow motion. Sevan tries to contact Darien but he stands his ground.

"There's nothing to talk about right now," he sends her a postcard from somewhere, "Maybe in the future..."

And the more she seeks his presence, the more he eludes her, sending her a casual postcard from time to time.

"Look at the beautiful view...I wish you could see it in reality. Love you, dad."

Several international television channels, among them CNN, are showing gruesome pictures and reporting about the horrifying terror attach that took place in our small town resulting in several casualties.

"Even now dad doesn't care about me! Why doesn't he call? Maybe I've been hurt? He wouldn't even know about it..." Sevan bursts out crying.

"Would you like to try and call him now, Sevannie? It's been six years since you last spoke..."

Sevan collects herself but asks that I stay nearby. She then calls him. To her surprise Darien picks up the phone.

His words come out casually, as though nothing transpired since he last hung up on her.

"I miss you daddy...I want to see you."

From the look on her face I understand that Darien's response is painful.

"Did you hear about the terror attack that happened here yesterday?"

"Yes, I saw it on TV."

"And you didn't care to know if I'm ok?"

I can hear Darien's sarcastic chuckle.

"I'm sure that if anything would have happened to you, someone would have already notified me."

Following a short silence Sevan asks.

"When can I see you, daddy?"

"It's inconvenient right now...I'll call you when I can talk."

Several months later Darien calls and updates Sevan.

"I've just sent you the flight tickets with express mail."

He gives her the details.

Sevan is ecstatic and anxiously counts the days.

As soon as she lands at the airport Darien hugs her.

"I'm glad to see you, Sevan...but what a shame... you just missed Oz by a day. He flew to Germany only yesterday to spend some time with my parents."

The following year Sevan again flies to visit him but asks ahead of time to allow her to meet with Oz.

"We'll see," Darien responds.

266

Sevan is exhausted by the time her long flight with its two connecting stops finally reaches its destination.

"I'm glad to see you," Darien tells her in the terminal, "let's grab something to eat before we get home."

Once they're seated he explains.

"You can meet with Oz but only if you follow the rules: you DON'T converse with him in Hebrew! You DON'T deliver any messages or letters to him from Israel! You DON'T show him any photos! You're only allowed to converse with him in my presence and strictly in English! If you try anything funny, you'll find yourself on the first flight back home! Got it?!"

***

Ten years have now passed since Oz' abduction.

I hear of another organization that helps locate and rescue Israelis in farfetched places around the globe. It seems as though the number of rescue teams are increasing by the day, with each boasting unique abilities.

The small structure located at the edge of the city, resembles a plain one story house with several rooms. I'm asked to join the group gathered in its central room.

"We have Tara Schmidt sitting with us today. Her son was kidnapped by his father. Tara, I'd like to introduce you to ..." the six staff members are seated in a circle, each one an expert in his field.

"Eyal is a former general with the Security Services. He's been with us for years. He helps where he thinks he can be of use. And this is Ze'evik, a field guy that I've known for years..."

By the time introductions are over I feel that maybe this time a solution might be found thanks to the professionals who work together as a team. Once again I repeat the story only this time I'm asked to do so in greater detail.

When I'm done the room is silent.

"I'm willing to back up Tara and try to help her!" Eyal turns to me, "your story really touched me… it's really cruel…and sad…terribly cruel…"

I cry. I find myself sitting among strangers wiping tears of gratitude for their empathy over my loss. Eyal takes the lead and raises several operational options and at once I understand that his services, albeit wrapped with good intentions and empathy, cost money. And quite a bit of it.

We decide to meet again at his office and go thoroughly over the details. Several meetings later, Eyal suggests that we both fly to the States and meet directly with Oz.

Two months later we're on our way to Dallas.

The city has changed considerably since I've last seen it. The main arteries of transportation crisscrossing the city have changed and widened with vast new highways added. I find it difficult to identify the area. After registering at the hotel we go about scouting the nearby locations as well as Darien's house, situated about fifteen minutes away from Oz'. Eyal decides to check out the route ahead of time and proceed the following day.

It's Saturday. Seven a.m.

The two of us are seated inside the parked car, fifty meters or so from Oz' place; it's a tiny dreary structure resembling a shipping container large enough to hold two cars. A dangling spiral staircase is connected to one of its sides overlooking a sandy trail in the midst of a neglected back yard. The entire area looks dilapidated. Tiny reckless looking structures are scattered on both sides of the street. Intimidating faces sounding raucous music and voices sit at this early hour of the morning inside gaping porches drinking and smoking. Someone notices us and points a finger towards our car. The entire gang bursts out laughing.

"Let's get the hell out of here before someone comes," Eyal starts the car, "all we need is for the police to show up ..."

The faces stare at us. Eyal drives away, makes a large circle then reaches the street from its other end and parks the car behind a tall tree that hides us.

"I have binoculars with me ...we'll be able to see Oz from here."

We sit and wait. At ten thirty we spot Oz as he carefully climbs down the spiraling stairs and advances on the dirt path towards the car. I flatten the hat on my head. Oz gets into the car and starts driving. We follow his footsteps. He drives very slowly with his head wandering sideways, every so often. I feel nauseous. After a fifteen minute's drive he reaches a large parking area next to a shopping mall. We park the car not too far from his.

"Stay here and don't move. I'll call you."

Eyal follows Oz. I remain standing near the car.

The air is chilly with tiny prickly rain drops that are relentless. A long half hour passes by, then another and by now I realize that the parking lot is full.

Eyal calls.

"Tara! Keep your eyes on Oz! He's moving towards his car! Make sure you locate his car...as soon as I get there we'll follow him."

I look around but I can't spot Oz' car. All the parking spaces are filled and I've totally lost its whereabouts.

Eyal comes running.

"Where's his car? Did you locate it?"

"I'm sorry...I..."

Eyal is tall. He stretches his head in the direction where he last saw Oz and points to him.

"There! We mustn't lose him now!"

Again we're in the car, keeping our distance from Oz' slow moving vehicle.

"I followed him inside the shopping mall...but he didn't even notice me. He wanted to repair something but he didn't quite know where to go to ...I stood next to him... elbow to elbow...he asked all kinds of questions but no one seemed able to help him. Then he went downstairs... near the fast foods and restaurants and asked one of the cleaners if he could help him. He seemed so...alone...so lonely...he was looking for something that he couldn't even define... like someone who's lost..."

We reach the next set of lights and Eyal overtakes Oz' car.

"Okay... it's clear now that he's heading back home... I'd like to get there before he does. Is everything ready?"

"Yes." I have both arms around a box I've prepared. Among other things, I've packed the special D.A.R.E. medal and certificate awarded him during his last year in middle school with some small souvenirs from home I thought he'd like to have.

"I'm just reminding you ...now's the time to be strong...this is your chance, Tara!"

Again we sit and wait for Oz outside his yard.

Moments later Oz drives very slowly into the yard.

"Go Tara! Go... and take the box with you!" Eyal prods me lightly. My legs are stiff.

"Tara! This is your chance! Go! Get out of the car!"

I get out wearing a wide brimmed hat. My hands are hugging the box. Oz' car finally comes to a stop at the end of the pathway. I advance towards him. The car door opens and Oz climbs slowly out of it. By the time he locks his car door I'm standing next to him.

"Ozzie."

He raises his head, recognizes me and starts running in circles around the car.

"It's me...Ima...I only want to give you the box...I have a present for you..."

Oz is terrified. He runs back and forth and all around, clearly agitated and confused just looking for a way out.

"I only came to give you this," I remain planted in place as I stretch my arm holding the box in his direction.

Oz continues to run. He crosses the street to its other side and by now he's facing a highway. I'm scared that he might continue running if he feels threatened. I move slowly in his direction. He tries dialing but the situation overwhelms him and he continues to stare at the phone, refusing to look at me.

"Ozzie... I miss you...I love you...I didn't come to harm you..."

He remains frozen in place.

I reach out slowly with my hand and touch his bare arm. His terrified eyes wander in front of him and he looks as though he's about to burst out crying. I place the box on the sidewalk, walk back to the car, and I can't stop crying.

***

Throughout the first years following Oz' abduction, Naomi refused to allow mother any communications with Oz simply because she kept in touch with me. But after I stopped communicating with mother, Naomi removed her restrictions and now, the mean hearted person that mother is, speaks daily with Oz but acts as a colander with its holes clogged up at one end. She sucks up tidbits about me and passes them onto Naomi but blocks me on the other side, refusing even a crumb of information about Oz to pass back to me.

Shortly before cutting my ties with mother, I paid her a visit.

"Did you speak with Oz?" I again ask.

"I asked him to talk to you but he said that you lied to him about the guardianship..."

"We've been over this a thousand times, mother! And you know the truth, so why don't you..."

"So what IS the truth?! Eh?! Let's hear it?!"

"You already know that the court granted me the guardianship so that I could sign his school..."

"So why don't you annul it?"

"Because it's an expensive legal procedure. Besides, since it was granted solely for the purpose of signing his school documents, now that he's no longer..."

"So annul it! And I'll make sure to let Oz know."

"Do you really believe that if I annul it, Oz will agree to renew his relationship with me?!"

"We'll never know until you actually do it! Will we?!"

I force myself not to respond to her but discuss it later with my attorney.

"I don't believe a word your mother says. It sounds to me like just another excuse..."

But I insist and pay my attorney a handsome fee in addition to the court fees. In return he forwards my request for the annulment of the guardianship to the court and petitions for its approval.

Several months later, the long awaited document is received in the post.

My hands are holding a copy of the original request sent to the court by my attorney. On that same copy is a two-word printed response from the court with a freshly stamped date above it.

"REQUEST GRANTED."

I drive straight to mother's house.

"Here! The guardianship is annulled!"

She blinks several times.

"Where does it say so?"

"Here's the court's response with a dated stamp..."

"But you need a proper letter from the court, not just a dated stamp with two words on it!"

"But that's the way it's done over here. The court doesn't issue a separate letter. It simply prints its response on the original request and then adds a stamped date with the court's stamp next to it... "

"It doesn't look authentic to me...but I'll pass it to Naomi and let her decide."

Two weeks later I again face mother.

"Naomi received the document and she claims it's fake. She had it checked by a friend of hers who told her that the guardianship hasn't really been annulled!"

"What are you talking about?!"

"But anyway...it's not gonna' help you because Oz doesn't' want to speak to you."

"So why did you tell me to annul it?!"

"Because Naomi thought that it might help. But you didn't do what you were supposed to do! That's your problem!"

My frustration threatens to explode.

"Why are you so mean to me?!"

Her hand releases the document. It falls on the floor.

"Now you're starting to aggravate me! I'm already old and I can't take this kind of pressure."

She shuts her mean eyes.

"But you're not too old to fly to Naomi twice a year and go on trips with her and Garry, right? If you really want to see Oz...if he's really that important to you..."

Her eyes are nailed on me. She stifles her voice and refuses to answer. When emotions spark up it's difficult to apply logic especially when I'm standing in front of the woman who bore me, the one person meant to back me up and support my wish to have contact with my own son.

Mother's soul is mean and ugly and when she senses a threat, her appearance changes. She spends her days on the phone, speaking with Naomi, talking to the poor girl who suffers from all the ailments in the world except for the mental illness that mustn't be mentioned. Poor Naomi is miserable because she doesn't have kids of her own so she's allowed to snatch Tara's child. Poor Naomi is in charge of managing the relationship between the mean woman and my son and dictating how to behave towards him. But I'm not allowed to complain. Not allowed to shout. Or to protest. I'm no allowed to remark. And especially not to ask unnecessary questions, a replicate of our childhood days.

"Mother, please...please help me ..."

"So... I'd like to understand ...do you prefer that Naomi cuts all ties with Oz?"

"But I'M HIS MOTHER! I'm the one that's supposed to be in touch with him! How is Naomi even connected to this?!"

"Well...it's up to you. You either agree that Naomi stays in touch with him... or no one else will! That's all there is to it!"

The fury stored inside my stomach wants to jump out and slap her face.

I can't bring myself NOT to hate her. I despise the mean quibbles that come out of her mouth wrapped up with Naomi's sickening demands.

A few months ago she left me a message on the recorder.

"I just want to let you know that Oz never wants to see or hear from you again...but I want to explain why. He claims that you were mean to him, that you requested the guardianship because you thought he's retarded. So don't even try calling him because he won't answer you. It's an open-and-shut subject!"

I can't understand how she calls herself a mother.

"That carcass only spawned him!" Naomi declares and the colander is quick to update me.

"Naomi said that Oz claims that you're only his biological mother!"

Only.

Only his mother.

Only the mother who spawned him.

***

Time holds its own rhythm as it hurries and trots and skips at top speed over the passage of years.

I find out that Oz is working is a large furniture store and decide to try and see him again.

I fly over to Texas where I meet with a friend from the past.

We're in the parking lot, stepping out of the car and walking in the direction of the store.

"Now remember what I told you...take a deep breath...I'll ask about him and see if he's actually working here. Anyway he's not gonna' recognize me...and once we see him we can decide what to do."

She hugs me and we enter the store.

A large, circular shaped customer service center is located at the entrance of the store. We're both rooted in our places looking around and taking in the tumult and the shopping crowds.

A woman's voice sounds over the loud speaker.

"Order for Mr. Roberts...your order is ready. Please advance to the customer service center."

A heavyset man walks over.

"Hi, I'm Roberts...my order..."

"Yes, here's your order," the representative hands him a document and calls out again, "Mr. Roberts' order...please come to the customer service. The order..."

My eyes register two teenagers exiting the storeroom located to the right of the customer service center. I immediately recognize Oz. He can hardly balance the heaviness on his slim shoulders. His face is strained. He bites his lower lip as the heavy furniture wobbles on both their shoulders.

"Move it guys... move it," the woman calls out, "the customer is waiting for his order."

I'm stunned. My hands close over my mouth. I scream silently hardly able to keep in the pain. My friend whispers in my ear.

"That's him! Right? It's Oz! I can't believe it's him!"

"Hey Oz! is that you?!" my friend calls out without giving it a second thought.

Oz turns his eyes and recognizes me. The furniture crashes to the floor and Oz starts running in circles around the service center.

"Oz!" I call him but my voice is broken, "Oz..."

A security guard appears from nowhere and blocks me.

"Lady! Don't move lady! I'm calling the police..."

"It's my son!" I point to Oz, "it's my son..."

My friend grabs hold of my arm.

"Let's all calm down," she faces the crowd that circles us, "there's no need to call the police or anyone else...let's all simply calm down... we're leaving the store right now..."

Her hand grips my arm firmly as she pulls me forcefully out of the store.

I turn around and see Oz standing behind the customer stand. His body is paralyzed with a terrified look on his pale face.

***

BREAKING THE SILENCE

The apartment. Night time.

Tall palm trees front the building, stretching their prominent fronds beyond the second floor balcony peeking at the blooming flowers. Below, in-between tall structures with heads grazing the sky, is a snaking anaconda, a winding path that twists across the length and width of the spacious complex. The city lights fashion a pink quilt cradling the wide sky and softening its threatening blackness. A thunderous silence engulfs the apartment. A nightly silence.

And at once piercing screams.

Stray cats drunk with lust wriggle around the thick vegetation surrounding the footpath, forcing the darkness to tremble as they sweep the universe into passionate nightly witchcrafts.

Then once again all's quiet.

Throughout those silent hours I'm in the living room staring at the reddish sky as it flickers through the glassed balcony door. The air is dense. I take a deep breath and follow the shadows of the oriental carpets spread on floors and walls and tune to the silent storm. Only few reminders are now left following Oz' abduction: some photos and sounds accompanied by oppressive thoughts that gnaw at me. Sevan's recently emptied room resembles a hollowed gaping mouth.

I wish to reach out and stroke my little girl's golden hair and hold her tightly to my heart, but the emptiness surrounding me is heavy and bitter and saturated with painful memories. The silence is harsh.

After rehashing past events and remembrances over long years, and feeling haunted by endless misgivings and self doubts, I reach the understanding that there's no way out but the truth. Its factual veracity cries out. I breathe in the air left behind by both my children and choose to entrust the truth into their hands.

I have nothing left but the truth despite its bitter harshness.

And so from the distance of time I now react, reach my hands to the keyboard and continue to reminisce.

***

By early morning, as in past mornings, I'm in the office. Long years have gone by since I first sat on the black chair fronting the faceless wall with the small flowerpot at its feet. The scrawny stalk with its meager foliage has stood the test of time thanks to my kind words and caring strokes.

The office.

My place of employment that enables me to continue life despite the circumstances.

Oz' image flashes in front of my eyes. I step into the corridor and stand by the open window.

What'll happen after Darien and I are gone?

Who'll even remember Oz? Who'll care or inquire about him? Who'll take care of him?! Who?!

I wipe my eyes, take a deep breath and return to the office and its black chair.

Time gallops when the office is busy: the phones ring, a fax machine spits out documents faster than fast and the attorneys are in a hurry to rewrite words and cushion them with disclaimers and stipulations.

And at five I tick off another day that brings me closer to my goal then rush off to the other place where I sharpen words.

At times my thoughts linger on the soul, on that obscure miniscule particle unable to defend itself for lack of proof of its own corporeality. Only the body holds the right to avenge its physical insults. And it's that precise distinction, as stated in the Latin law and its clause for proof, which triggers my anger.

"Corpus delicti" –there's no murder without a body, says the law.
But what about the soul?!

I stare at the nothingness within the room and wonder what's with those suffering wretched souls? What happens to them?! And at once I'm reminded of the helplessness of the court in the state in which Darien committed his crime.

Three judges mulled over the case relying on the archaic laws of the state which were never clearly defined. The judges detailed the severity of the crime and the hefty price that Oz will be forced to bear for the rest of his life, as a result.

According to those backward laws, a kidnapping is defined as such, only if a person enters someone else's domicile and drags them out forcefully and against their will. But if a person is threatened or held forcefully under duress by another and is prevented, as a result, from acting on his own free will, that doesn't constitute a kidnapping offense.

It might seem strange to think of success in terms of smell, but the first time I smelled Darien I realized his scent differed from others. There's something indefinable in the smell of success or any outstanding accomplishment, but the sweet fragrance of financial success is most perplexing. Perhaps it has to do with the perfumed odors announcing financial prosperity, a magnetizing fragrance that strongly contrasts the countless smelly bank notes touched along the way by many strange hands; and maybe the fragrance of financial success is a combination of the pungent stench of its prior disappointments when mixed with the fragrance of its triumphant outcome.

And all at once and without reason, the office is flooded with the smell of my planned scheme, much like a rare book buried deep in an abandoned archive that's about to unveil itself.

The attorney's door is wide open and I'm able to hear the conversation. A widower and former high ranking army officer, who has several properties listed in his will in both his children's names, has come to consult with the attorney about one of his sons who's suspected of the kidnapping and possible murder of his two year old child.

The man is devastated. I follow his voice through the open door and listen to his painful words that reflect his stance on the proportionality of justice.

"You need to understand," his eyes water, "I'm only talking about the acts, the actual acts... and I'm not debating now whether or not they were actually committed... and hopefully they were not, but..."

The short silence allows me to enter the room and place a glass of cold water in front of him.

"Thank you," the man says and continues, "If they'll prove that he actually committed this crime, I'll never be able to forgive him! Never!"

He takes a gulp and goes on.

"I've witnessed some horrific things in my life time, believe me... in all the wars and the actions and the places I've been to... and it's not as though I've never heard of such acts, but I'm unwilling to accept the fact that one of my sons...my own flesh and blood committed such a crime. I'll never be able to forgive him! Never! But now I'm only saying this quietly ...as you can see...because what I'd really like to do to such a bastard is hang him by his balls! Upside down! Like this ...until his last breath is out! D'you understand

what I mean?!" his voice is now louder, "I'd grab him like this...
like this...with my own bare hands." He holds up two massively
clenched fists, "like this! I'd strangle him like this... but slowly, not
at once! I'd want him to suffer ...d'you get what I mean? I'd have to
make sure he suffered!"

The attorney nods his head and I shut my eyes and join the man's
bitter anger and his tears about the proportionality of justice.

I feel a sudden flush of heat. I take off my sweater and my thoughts
drift to Darien. My hands are busy with the documents on my desk
but my mind is elsewhere, occupied with matters far removed from
my work place.

The fax rings, interrupting my thoughts and forcing me, once
again, to reality and to the presence of the office and the well orga-
nized world that helps me block the turmoil from within.

***

It's now morning with twenty-five degrees outside but I'm cold. I
put on a sweater and hurry to the office for another day of work distancing myself from the memories that lurk inside the apartment,
much like Darien's frequent escapes to the office to avoid me and
the children.

"I'll be home in a little while...I've got an urgent meeting... need
to finish the deal..." always in the evening with a promise to be back
on time to see the kids before they're in bed. But rarely did he keep
his promises. The children learned quite early on that they shouldn't
rely on him, which is why I'm amazed at the ease with which he
managed to convince Oz with his lies, especially those pertaining to
the guardianship.

"Let me explain to you, Oz! I want you to understand why your
mother asked the court to grant her this document...why she
requested this guardianship. She simply wants to use it against

you...she wants to control your life and harm you ...she wants to kidnap you and throw you in jail! Got it?!"

Time becomes an elusive dimension with its own unique twists. On ordinary days when I'd like it to hurry, it crawls and I find myself checking its beats every few minutes probing it to move faster, but it dawdles as only clocked droplets know how to dawdle.

On my way home I try to sort out my thoughts because I need to understand how to continue documenting the events.

My remembrances weigh heavily on my heart and sadden me. I wonder when will Sevan finally wake up and realize the roll my mother is playing within the complicated tangle she'd helped create.

I think about the complexity of our family's entanglement, and my father's image floats in front of me. Twenty three years have passed since his death, years filled with villainous acts enabled simply because he wasn't alive to stop them.

I study my father's hands, the hands of a farmer, very large and heavy with coarse skin scorched by sun; hands of tremendous strength able to carry heavy weights, yet their touch is as soft as a baby's new skin. Father's hands mirror the extraordinary blend of his soul: a fusion of polarized elements holding strength and delicacy all in the same breath.

With his enormous hands he washed dishes, loaded heavy cement sacks, stroked Oz' hair, hugged both kids and brought calmness into their lives. His hands dug watering holes, helped save an injured bird and piled on his broad shoulders the lives of many strangers and family members who sought his help. His abilities reflected extraordinary mental strength combined with great sensitivity; a quiet person allowing for a relaxed conversation with any adult or small child. His kindness of heart reflected the way he saw the world, gazing at it through the pure innocence of a child's eye and the excitement of the newness of life, a rare combination of a very wise and thoughtful man who was also very funny.

Darien too loved him very much and appreciated his sharp mind, his wonderful sense of humor and unrelenting optimism, a man whose very existence opposed that of his own father, Helmut. And all at once I miss my dad, the strong pillar of resilience I could always lean on. I try not to mix the two inside my head but it's like ground waters that ultimately always mix.

I'm inside a shopping mall staring at a large display window heaped with newly titled books. Several people pass me by as they come and go much like the shadows reflected on the other side of the window.

I enter the crowded store hoping to find some kind of guidance or hint which might spark up my imagination, be it in the form of a new title or illustration. Given my preoccupation with the horrid story, I sense that life has alienated itself from me; as though its pulsating heart is squeezed tightly into a corner trying to avoid touching me so as not to be infected by my ailing preoccupation. When I walk down the street I imagine that the passersby are able to sense the illness rooted inside of me. Their faces turn serious as they stare then drift sideways. I can understand their wanting to shy away and avoid close proximity with someone who's already agreed to exchange his life with death and only longs to reach the end and rid himself of aches and pains.

On rare occasions, and only when I'm snailed deep within myself and my soul, only then do I dare hope for a new love. I long to know its sweeter sides, get a taste of true friendship, passion, a kind smile, feel softness and experience the newness of a love void of secrets and distortions. I yearn for a second chance and long to reveal my love to another man and enjoy his love of me, a man who will contain my soul and allow me to share his. But there's hopelessness at the end of any such wish. My soul is hollowed from too many painful longings, and there isn't a man who would wish for himself the pains of a hollow-hearted woman who's lost her son.

The days crawl in a systemic rhythm ticking away minutes and hours to perfection. I spend my mornings at the office and by the end of eight hours return to the apartment, make some phone calls, last minute chores and listen to the newscast sum up the day.

Time drags itself and there's no end to the story. I'm dispirited from the overwhelming thoughts and dammed remembrances all of which are colored in black. And by late evening, once again, I find myself in the living room rummaging through the past and staring at faded lives while trying to re-sprout exhausted memories that refuse to be forgotten.

***

A good friend of mine calls to ask how I'm doing. Twelve years ago her son was killed in a car accident leaving her and her husband with three adult children. Besides asking 'how are you?' and 'what are you up to?' she wants to know how I'm coping with the emptiness in my heart and if I've found new interests to latch onto that can help me in daily life. Over one of our late night conversations, shortly after Oz' abduction, she said to me.

"Don't misunderstand me, Tara. After Meir left us, I went absolutely nuts and so did Danny ... and even now he speaks to Meir as if he can actually hear him. But at least we reached a closure... there was no other choice... we had to come to terms with his death and accept the fact that Meir is no longer with us ... that he'll never return. But in your case...to go through an emotional seesaw ... while knowing your son is alive but out of reach...I can't even imagine such a situation. I don't know what I would have done. We at least have Meir's special place where we visit him three, four times a week and we have the park in his memory and the garden around his grave ...it's a place where we can fall apart, you know...a sort of... well, a parking place where we can park our grief for an hour or two. And when we leave the cemetery we know that he's safe until the next time ...but we don't stay there all the time because we want the other children and grandchildren to be close to us...and that pain...

you know...that pain kills the soul. But in your case...you don't have the luxury of parking your pain on the side...not even for a second, because if you do that it's as though you've given up on Oz and on the hope of ever seeing him again...and I know you'll never give up on him...I don't think I could have survived a kidnapping of one of my children..."

***

I wonder about the powerlessness to control our lives and the nullity of our actions in the face of unexpected circumstances, eventualities beyond our control that simply occur trailed by unforeseen consequences that divert us from our path. We can never predict for certainty the outcome of an un-birthed moment prior to its actual birthing, or guess at the time of its occurrence that a specific event will, in retrospect, be viewed as a turning point in our lives. Nor can we foresee in advance that the lullaby we sing to our baby or our breast feeding him will prove to be the last time we ever get to do it, much like the hug I gave Oz at the airport that proved to be the last hug I ever gave him. Only hind sight can determine the significance of a past event and magnify its long term consequences, similar to clues that surfaced in the past and are meant to clarify the present; or same as pointing at past hints that were supposedly meant to predict the imminent hour of a person who has recently passed.

My thoughts swerve to the last time Darien hugged me and the last touches that passed between us; there were so many painful moments that could have swerved our thoughts or changed our decisions, had we only been aware that it was their final hour and opportune moment, a crucial time that would never again cross our paths.

Wonderments beyond my control spring out of nowhere to create delusionary hypotheses. Maybe I could have found refuge elsewhere and chosen differently other than divorcing Darien. Maybe.

Luck, Mazal, they all say, everyone needs luck on their side. I try to decipher the meaning behind that elusive word assigned, as per the calculation in gematria (the method of assigning numeric values to Hebrew letters), the number seventy-seven.

Perhaps thanks to those tiny luck trinkets that came my way many years ago, perhaps thanks to them I'll succeed, this once, in changing the course of my luck?

Perhaps.

***

In the evening I meet with the girls. The five of us met in high school when our daily lives were colored by the honesty and innocence of teenage hood.

An enormous ficus tree with branched roots marking its surroundings stands tall in the entrance to the coffee shop. I look around for a place to sit ignoring the two women closest to me. They giggle out loud then whisper like the girls we once were and at once one of them nods her head and we recognize each other.

The other two join us as we sit crouched together immersed in sights and sounds that resurface from the distance of many years and we're now teenagers again laughing and chatting as though we've never parted.

But it's only as though.

Minutes pass then an hour and two and by then time runs its course and the giggles make room for sorrows and tears and lives tinted with disappointments.

And again I look around me with sheer amazement, unable to comprehend how my teenage friends, those same girls-women-mothers-grandmothers are able to continue smiling and skipping over the potholes of their lives, wondering how they were able to survive successfully the heavy loads of their daily existence.

They then turn to me.

"And what's with you, Tara? Do you have any kids? And where did you live? Oh! So how are you managing without them ...? Oh...that's terrible...absolutely awful... and what will you do now? But why...? And why not...? And when...? And how exactly did it happen...?"

I burst out crying knowing that it's too late.

They all want to comfort me trying to find the right words for my impossible situation.

I leave the reunion with a deep sense of failure.

My return home is fraught with tears, salty sprinkles that burn my eyes and disrupt my vision. The rain is relentless with glittering lightning. I'm blinded by the car lights that force me to hurry up, urging me to continue uphill on the path of life, to persevere, to prolong the pain of loss, shake off the hardships, keep going, hurry up, disregard the thunderous roars and blue lights as they crack open the sky and blind me.

And at once I feel beaten and exhausted.

A split second before it all falls apart I stop the car on the side of the road and think of Sevan.

When I hug her close to my heart, shut my eyes and smell her familiar sweetness, my head swoons with other thoughts all of which are connected to my mother, jumbled notions that form a malleable mosaic with changing colors and shapes.

My mother's voice never lets go; deep sounding and cracked from long years of meanness and smoke, it continues to spit out the usual abominations.

"Poor Naomi...she doesn't have kids of her own...such a shame... she has so much within her to give..."

"Do you even understand what you're saying?!"

"Of course I do! But I also understand your frustration. It's really difficult..."

"Did you say frustration?!" my throat threatens to explode, "MY SON WAS KIDNAPPED! IT'S MY SON! MY SON! NOT NAOMI'S!"

"So how do you think I feel? Just imagine...he's MY GRANDSON!"

"But he's first of all MY SON!"

She's relentless.

"Okay.... but there's nothing we can do about it... you need to move on..."

"What do you mean move on?! Where to?! Where am I supposed to move onto when I know that Naomi doesn't allow me any contact with my own son and poisons his mind and soul?!"

"But she has a lot within her to give ..."

"Madness! That's what she's got within her! Madness and meanness just like yours!"

"Shame on you! Shame on you... I was so worried about Oz and the problems you had with him... do you even realize how worried I was about him? You can't say that I didn't love him."

"Yes! But you loved him from afar! And you're even satisfied calling him once every two weeks...or once a month...and with that you've done your duty!"

"Not true! I speak with him a lot... in fact we speak daily. He calls me nearly every day..."

"Oh! So how come you never told me about it until now?!"

"Because it's useless...because he's not willing to speak to you."

"Of course not! Because Naomi doesn't allow him..."

"It's useless to go on with this...all you do is blame Naomi and she only wants what's best for him..."

"What's BEST for him?! By inciting him against me?!"

"It's not nice of you to say such things about her..."

I'm sitting in front of her crying my heart out over the disappearance of my son from my life and the awful things he's experiencing.

"It's really very sad...very sad..."

"So why won't you help me?!"

"What do you want me to do?!"

"Do you even love Oz?! Do you care about him?!"

"Of course I care about him, but I'm not willing to give up Naomi for him."

"How much is his life worth to you?!" I again ask her.

"Ah! Don't even compare him to Naomi!"

"How can you be so ...so heartless?!"

"It's what Naomi wants! And I'm not willing to fight with her because of him!"

And I can't stop crying.

***

Today is Valentine's Day. A day dedicated to the noblest of emotions. Love.

An inner feeling overwhelms me and calls for my remembrances.

My first love to a man ended in a disappointment leaving an ugly scab deep inside my heart which I carried with me over long years. But unlike my bitter experience of that painful love, I was lucky to know another kind of love, a pure love, totally unblemished and crystal clear, an unconditional love of both my children.

A mother's love.

I loved their every tinge of excitement, their feather soft skins, their smells, their throaty gurgles and excitement at the first moment of unveiling the world; I loved their fascination of newness, the trust built between us, loved their varied likes and dislikes, their pauses and questions, the naiveté and wonderments they shared with me, their excitement over nature and daily events; I loved their unique needs, the dialogues we had, the discourses we exchanged, loved the new worlds we created together woven with the marvels of childhood freshness.

But most of all, I loved loving them and enjoyed their love of me.

"Ima," Oz calls me from the distance of the long years that now separate us.

I recognize the tone of his voice and feel warmth in my heart as I hug him through the tearful eyes of my remembrances. But my thoughts have a mind of their own as they skip to my mother, to the woman who doesn't want me.

"Ima," I call her but she doesn't respond.

She only stares at me with those mean eyes of hers that refuse to wink, "please, Ima...please help me...I need your help..." I beg of her.

I can sense her frail spirit from behind the murkiness of the old eyes. Her thinning lips move noiselessly, amplifying the silent words of the woman who always instilled a sense of fear and mightiness in me, the one who presumed to oversee our family.

Once again I listen to sounds. And recall names. And remember events. Syllables in varying shapes create words that are shortened and thickened to form sentences. The words retain their freshness of force and precision due to my unwavering determination to document the events, though it doesn't make the telling of the story any easier.

Darien and I are in bed. Two separate worlds.

"Why don't you want me to touch you?" his arm under my neck.

"It hurts when you scream...it's frightening..." I cry.

"But you know I don't mean it..."

"You shout...and curse...you're so angry..."

"I don't do it on purpose... it's only that... you're so...so stubborn..."

And from there, without any order or reason, I find myself staring at my wardrobe bursting with fur coats, scarves, hand bags, jewelries, frightfully expensive gifts with which Darien is hoping to win my heart and love; in exchange, he hopes to erase from within me that tiny particle which he views as the obstructive force that stands in the way of our togetherness.

***

The change occurred on my mother's eighty-seventh birthday when

290

I came over to congratulate her but as always, within minutes, our dialogues turned sour.

"You don't act like a mother. How can you simply ignore the situation and not want to help me with Oz?" I burst out crying.

My loud cries and back and forth uproars reached Bilha and Chris' ears. With only three meters separating both houses, they came into mother's house to check what's going on. It was the first time they'd heard about Oz' kidnapping. Throughout the long years of Oz' disappearance, my mother fed them lies, blaming me for committing unjust evils, for being stingy and mean and any other blame dictated to her by Naomi. But she never told them the truth that Oz was abducted by his father and forced to remain with him in the States.

After hearing details of Oz' disappearance, the situation changed rapidly; within days the three of us decided to renew our relationship and together we approached mother and asked her to help us communicate directly with Oz.

Mother refused.

"Oz doesn't want to have anything to do with Tara."

"Rachel! What are you talking about?!" Chris was enraged, "You know his situation! You also know how he got there. He was FORCED to stay there! And you also know that Naomi's been poisoning him! I was in a similar situation! You know what I went through..."

"There's nothing we can do about it! He simply refuses to have anything to do with Tara!"

Chris, who was born in Italy, was very perturbed by Oz' abduction and kept asking for additional details. When his parents divorced, Chris' father decided to split the family apart by severing all ties between both his sons who remained with him, and their sister who remained with her mother. Over the course of eight years he punished his sons, fed them lies and poisoned their minds and souls. By twisting their childhood memories he planted in their hearts and minds a deep hatred for their mother and sister. By the time he understood the terrible mistake he'd made and allowed for their reunion, it was too late. The rift he'd created was so deep it lasted on for several more years. Chris eventually immigrated to Israel all by himself. While working as a physiotherapist in a hospital, he'd met Bilha who was recovering from her accident and a year later they were married.

Over the years Bilha continued struggling with the long term affects of the accident and was only dimly aware of the overall dynamics at home; Chris didn't have the time or strength to face the daily problems and leaned on my parents for support relying on their help with Bilha and the children. The proximity of my parents' house suited everyone enabling Naomi and mother to meddle in Bilha's affairs and basically manage her household.

Mother who enjoyed stirring up family turmoil, constantly complained about me and the kids.

"Tara is driving me nuts," she'd say, "absolutely nuts. She got it into her head that I helped kidnap Oz and now she wants me to help her reconnect with him. I don't know what she wants from me?! I wish she'd leave me alone..."

But when Chris and Bilha caught her lying and demanded explanations, mother began to complain that it's not fair, that they can't force her to say anything, that the situation can't be changed, that Naomi is miserable, that she doesn't have any children, that she has a huge heart and that she only loves them and their children. She told them they should be grateful, remember all the presents Naomi gave them and be supportive of those who provided for them over the years and helped build their spacious house; she said they should show gratitude for the things they've received from my parents and simply shut up! Stop annoying her with bothersome questions! Things happen in life! And they need to respect Oz' wish not to want to see Tara!

"She's not at all what she seems ...you simply don't know her.

She's crazy...she needs to be institutionalized...she's mean...and she's been mean to Oz...just wait until she starts bothering you... then you'll know...and understand...and then you'll stop collaborating with her..."

Within a few months, even Chris and Bilha's teenaged children understood the situation. They severed their ties with Naomi and shied away from their quarrelsome grandmother, a fact that irritated and entangled her further with her own lies.

Chris calls me up one evening and tells me about a conversation he'd had with mother. Mother had always assumed that Chris would be the one to take care of her when she'd need assistance, just as he'd done with dad until his dying day. She asked Chris to come over and discuss it. Chris clarified that he had no intention of assisting her, unless she helps me reconnect with Oz.

"But he doesn't want to hear from Tara. He claims that she's only his biological mother..."

"So you should speak to him differently and tell him about Naomi's lies!"

"Naomi's already agreed to do what you've asked her...she's always willing to give in, even now, poor girl, she's willing to stop communicating with Oz as long as she's not accused of poisoning his mind..."

After mother agrees to release Oz' phone number, Chris calls him directly.

For the first two weeks Oz remains suspicious; he wants to know why Chris is calling him, where he's calling from, does he have any connection with me and if so why? Does he ever come to the States? And how are the children? And where are they? After a while he feels comfortable enough and begins calling Chris more often. We all cling to the hope that maybe Chris will be able to gain Oz' trust and eventually fly over and visit him and perhaps even persuade him to renew his ties with me.

For the next six months Chris and Oz communicate regularly. Sometimes Bilha also joins the conversation. Oz continues to show an interest and inquires about the family members and at a certain point agrees to meet with Chris.

We're all excited when Chris flies over to Texas.

As soon as he reaches the hotel he calls Oz.

"I just landed in Dallas...and I'm looking forward to seeing you tomorrow as we planned..."

"Great. I'm already excited to see you too, Uncle Chris."

The following day Chris reaches the rectangular shack, climbs up the winding stairs of the tiny structure and knocks on the door.

Silence.

"Oz! Are you there Oz?"

"I'm not opening the door...I'm not..."

His voice is dim. Unclear. Behind the locked door Chris hears whispers. Oz' voice sounds hoarse with fear.

"I'm not going to harm you," Chris tries to calm him, "I only came to visit you. I brought you a present... something special... something you'll like...from the entire family and from the kids. Please Ozzie, please open the door. I flew over here especially to see you. Please Oz, I really want to see you..."

Oz remains silent behind the shut door.

Chris returns to the hotel and calls up Naomi.

"You horrid woman! What have you done to Tara's poor son?! And why?! You're crazy! Why do you fill his head with mean thoughts? You mess up his mind and make him feel bad! You're a liar! You're sick in your head!"

He then calls up mother.

"Oz refused to open the door! I stood outside but he was too scared to open it! Why didn't he open the door?! He was so eager to see me. We spoke a lot about it and he was so excited ...I flew here especially to see him. Why didn't he agree to open the door and let me in? Why?!"

"It's obvious why he didn't want to open the door! You frightened him! And you didn't coordinate it with Naomi! That was your mistake! You should have done so ahead of time, then she would have agreed and you could have seen him!"

"You're as crazy as your daughter!"

"But that's how it works! Naomi knows how to manage things! She warned Oz to hide inside the closet ... she told him you might bust open the door and kidnap him!"

At this point Chris understands the deeply rooted illness of mother's soul, a disease identical to that of Naomi's, and stops communicating with her all together.

***

Today is Oz' forty-first birthday. Twenty-two years have passed since his abduction. My heart is aching to see him, to hold out my arms and hug my beloved son.

Despite all the years that have since passed, when I shut my eyes I can still relive my last brief moment with him and feel the skin on his arm. But I have no idea of his recollections of our meeting.

Would he want me to revisit him?

I consult with professionals who explain about the trauma Oz experienced and its severe consequences on his emotional state of mind. They give it a name and elaborate on Stockholm syndrome, a psychological response that serves as a coping mechanism in abusive situations: if a person is abused, kidnapped, taken hostage, imprisoned or forcefully held against his will. In order to survive the trauma of his imprisonment, that person must identify emotionally and mentally with his captives.

"It's very difficult to recover from it, Tara... even after the person is released. The trauma of the actual imprisonment remains deeply rooted inside his heads for a very long time...sometimes even years..."

"So what you're actually saying is that... I either agree to let go of things... and basically never see him again or ... that if I insist, I might cause him further trauma?"

I'm debating. On the one hand my heart refuses to harm Oz and add to his already traumatized condition but on the other hand I'm unwilling to give up on him.

I'm haunted by The Judgment of Solomon that constantly debates the question of justice which can never be resolved. The pain involved threatens to choke me.

I'm surrounded by so many good-doer souls who buzz around advising me on the concessions I need to make. They all want to demonstrate their overly clever ability to find a perfect resolution for the situation.

"You can't always predict someone's reaction or behavior ahead of time ... or even their logic... and because we're dealing with Oz there's an added problem," the specialist explains, "which is why I would recommend a different approach..."

Only when I'm alone in the apartment, only me with myself in the deepest of darkness, only then do I allow the awful sadness to flood my entirety, releasing tears and submerging myself into the deepest of sorrowful remembrances, those that have been gnawing at me for years.

The silence inside the apartment is painfully dense. My eyes rummage through its emptiness, looking but not seeing, trying to recount the long hours I've spent writing.

My memory releases intermittent flashes, tiny instances with terrifying visions all bunched up and crammed inside secreted rooms connected to endless corridors. There's pain everywhere with wailings and bleary eyes and a bitterness that fills my mouth.

Then the awful heavy silence returns.

My temple throbs. I shut my eyes briefly then move again through the empty rooms hoping for a moment of tranquility, wishing to erase the bad memories. I undress, throw my clothes into the dirty laundry basket then step into the shower under the hot water, determined to wash away the nausea.

My cursed conscious creeps up my throat. I vomit. I vomit the ME that's inside of me, the hatred, the meanness, the filth and the scum of the past years, releasing from within the darkest of secrets along with the rot of intrigues and conspiracies; I drain my head of any thoughts of Darien, the conversions we'd had and the touches, repelling any wants of vengeance and disgust, but I remain with the one thing I can't get rid of: my own soul.

And the following day I get up to the start of a new day and my job at the office.

The pain of Oz' loss is constant and relentless. I'm scared of reaching the end of my path carrying with me a sense of defeat that will crash my heart. I keep thinking about the power of words and wonder what will happen if my words fail? Or if they prove insufficiently powerful and Darien, once again, escapes justice as he always does? I don't care if he lives, dies or rots. I only want him to release Oz from his grip. I've got to reach Oz, leave everything behind and reach him...

My deliberations resemble whirlwinds that threaten to drive me crazy. I have no way of getting rid of them or sharing the horrors that live inside my head. I simply continue working on the facts until they become a cohesive manuscript. Again I pause and make room for hesitations until I finally send it off to a publishing house.

And all I'm left with now are wonderments whether or not it'll reach its final destination.

I'm totally reliant on the factual truth and the power of its words but I don't forget, not even for a split second, the unpredictable hand of fate that already hinted at me in my past. All that I still have left are the hopes and wishes of a mother's heart. I want to hug Sevan and strengthen her with the words of solid truth and clarify the facts to Oz. Perhaps my words will reach his understanding and he'll be agreeable to reconnect with me.

As I rehash past events, I'm reminded of the foul bird droppings that landed on my head years ago in Paris when I'd come to tour the city after my military service. It was on my second day that I'd met a dark eyed Parisian who courted me with charm, sent me flowers, bought me chocolates and knew how and when to tease my waistline.

On that ill fated day the air exploded with the sweet scents of May, silvery spring blossoms of bushes mixed with colorful happy faced flowers that winked at the lovers in the Champ de Mars Park in the seventh quarter. We sat on a small bench, our heads leaning against each other's with our hands knitted together, enjoying the blue sky above.

The wet thrust made me jump.

"Ah!! Bird poop! I just washed my hair."

"Is a sign of good luck!" he burst out laughing, took a handkerchief out of his pocket and began scooping up the white foam that quickly melted between his fingers. Within seconds my head turned into a green stench.

"I've got to go back to the apartment!"

"No...no..."

His hand continued to brush my long hair.

"Is not bad... you know... is soon dry... no worry...I take you like this... is okay...with all the shit..."

At that very split second I was again bombarded.

"Merde! Now is serious!" the stench changed the expression on his face, "two time is Merde! Is bad luck!"

The event itself, humorous as it may have seemed brought tears to my eyes and put an end to the stormy romance in the heart of

Paris. In the years that have since passed I tried to imagine what would have happened if...

If I could have avoided that second whipping, simply left the bench and moved elsewhere, would it have found me regardless? And what kind of twisted paths would it have chosen for me? And would they have changed my life? Is it at all possible that those fateful winks were sheer coincidences void of any significance or intentions or were they simply trying, in their unique ways, to forewarn me of my future life and of Oz' abduction thirty one years later?

My life's path is strewn with tiny luck-intended hints, all of which were meaningless at the time of their occurrence like the one hundred dollar bill that I found on the sidewalk, or the gold Krugerrand which I found in the entrance to a bank in Amsterdam and the three coined Belgian francs found within one hour of each other at three different locations in Brussels.

And there were other signals such as coincidental meetings with strangers which, at the time, seemed unimportant. Only in retrospect did I understand the reasons behind them.

Life's fragility is recognized in retrospect and measured by verdicts lacking corporeal presence; which is why I am unable to let go of the notion that the same higher power which was responsible for releasing the stink bomb on my head, was merely hinting at things that have since happened, and of those still awaiting me. Otherwise, there's no explanation for all the events that took place following that bird's droppings.

A gentle breeze flutters through the tree branches caressing my face. I'm seated on a shady bench, my eyes scouting the humming pigeons as they tiptoe on their tiny feet with their sharp toenails pecking seeds. My thoughts, as always, are elsewhere in far places across the ocean.

The phone rings.

"We're calling from the publishing house...we're impressed with the manuscript you sent us and we'd like to publish it. There's great importance in exposing the story... if only to prevent similar cases from recurring in the future..."

My eyes well up.

It's the first time in over two decades, that someone encourages me to release the truth.

***

EPILOGUE

The birthing of my book was stalled due to the COVID pandemic as the entire world came to a near standstill. When the pandemic began to subside the media, echoed by the global public discourse, sounded new voices in response to the long term social seclusions that were imposed worldwide. People sought to express their life's experiences and hardships through literature and other forms of art. The release of my book happened to coincide with this new reality.

When the book was first published in Hebrew, it aroused emotional reactions and evoked questions associated with the current discourse about crimes and violence committed within the family. It strengthened my decision to use the power of my words and the intensity of their veracity to tell the story of my own fractured family.

I hope that the exposure of this haunting story will free my children from the burdens of lies and secrets and enable them to see the truth.

I translated the book into English for the sake of availing it to my beloved Mickey & Nooshi.

I love U lots and miss you millions. ‿

Ohevet...Ima

Printed in Great Britain
by Amazon